# HITCHED TO THE
# GUNSLINGER

# HITCHED TO THE
# GUNSLINGER

# MICHELLE
USA TODAY BESTSELLING AUTHOR
# McLEAN

Entangled Publishing, LLC
10940 S Parker Road
Suite 327
Parker, CO 80134
Visit our website at www.entangledpublishing.com.

Amara is an imprint of Entangled Publishing, LLC.

Edited by Liz Pelletier & Lydia Sharp
Cover design by Elizabeth Turner Stokes
Couple photography © Period Images
Town © SchubPhoto/Shutterstock
Interior design by Toni Kerr

Print ISBN 978-1-64937-022-8
ebook ISBN 978-1-64937-035-8

Manufactured in the United States of America

First Edition September 2021

AMARA

ALSO BY MICHELLE McLEAN

*To my loved ones who will probably not read
this book because of the naughty bits,
but who will be my biggest cheerleaders
anyway because you love me.*

*Hitched to the Gunslinger* is a historical Western rom-com full of humor and heart that ends with a happily-ever-after. However, the novel includes some elements that might not be suitable for all readers. Gunfire and shoot-outs, blood and death, and alcohol consumption and drunkenness appear in the novel; there are also mentions of the deaths of family members in the characters' backstories. Readers who may be sensitive to these, please take note.

# CHAPTER ONE

Gray Woodson didn't know much, but he knew one thing… Life had been a lot easier when he was killin' people.

This whole retirement thing, on the other hand, was a pain in his saddle-hardened ass. It had taken all of two days for him to be recognized in a new town this time. He hadn't thought his face would be so well-known way out here. It wasn't much to look at. Nothing he'd call memorable. Now, his trigger finger? Sure. He was the fastest draw in the country, after all. Gave him some bona fide bragging rights. But it wasn't like he was wandering down the streets of town, drawing his gun on complete strangers.

But people still recognized him. All it took was someone's uncle's friend's little brother's cousin who happened to be in that one town that one time something had gone down, and that was it. Notoriety for life. Lucky him.

And now it looked like he'd need to move on again sooner than he'd hoped.

Gray repressed a sigh as the barkeep's shaking hand sloshed more mineral water — only dead gunslingers ordered whiskey, in his book — on the counter than made it into his glass. The man stuttered out an apology and then filled the glass almost to the brim, pushing it toward Gray with the air of a man feeding a starving coyote.

"It's on the house," he said.

Gray shook his head. "That's not necessary."

The man's face paled even more, if that were possible. "Don't sell much mineral water 'round these parts. I mostly keep it in stock for mixing drinks. I'm happy to get rid of it."

Yeah, people always said things like that when Gray objected to special treatment, and then a week later the gossips were clucking about the big bad gunfighter who was terrorizing honest men out of their hard-earned money. No thank you. He wasn't playing the game anymore. He was retired.

Gray slapped his money on the counter. "I pay for what I take."

The barkeep accepted the coins with trembling fingers. "Th-th-thank you, Mr. Quick Shot, sir. You're very generous, sir."

Gray grit his teeth to keep from snapping out a retort. The last thing he needed was for the man to drop dead at his feet. "It ain't generous to pay what I owe. And the name is Woodson."

The barkeep's face drained of all color. "Yes, sir. Sorry, Mr. Woodson, sir."

Gray didn't bother hiding his eye roll as he took his drink back to the table in the corner, as far away from prying eyes as he could get.

Didn't matter how far in the shadows he sat, though.

"My reputation doth precede me," he muttered into his glass while he watched the other patrons shoot furtive glances at him.

"Well, it *is* quite the reputation," a familiar man in his

early twenties with dark-brown hair said cheerily as he pulled out a chair and sat at Gray's table.

Gray scowled. "Sunshine."

Jason Sunshine—and yes, the man was every bit as irritating as his last name implied—tipped his hat in greeting, ignoring Gray's foul mood. He leaned in and squinted at Gray for a moment before sitting back. "You're looking a little crusty, if you don't mind me saying so."

Well, that's a fine way to say howdy. He scraped his hand across only a coupla days' growth of beard. "I do mind. Go away."

Jason grinned, his smokey brown eyes twinkling. "But I've only just found you."

"Lucky me," Gray mumbled, still glowering. "You're not lookin' so fresh yourself, you know. I think you've been on the road too long. Maybe you should go back to school, teachin' or tutorin' or whatever it was you did in your fancy city before you decided to start houndin' me."

Jason didn't rise to the bait, too busy watching everyone else watch them. "Tell me, how does it feel to command the respect of everyone in the room the moment you mosey on in?"

Gray clenched his fist around his glass, glaring at the only man who'd dare invade his space, uninvited. His free hand itched to go for his gun, but he checked himself. Even *pre*-retirement he hadn't killed a man just for sitting at his table.

Well… Okay, maybe once. But there had been extenuating circumstances. Honest.

And had the irksome little prat sitting across from

him now found him a few weeks earlier, Gray might have made an exception in this case as well. Jason had been pestering him for weeks, trying to get Gray to teach him his "trade." Gray's surly refusal hadn't dissuaded him one flat bit.

"It's not respect. It's fear," Gray said. "And it doesn't appear to work on everyone in the room." He gave Jason a significant look that the much younger man brushed off with a grin.

"Oh, it works on me. I've just decided that the possible benefits outweigh the risk of you putting a bullet through me."

"Might want to work on your decision-making skills." He drained his glass and slammed it on the table. "Anything I can do to dissuade you of that foolish notion, you just let me know."

"You haven't killed me yet," Jason said with a smirk.

Gray narrowed his eyes. "The day ain't over, Sunshine."

"You keep saying stuff like that, but you know, in all the weeks I've been following you, you've never once tried to kill me."

He shook his head at the youngster's outrageous lack of common sense. "What a spectacularly ridiculous reason to continue to annoy me."

Jason shrugged. "I think you kinda like me."

Gray snorted. "Yet another reason why I've never once considered intelligence to be your strong suit."

The barkeep was at his elbow, refilling his glass before he could make a move to get another. He appreciated the service, but he hadn't even heard the man move from behind the bar. Maybe he should put a bell on the guy's belt buckle. He didn't like people sneaking up on him and two had managed it in the last five minutes. He must be losing his edge.

"See," Jason said, pointing at the glass. "It has its perks."

Gray snorted again. "If you want to build a reputation as a gunfighter for fast drink refills, you're definitely gettin' into the wrong game."

Jason waved that off, too. "It's not just that. Look around," he said, nodding at the men sneaking nervous glances at them. "There's not a man in here who'd willingly cross you. It must be satisfying being the one who's feared instead of being the one afraid, is all I'm trying to say."

Gray shook his head in disgust. "You know nothin'. And I don't have the patience or desire to remedy that."

He sat back in his chair, irritated that Jason had managed to get under his skin again. The bothersome little shit was a city-bred adventure-seeker barely old enough to shave and raised on sensationalized tales of the Wild West. His quest for excitement made him over-eager to sign his own death warrant. His enthralled face every time he brought up some tall tale, the smattering of freckles across his cheeks, making him look so much younger than he probably was, just made Gray…sad. And tired. So very tired.

Jason just didn't get that the gunslingin' life wasn't all it was cracked up to be.

Sure, Gray's reputation as the fastest gun this side of the Mississippi might afford him some protection. And

Gray wasn't so much of a knucklehead that he didn't get why that might appeal to Jason. Most men gave him a wide berth. Most wouldn't dare threaten him. But most also wouldn't befriend him. Most wouldn't allow him to court their daughters, let alone marry one. Most would do whatever they could to make sure he stayed far, far away.

It was a lonelier existence than he could have anticipated. Not that he loved the company of other people, mind you. Generally, he was content to be on his own. Still, it wasn't the life he'd set out to build for himself.

And then, of course, there were the odd few men who wanted to gain a reputation of their own by taking out the best. Which painted a target on his back the size of his logger grand-daddy's prized pecker poles. And those who had tried, and failed, to best him...their faces would haunt his memories for the rest of his life. Each and every one of them.

What a glamorous life, indeed. No. He wouldn't help Jason become one such as him.

He wouldn't condemn another man to this life, no matter how much the jackass wanted it.

Gray downed the last of his drink, then slammed the glass down and pushed away from the table. He marched to the center of the saloon where a poker game was going on and made a slow circuit of the table, taking stock of each man.

He narrowed in on an exceptionally gangly-looking fellow who had that drawn, haggard look about him. The one that suggested he had precious little money to lose. Spending his time at the gambling tables was a travesty of judgment on the man's part. Especially considering his quickly dwindling pile of money. But there always seemed to be one at every table. Men who just didn't know when to quit.

Gray sighed deeply. He knew he should just walk away. But he'd never been much good at that.

Decision made, he grabbed the player by the scruff of his shirt and pulled him from his chair. The man sputtered and blinked his bloodshot eyes, his gin-sodden brain taking a few moments to catch up with what was happening. Gray swung him around and shoved what few coins the man had left into his shirt pocket.

"If you're wise, you'll take that home to your probably long-sufferin' wife and keep away from the gamin' tables until you can actually afford to lose."

Gray dropped into the man's seat and rapped his knuckles on the table. "Deal me in."

The farmer he'd displaced began to stammer an objection, echoed by the other men at the table. Gray didn't look at any of them but yanked his gun out of his holster so fast that none of them had time to draw breath. He didn't even aim it at anyone, but simply laid it on the table beside him.

The man whose seat he'd taken held his hands up and backed away muttering, "It's fine, no problems here," and went to nurse his bruised and frightened ego at the bar.

Jason unfortunately wasn't spooked by Gray's antics. He shook his head. "Well, now, that was just rude."

"I saved him from losin' his shirt."

"True, but you could have been nicer about it."

Gray didn't look at him but threatened under his

breath, "You're gettin' perilously close to discoverin' what it takes for my patience to run out."

Jason opened his mouth to reply but made the wise choice for once and shut up. He perched in a chair at the table nearest to Gray's. Not an ideal situation, but as long as he kept his mouth shut, Gray wouldn't fuss about it.

He gathered up his newly dealt cards and joined in the game. The other men playing didn't dare object. After a few hands, they seemed to realize that Gray wasn't going to kill them if he lost, and he actually got some decent play out of them. Even better, he won several good hands. The money would come in handy. It was definitely time to move on. But in the meantime, he intended to enjoy an evening of good cards and piss-warm mineral water.

The night dragged on long enough that Jason fell asleep at his table. Gray smiled, startling the man who sat nearest him. He resisted the urge to grumble. He smiled occasionally. People acted like it was the second comin' of God or something if he happened to show his teeth.

Now the reason for the smile *was* a miracle, if a minor one. He'd been prepared to tie Jason to the table leg in order to escape him if necessary. Leaving while he slept would be much simpler. Not that he was sneaking out by any means. Gunmen of Quick Shot's caliber did not sneak. But he also preferred to keep his life as simple as possible and having to lose Jason was a tiresome complication. Removing that complication without having to kill the little shit was a reason for celebration.

Gray nodded at the barkeep for one last drink.

He was parched but still should have known better and high-tailed it out of there the second things had started going his way. But no, he had to push his luck.

And now the argument that had sprung up behind him had turned into a full-blown fight. Gray stared into his cup while the sound of fists meeting flesh echoed behind him.

"Why don't you do something?" Jason said, skidding to a halt beside him.

Great. Now the kid was awake and breathing down his neck again.

Gray shrugged. "Not my fight."

Jason opened his mouth to argue, but Gray held up a finger and finished his drink while Jason watched, mouth hanging open.

Gray glanced over Jason's shoulder at the commotion. "Duck," he said.

"Wha—?" Jason gasped and ducked half a second before a chair flew over his head and crashed into the bar.

Gray decided to take advantage of Jason's distraction and gathered his money and gun and walked out right through the middle of the chaos. The seething mass of fighting townspeople paid him no mind, parting around him to open a path like Moses had when parting a particularly unruly sea. Even in the midst of their drunken and distracted foolishness, their instincts kept them from provoking the biggest predator in the room.

Okay. Maybe the kid had a point. There were a few perks to the whole "infamous gunslinger" bit.

Gray took a few moments to tie the reins of Jason's horse in an exceptionally tenacious knot. It wouldn't stop him, but it'd slow him down enough to give Gray a head start. He had several good hours of light left before he'd need to hunker down for the night. With any luck, the kid would have no idea in which direction he'd gone and would have reservations about traveling only a couple of hours before dark. Gray would be up at the first sign of light, too.

He untied his own horse and tried to turn her head from the clump of grass she gnawed on. But the old nag wasn't having it.

"You're gettin' to be more trouble than you're worth, girl, you know that?" he said, yanking on the reins again.

The horse's only response was to toss her head hard enough to jerk the reins from his hand so she could go back to her grass. Gray briefly debated leaving her where she was and taking Jason's horse instead. But horse thieving was a sin even a gunfighter, at least this particular gunfighter, wasn't willing to commit.

He gripped his horse's bridle and brought his face close to hers. "All right, Birdie, listen up. I'm goin' to mount, and you and I are goin' to ride our asses outta this town before that snot-nosed little weasel makes his way out of that saloon, or I'm going to drop you off at the first glue factory I come across. Got it?"

Birdie blew a nostril full of hot air into his face, but she didn't go back to her patch of grass, so Gray assumed she understood. He mounted up and turned her west. Thankfully, she didn't test him further. She was all smoke and hot air. Exasperating, stubborn nag though she was,

Birdie was about all he had in the world that was truly his. They'd been through a lot together. Probably why she hated him. But he'd hate to lose her, so as long as she continued to drag his sorry butt where he needed to go, they'd get along just fine.

There was no need to stop at the boarding house where he'd been staying. He'd paid for a week in advance and preferred to let the old woman who ran the joint keep the money than risk being waylaid on his way out of town.

As for his belongings…everything he owned was in his saddle bags. He traveled light. Had never been in one place long enough to need more than he could carry with him. Hopefully, that would change one of these days. If he could ever find a place to settle.

He let Birdie have her head while his mind wandered, drifting back to what Jason had said. If Gray was honest with himself, something he tried never to be, for a variety reasons, he would admit that in his more ignorant youth he had enjoyed several aspects of his notoriety. It didn't hurt to have men fear you when no one had your back. And there were always the ladies who enjoyed a dangerous but charming man.

But it had gone on long enough. Hell, most gunfighters were dead before they hit thirty-five and he was several years past that. If he wasn't gonna die in some street somewhere, he needed a good place to live out the rest of his days.

About the time his butt started going numb, Birdie crested a hill that overlooked a small but seemingly neat and tidy town. Gray pulled the mare to a halt near a sign that hung half off its post. The word DESOLATION had been burned into it, and he chuckled. Maybe it was named that to discourage people from visiting. Definitely sounded like his kind of place.

Then again, it wasn't much to look at, from the distance where he sat, at least. There was a street of sorts boasting the kind of buildings that'd be found in any town. Nothing particularly ramshackle about the place, but nothing overly nice, either. Still...he took a deep breath and tilted his head up to the blue sky. Something about the place called to him. Maybe because he was already well acquainted with desolation. It just felt... right.

Suddenly, Birdie took off in a trot, and Gray opened his eyes and gripped the reins.

"What the hell... Oh." The nag was heading right for an orchard of apple trees a ways down the hill.

Gray sighed. Apples were not his favorite. In fact, he usually avoided them at all costs. However...his stomach rumbled. It had been a while since he'd eaten and frankly, he didn't want to try and change Birdie's mind. She would rather chew her own leg off than do what Gray wanted under most circumstances. He really didn't want to see what she'd do if he tried to keep her from an orchard full of treats.

So. Apples for dinner it was.

His optimism over his dinner choice faded even further after he'd slid out of his saddle and taken the first bite. The overly tart juice flooded Gray's mouth and puckered his cheeks.

"Ugh," he said, tossing the apple over his shoulder.

Birdie, on the other hand, had no such complaints and was happily munching on her third apple. Gray debated the wisdom of pulling her away from her treats so he could go into town and find his own supper, when the sound of raised voices floated over the breeze.

He nudged Birdie closer to the commotion, taking care to keep hidden behind the trees. In a small clearing next to a grave, a stern-looking woman stood, hands on her hips, facing off against a group of men. They weren't physically harming her, but it was obvious she was not happy at their presence.

Something about the way she stood her ground, her whole demeanor poised and ready for a fight, sparked an admiration in Gray. He wouldn't call her beautiful. In fact, he'd never quite understood how men found women at their most attractive when they were angry. The women he'd known had been much prettier when they were smiling and batting their eyes at him. Not so much when their faces were blotched from anger and their claws were out.

This woman was definitely in a high dander. She reminded him of a hissing cat being forced into a bath. All prickly fur and bared fangs. Her hair was a nondescript light brown pulled back in a messy bun at the nape of her neck, despite a large portion of the apparently untamable curls escaping the knot. The rest of her, though, looked highly starched, impossibly clean, and neat as a pin. And radiating fury. Attractive, at that particular moment, she was not. However...she did look every ounce the queen ready to defend her territory. Quite mesmerizing.

He had no doubt she'd do just fine on her own, and he had no intention of wading into a mess that wasn't his. Heck, he hadn't even made it to town yet. Not that she needed his help in any case. She looked ready, and more than capable, to start knocking a few heads together. An admirable trait in a woman, he'd always found. But not one he wanted aimed at him. Now seemed like a great time to head the other direction into town and find a place to lodge for a few days.

He turned to grab Birdie. Only…she was no longer there. He spun in a circle, searching for her. She wasn't far away, but…

"Damn it all to hell," he muttered.

The miserable beast had abandoned her apple feast and was trotting straight for the arguing group. Damn useless animal.

But there was no help for it. He'd have to go bring himself to the attention of the squabbling folks by the grave unless he wanted to abandon his horse. Which was sorely tempting, but everything he owned in the world was in her saddlebags.

He sighed and made his way down the hill.

His mama used to tell him that burdens were a blessing. Well, if that were true, he really wished God would bless him a little less.

# CHAPTER TWO

Mercy Douglas calculated her odds of escaping a hanging if she did the world a favor and rid it of Josiah Banff.

Since the sheriff stood right behind him, watching their disagreement unfold, probably slim to none. *Blast*.

Josiah, the biggest landowner in the area who'd been an aggravating thorn in her side since the day he'd seen her—and her land—nodded his head at the grave beneath the nearby tree. "It's just not right, Miss Douglas. A beautiful woman like you, all alone in the world."

Mercy raised an eyebrow. No one had ever referred to her as beautiful before. Sturdy, maybe. She'd heard *robust* a few times. And Frank Revis, the town drunk, had once told her she had a strong countenance and ample backside, which seemed to be a compliment to him. Her lack of beauty usually didn't bother her much. A quick mind and strong body were much more useful to her than a pretty face.

So, she had no doubt any man laying on the flattery that thick was doing nothing but blowing smoke up her ass and telling her it was rainbows.

She gave him a tight smile. "You shouldn't concern yourself, Mr. Banff, with my circumstances. I'm perfectly happy as I am."

One of his men snickered, and Josiah looked skeptical. "There's no need to spin tales for me, Miss Douglas. You must be absolutely bereft."

She gritted her teeth, hating to admit he was right. She'd give anything if her father were alive again. She'd be willing to bet that the unfortunate accident that had killed him hadn't been an accident at all. But she had no proof of anything. No proof Josiah had murdered her father, though she knew deep in her bones he had. And she was done playing nice. Even if that meant provoking the loathsome man. Anything was better than this nauseating dance she'd been doing with him since the day she and her father had arrived in Desolation and taken over a distant relative's abandoned homestead.

Mercy took a deep breath and steeled her resolve. Grief clenched her heart as she stared down at her father's grave. She'd never been one to wish her circumstances were other than what they were. There was no point in doing that. But right at that moment she wished more than anything that her father was still there to stand with her against Josiah. Because no one else would.

"You're right, Josiah. I am absolutely bereft."

He perked up at that, his already slightly bug-like eyes widening hopefully, but his optimism was short-lived.

"You've been sniffing around my land since the day my father inherited it, and I'm heartily sick of it."

Josiah's mouth dropped, but she was just getting started.

"You seem utterly hell-bent on buying, stealing, or marrying my land right out from under me. *Why* you are so keen to get your hands on it, I have no idea. Don't care much, either. The fact that I have repeatedly and vehemently answered *no* to every proposal of every kind that you've delivered doesn't seem to mean anything to you. You want this land and you're determined to get it, no matter my opinion on the subject."

"Now see here, Miss Douglas—" he started, anger burning away the pleasant facade he usually donned when speaking to her and making what might have been a semi-handsome face plain unpleasant.

"No, *you* see here, Mr. Banff," she interrupted. "I wanted just a few days of peace to mourn my father. I see now I was foolish to hope you'd show some common decency. You're nothing if not persistent, I'll give you that. But I'm going to tell you the same thing I told you yesterday when you showed up at my home only an hour after my father's funeral, offering to solve all my problems with money or marriage if I'd just part with my property. The answer is *no*. The answer is always going to be *no*. It doesn't matter how many times you show up with the sheriff and your cronies in tow. Though ambushing me at my father's gravesite is particularly loathsome, even for you."

The sheriff at least had the grace to look sheepish at their intrusion, though the rest of Banff's men surrounding them didn't have the same decency. Even if they didn't like what he was doing, it wouldn't stop any of them from following Josiah's lead. Which was apparently to aggravate her into giving in.

It wouldn't work. He hadn't even seen stubborn yet.

The sheriff stepped up after a glare from Josiah. "Now, Miss Douglas, it wouldn't hurt to just hear him out." Her glare had him scurrying back like the spineless creature he was.

She returned her attention to Josiah. "I don't need to hear you out again. I've heard more than I ever care to hear from you in a lifetime."

"Like it or not, missy, things are different now that your father is dead. A woman alone is—"

He waved toward her homestead with an impatient gesture. "What are you going to do out here all on your own? Take care of all this land by yourself? It's going to waste without the money and resources to make it truly profitable. Now, if you'd just see reason... I'm offering well more than what the land is worth, and you know it. You could take the money and move back east."

"Why should I move when I'm perfectly happy where I am?"

He got that glint in his eye that she detested. "Then marry me. I'll take care of you. I'd even let you continue to rent out your little bungalow like you've been doing and keep the money for yourself."

He'd *let* her. She opened her mouth and pressed her hand to her chest, as though she were overcome by his generosity.

"You mean you'd let me continue to do something I'm already doing and keep my own money to boot, instead of handing it over to you? Why, sir, you are generous to a fault." She batted her lashes at him a few times with a sickly-sweet smile. When Josiah smiled in return, she rolled her eyes. He couldn't possibly think she'd been serious.

"What are you playing at?" he asked.

"Oh, for the love of God, it's called sarcasm, Josiah!

I'd rather sleep in a pit full of vipers than spend one moment as your wife."

One or two of his men not-so-casually rested their hands on their guns, their eyes flashing indignation. But a few of his men gasped, their eyes darting between one another and their boss. Apparently, they weren't used to anyone speaking to him that way. Well, they'd better get used to it, because she was just getting started. And she wasn't afraid of anyone.

Josiah sucked in a deep breath and his chest puffed out far enough he was in danger of losing a few buttons. It would have been comical…if not for the rage burning behind his eyes. His hand edged toward his gun, his men echoing his movements, and she instinctively took a step back.

Still, Josiah needed to get it through his thick head that she wasn't going to cave to his demands. The sooner he accepted that and moved on, the better.

She stepped forward again, though she kept one eye on his trigger finger, and opened her mouth to tell him what he could go do with himself—

A soft snuffling sound followed by horse hooves thumping the ground interrupted her, and they all turned and stared as a horse wandered into the clearing. Mercy froze as it came right up to her, breathed in her face, and then nuzzled at the pocket of her skirt.

She choked out a laugh and pulled out the apple she'd dropped in there earlier.

"All the apples in the orchard and you want the one in my pocket?" she said with a smile, momentarily distracted from her other unwanted visitors.

"Who does that horse belong to?" Josiah asked, frowning.

"She's mine," a man said, strolling toward them. He glanced around at all of them, his brow furrowing slightly as they continued to stare at him, open-mouthed. "Don't get many visitors here, eh?" he said, reaching over almost leisurely to take the horse's reins.

He dodged a poorly aimed nip from the horse and gathered her reins more tightly, scowling at her. "I saw that," he muttered.

"Were you thrown?" Mercy asked, though she should have probably been polite enough to introduce herself first.

The man frowned. "No. Why?"

Her cheeks flushed. "Oh…no reason…I…" She stammered to a stop, looking him over again. Maybe it had been a rude question, but what else was she to think? The man looked as though he'd rolled in several bushes and been dragged a few dozen yards. His hair was cut short but still managed to stick out in odd places from beneath his hat, and his clothing was rumpled, though upon closer inspection, not dirty exactly. Not clean, either.

Her eyes met his and her cheeks flushed hotter when his eyebrows rose a notch. Then his gaze very obviously roamed over her. She sucked in a scandalized breath and stepped back. He rose one mocking eyebrow and shrugged.

Well, she could hardly berate him for doing the same thing she'd done. Though she was sorely tempted. His perusal had been borderline salacious. She, on the other hand, had merely been curious. He was handsome. If she looked closely enough. Tall enough to be a commanding presence without being so tall she'd get a crick in her neck from looking up at him. Muscles that spoke of years in the saddle…though they were perhaps blurring a bit at the edges. Toffee-colored eyes lined with long, dark lashes that many a woman would kill for. By far his most attractive feature. Behind the silver-sprinkled scruff of his whiskers, the lines of his face weren't quite as deeply etched as she'd first thought.

She knocked a few years off his age to late thirties. Then added a few back on when he let out a grunt as he bent to retrieve something that had fallen from one of his bags.

Josiah glanced at him with annoyance. "Is there something you needed, stranger?"

Mercy started at the question. She'd almost forgotten Josiah was even there. Something he'd certainly noticed and did not appreciate if his glare were any indication. That was a definite mark in the stranger's favor.

"Nope, just retrieving my horse and I'll be on my way," the man said.

But a gasp from one of Josiah's men drew all their attention. The disheveled man sighed as Josiah's man whispered something in his ear.

"Here we go," the stranger muttered.

Josiah's eyes widened and looked at the stranger with much more interest. And a flash of fear. Mercy frowned a little. What was going on?

Josiah drew himself up to his full height and squared his shoulders as he faced the stranger.

"Now, see here, Mr. Woodson, we don't want none of your kind of trouble."

The sheriff's face drained of color so quickly that Mercy thought for a moment he might faint. "Quick Shot Woodson?"

The stranger grimaced. "My mama called me Gray." Then he turned to Josiah. "You have a problem with me bein' here, take it up with ol' Birdie. She's the one who decided to interrupt your little discussion."

He bent to pick up an apple from the ground and waved it in the direction of his horse, who studiously ignored him. He didn't seem to care at all about the armed men in his midst.

Mercy raised a brow. So, this was the infamous Quick Shot. Her father had told her ol' Quick Shot had once taken out four men in El Paso before any of them even had a chance to aim. Hard to believe, looking at the man in front of her. He didn't look like he could dispose of the apple in his hand.

Then again, Josiah and his men were already behaving much better with him here. Most of them had taken a step or three back, and Josiah hadn't looked in her direction once since old—emphasis on the *old*—Quick Shot showed up.

Maybe he could be useful after all.

It wasn't like she had many other options. Or *any* other options, really.

Before she could change her mind, she blurted out, "Plans can change, though, can't they, sweetheart. Depending on the circumstances." She ignored the shock on Quick Shot's face and turned back to Josiah. "I see you men have heard of my fiancé. Good, that'll save me the introductions. And the warning."

She glanced at her new "fiancé" and said, "Supper will be ready in an hour, dear."

Then she turned and headed down the hill to her house, not caring how any of the men were reacting to her declaration.

If Quick Shot refuted her claim, and frankly she fully expected him to, then at the very least she'd bought herself a few minutes to get away from Josiah and back into the safety of her locked house. If he didn't refute it, if he actually went along with the outrageous lie she'd just announced, then... Hell, she had no idea what she'd do.

But she'd better figure it out quick. Before the most infamous gunslinger in the country followed her home.

# CHAPTER THREE

Gray stood, plum speechless, as the woman marched away.

The men across from him were just as flummoxed, if their slack-jawed expressions meant anything. Well, what the hell was he supposed to do now? He'd only wanted his horse. Now he had a fiancée? He could call her obvious bluff, but he had a feeling that would make the men who were nervously shifting their feet around him a mite too happy. And he wasn't in the business of making anyone happy.

His old nag of a horse didn't seem to have any confusion and was already trotting after the woman, whose name he'd never caught. Useless animal. The woman had smelled disarmingly like she'd been bathing in a vat of cider, which was probably what Birdie saw in her.

He glanced at the men once more and blew out a breath. This was what happened when he stepped into shit that wasn't his.

He sighed. Ah, the hell with it. It was getting dark, he was hungry, and he hadn't had any better offers. She'd mentioned supper, after all. Maybe he could at least get a meal out of her. He turned on his heel and followed the woman down the hill, admiring the view as he went. His new fiancée might have a bad temper and some impulse control issues, but she had a fine, plump backside that under other circumstances he'd be delighted to follow around.

When the woman got to her front porch she paused and turned, her eyes widening a little when he entered the yard.

"Did you not expect me to follow you?" he asked.

She shrugged. "Wasn't sure what I expected, to be honest. I hadn't exactly been planning to announce an engagement to the whole world."

He raised a brow. "I take it you aren't really after marryin' me?"

Her cheeks flushed and her eyes—deep blue, the color of overripe blueberries, a surprising combination with her brown curly hair—flashed with the sudden color.

"Not particularly." She looked him up and down. "Before I let you in, what exactly are *you* after?"

"Supper."

Her mouth opened in surprise, but she glanced over his shoulder, and he followed her gaze. The sheriff and his men were still standing in the small clearing in the orchard, watching them.

"Let's go inside," she said.

Gray grunted, taking a moment to tie Birdie's reins to the porch post near the rain barrel. The woman held the door open for him and he moseyed inside, taking his time to peruse his surroundings. The house was small but looked cozy enough. A small fire crackled in the hearth. A couple comfortable-looking armchairs were positioned near it, while on the other side of the room a dining table and four chairs sat in the light of two large windows. Two doors on either end of the house led to what he presumed were the sleeping quarters and kitchen. Quite a decent setup.

The woman glanced down at the trail of dirt left by his boots, her brow furrowing. A small spark of guilt at marring the overwhelming cleanliness of the place nagged him, but he didn't let it bother him too much. He glanced back over to where she still stood by the door. She seemed wary but not overly afeared, which was a welcome change.

She blinked after a moment and gave him a tight smile. "Have a seat," she said, gesturing to one of the armchairs in front of the fire.

He sank into it with a grateful sigh. Now that was something he could get used to. Much better than bouncing around on a saddle all day. He tilted his head back, his eyes already starting to close.

"Aren't you wondering why I declared you my betrothed?" she asked and sat in the chair across from him.

He cracked an eye open. "You got your reasons, I expect," he said, closing his eyes again.

"Don't you want to know what they are?" she asked, her tone exasperated.

He sighed and pushed himself up straighter in the chair. He was curious, he had to admit, but frankly all he really wanted at the moment was a nice nap followed by a hearty meal. Her reasons for what she'd done could wait, in his mind. But she apparently disagreed.

He waved at her. "All right, then. Go ahead and tell me."

She frowned and her mouth opened and closed a few times, like she couldn't quite find the right place to start.

Or maybe she just wasn't quite sure what to make of him, because her brow remained furrowed, her mouth drawn in a confused frown.

He held up a hand. "Let me make this easy for you. Everyone I meet tends to want one of three things from me. They want to kill me, they want me to teach them how to kill, or they want to be protected from someone who wants to kill them. I assume you fall into one of those categories, most likely one of the last two, since you don't know me well enough to want to kill me."

"Bold assumption."

He almost smiled. "I won't be doin' any of those things."

Her frown deepened. "What do you mean?"

"I'm retired. I don't think you mean to be killin' me, but I'm not teachin' and not protectin'. So don't ask."

Her eyes narrowed with a flash of anger. "I don't want anyone killed, Mr. Woodson. Or do you prefer Quick Shot?"

He scowled. "Gray."

"All right. As for the other…" She shifted in her chair as if she were uncomfortable. "I suppose it's not too hard to determine from the little scene in the orchard that I could use…some assistance. Not protection, exactly, but—"

"No," he said, stopping her before she got too far.

She blew out a frustrated breath. "Then why did you agree to be my fiancé?"

"I didn't agree to anything. All I did was keep my mouth shut and follow you down here, and that was mostly because my horse had already done so. And there was some mention of supper..." he said, rubbing his stomach.

She rolled her eyes. "You haven't even heard me out. You'd barely have to do anything."

He pushed himself out of the chair with a grunt. "Look, lady—"

"You said I could tell you my reasons," she said, standing to block his exit.

"I just said that for the food. And frankly, judging by the smells coming out of your kitchen, it's not worth it."

She grimaced. "You have to at least listen."

"Don't need to do anything I ain't interested in, and I ain't interested in what you want." He moved around her and made it to the door.

"I'll pay you."

He stopped and looked back over his shoulder at her. "Well?" she said.

"I stopped, didn't I?"

She seemed perplexed by that, though a degree of relief was mixed in. Still, her eyes narrowed.

"You'd take money from a woman in need?"

"I'd take money from just about anyone willin' to give it away—as long as it don't require me to be killin', teachin', or protectin'."

She gave her head a little shake but inhaled a deep breath and retook her seat by the fire. She waited for him to follow. Great. It would be a long tale, then. He swallowed a groan and dropped back into his chair.

"Ever since my father and I moved here, Josiah Banff—he was the one doing most of the talking out there—has been trying his best to get his hands on this property. When we wouldn't sell, he resorted to threats, in between the odd marriage proposal, which I of course always turn down. The sheriff… You know which one he was?"

Gray raised an eyebrow. "Squirrely little weasel with a badge on his chest?"

Her lips twitched. "That's the one. Anyway, he's not much help. Josiah pretty much runs the town unchecked and…"

The chair was the most comfortable thing he'd sat upon in weeks. He shifted his butt around, sinking into it deeper. Yes, that was almost perfect, and he closed his eyes. It took a minute to realize the woman had stopped talking, and he cracked his eyes open a bit. She stared at him, incredulous.

"What?" he asked.

She shook her head. "I just can't figure you out."

Gray leaned back into the chair, getting even more comfortable. Hell, a man could sleep all day in this chair. "There's not much to figure. What you see is what you get."

Her eyes raked over him from hat to boot. The view did not appear to ease her mind.

"Don't like what you see, darlin'?" he asked.

She grimaced at him. "I really don't get it. A woman you don't know declares you her fiancé and instead of protesting, or at least wondering why, you just walk into her house and immediately try to take a nap."

Gray blew out a long breath. "I'm tired. It's been a long day."

The woman sat back, folding her hands across her

middle. "That it has."

"And you're making it even longer."

She ignored the comment like a champ. "I would have thought what I had to say would be interesting enough to keep you awake for at least a few minutes."

He shrugged. "Doesn't seem too complicated. He wants your land. You don't want to sell. Don't want to marry him. Havin' a man on your side stops the marriage proposals. Havin' a man like *me* on your side makes them hesitate to take matters into their own hands."

She nodded. "So you'll help me, then."

"I don't recall sayin' that," he drawled, pushing his hat back a bit. "Unless you've got a sack of gold hidden somewhere in this house, I don't think you can afford my services. Seems a mite too involved for me."

She threw her hands up. "If you weren't interested in helping, then why did you bother following me down here at all?"

"Like I said, supper."

. . .

Mercy's mouth dropped open and her hands clenched the arms of her chair.

The man couldn't be serious. He'd gone along with everything she'd said in front of the other men...just so she'd feed him?

"You want me to feed you and then let you go on your merry way? And what am I supposed to tell everyone when they wonder where my new fiancé is?"

He shrugged. "Not my problem."

She narrowed her eyes and took a few deep breaths. Like it or not, she needed this rumpled-up old has-been. Though she'd never met anyone *less* like an infamous gunslinger in her life. The man almost fell asleep the second he sat down, and if he did happen to move, he did so at the pace of a glacier going uphill in January.

But his name alone had gotten Josiah and his men to back off. Hell, the sheriff had nearly wet himself. Then again, Josiah was a persistent man, and Mercy doubted even Gray's presence would keep him at bay for long. Maybe she could pick up a few tips from Gray so she could at least defend herself next time the posse came around. She certainly couldn't depend on Gray himself to help out. If he stuck around longer than the next hour, that was, and she needed him to. Which meant she needed to find out his price. Everyone had one.

"What are your plans in Desolation, Mr. Woodson?"

"Gray." He frowned a little. "Don't see what concern that is of yours."

She pinched her lips together to keep from cursing at him, then forced a smile. "Maybe we can help each other out. If I know what it is that you're after…"

"I don't know why you don't believe me. All I'm after is a moment or two of silence so I can get some sleep," he said, pushing his hat farther down over his eyes. "And supper."

This man would drive a saint to drink. She tried again. "I meant in Desolation. What brings you to this town? Nobody comes here."

Gray snorted softly. "I can see why. A bit out of the way, isn't it."

"Maybe. But we like it that way. How did you find us, anyhow, if you weren't planning on coming here?"

Gray shrugged, watching her from under his hat. "Got on my horse and let her ride west. Useless animal probably followed the scent of apples," he said sardonically.

Mercy's lips pulled into a small smile. "We do have plenty of those. Are you just passing through?"

Gray shrugged again, a gesture that was beginning to get on her nerves. Then again, shrugging was the most movement she'd seen him make. Without the shrugs, she could easily mistake him for a dead man.

"I haven't decided yet," he said. "I'm looking for a place to settle. Could be here. Could be somewhere else."

Mercy watched him again for a few more moments, her jaw popping as she gritted her teeth. Gray's lips twitched a bit, as if he knew exactly how vexing he was being. And enjoyed it.

"Let me be plain, Mr. Woodson. There's nothing here. The town is small, most folks live farther out in the countryside. There's no inn, no hotel. Just a saloon. The only lodgings available in town are at Madam DuVere's parlor house. And if you want to sleep there, you'll be paying for a bedmate. You might not object to that, but Madam DuVere isn't known for taking on long-term lodgers. Even if she agrees, you'll be paying a pretty penny. You want her to feed you, you'll be paying even more."

Gray sat forward and leaned his elbows on his knees. "What are you gettin' at, Miss…"

"Douglas. Mercy Douglas."

No *pleased to meet you* from him. He just grunted.

She waited for him to say something else, but he only stared at her. She resisted the urge to squirm under the direct gaze of his surprisingly lucid brown eyes. Fine. She'd say what she had to say, then.

"What I'm getting at, Mr. Woodson, is that if you want a place to sleep and food in your belly for an affordable rate, I'm your best shot."

"Is that so?"

She nodded. "I've got a bungalow out back. And I'm willing to throw in meals with your lodging."

She was a horrible cook, but he'd find that out soon enough.

"This is a small town. I'm sure by now everyone's heard that Quick Shot Woodson is here. And let's face it, men of your…"

He raised an eyebrow, and she swallowed down the spark of fear that zinged through her.

"…your reputation, aren't always the most welcome in small towns that value their peace and quiet."

He studied her for a few moments and then sat back, a half grin tugging on his lips that sent a spark of a different, and far more surprising, kind zinging through her now.

He stood. "I believe there was a mention of payment."

She jumped up to block his path again if need be. "Free room and board."

He cocked his head and took a step closer. "For how long?"

"As long as you need it," she said, backing up a step.

He took another step closer and again, she backed up. Once more and she'd be up against the door.

His gaze roved over her. "And in return I just have to forfeit my virtue?"

She sucked in a breath, heat burning her cheeks. "Of course not! I'm only proposing a pretend engagement. Temporary. Just until Josiah gets it through his thick head that I'm not going to marry him or sell my land."

Gray's eyebrow quirked up again. "Seems like you're gettin' the lion's share of this little deal."

Mercy shrugged this time. "You're getting what you've said you want."

"True." He contemplated her a few more moments. "Fine. Deal."

She broke into a grin, relief and excitement shooting through her.

Gray turned and dropped back into his chair. He sighed deeply, every inch of him exuding weariness. "I'll stay, but don't expect me to be doin' any chores around this place or goin' after Josiah or the sheriff. I'm not lookin' to cause any trouble."

She nodded, hoping that if it came down to it, he wouldn't be as averse to helping her as he seemed to be right now. Surely, he wouldn't stand by and watch if she were in real peril.

One more thing was troubling her, though. She didn't want to bring it up, seeing as how he'd finally agreed to help and all...but...

"I just have one...I mean I just need to know...how many..."

Gray's amusement faded. "Yes?"

He was really going to make her ask? Fine. "How many men have you killed?"

His eyes shuttered and he sat back, his lips tight. "None that weren't tryin' to kill me first."

She cocked her head. "Is that typical for famous gunfighters? I assumed men like you were always out looking for trouble."

Gray shrugged and frowned. "I don't know what's typical. I just know me."

"And you don't know how many men you've killed?"

"Never cared to keep count."

Well, that wasn't ideal. But then again, it wasn't his past that she worried about. It was his future intentions. "Planning on killing any more?"

Gray shrugged again. "Never planned on killing any of them. But if you're wonderin' if I plan on riding into town, looking for a fight, it won't happen. I'm retired."

"Retired?" she said, eyes wide in evident disbelief. "Never heard of a retired gunfighter before."

He raised an eyebrow again, and she blanched at the foolish remark. Of course she hadn't heard of a retired gunfighter before. Because they didn't retire, did they? At least not willingly. They just got killed. The fact that he was sitting there, into his forties if he was a day, meant he really was as good as the stories about him. Despite all appearances to the contrary.

"As I've said, Miss Douglas, all I want is a comfortable chair to nap in and a little peace and quiet. And regular meals wouldn't be amiss, either. You provide me with that, I'll go along with your little scheme, assuming it doesn't require anything on my part but my presence."

She nodded and stood. "Well, then, Mr. Woodson—"

"Gray."

She paused for half a second before nodding again. "Gray."

His full lips pulled into a small but genuine smile that did odd things to her belly. She cleared her throat. "I'll go get started on your supper."

He nodded and closed his eyes again, probably about to make good on his first nap in that chair. Good. The more comfortable he got, maybe the longer he'd stay. And of course, the longer he stayed, the more likely she could convince him to use his particular skill set to teach her how to get Josiah out of her life once and for all.

She walked into the kitchen, closed the door behind her, and sagged against it, feeling some small measure of relief for the first time since her father had died. Her troubles weren't over by a long shot. But she'd get the protection—scant though it may be—that Gray's name seemed to be providing.

Like it or not, Gray had hitched his wagon to hers and he'd have to see it through.

At least, that's what she hoped. With that man, though, she was starting to realize he was unlikely to do anything expected.

# CHAPTER FOUR

"Breakfast!"

Gray cracked an eye open and rubbed a hand over his face. His new fiancée had the lungs of a rooster getting his feathers plucked. He slowly pushed himself upright, pulled his suspenders back onto his shoulders, and shuffled out the door of the small bungalow that sat behind Mercy's house.

It didn't contain much more than a bed, a small dresser, and a chair, but that was all he required. It was quiet, separate from Mercy's house, close to the outhouse, and even had little window boxes. Maybe he could plant some daisies. He'd always loved daisies, and he'd had a fair hand for gardening once upon a time. It was relaxing. He could use some relaxing. Best yet, the structure sported a small porch on which sat a rickety, but quite comfortable, rocking chair. He could live and die there a happy man.

"Are you coming?" she called.

Gray grimaced. The whole dying happy thing of course hinged on his landlady—sorry, fiancée—leaving him in peace. Which she seemed less and less likely to do.

Still, it was hard to complain too much when he was getting free lodging and free food. Well, such as it was. Dinner the night before had been blackened chicken with blackened beans and rice and hard biscuits. A choice he thought she had made on purpose.

The smoke billowing from the kitchen this morning, however, suggested otherwise.

He shuffled into the house, running a hand through his knotty hair. Mercy glanced up at him, her forehead creasing with a frown as she took him in.

"What?" he asked, looking down at himself but finding nothing out of the ordinary.

"Did you sleep in your clothes?"

He shrugged and slouched into a chair. "I was just gonna put them on again, anyway. Sleepin' in them saves me some time and aggravation."

She opened her mouth to say something and then blew out a breath, instead going back into the kitchen, to reappear a few moments later with a pan of what he thought might be scrambled eggs. They were the right size and shape, though the color was more of a light brown than fluffy yellow.

He raised his eyebrows but didn't say anything as he loaded his plate. He gave it an experimental sniff and then shoveled a forkful of the mystery meal into his mouth. He chewed, contemplating for a moment, and then shrugged and ate another bite. Didn't taste half bad if he didn't concentrate on it too hard.

Mercy watched him eat for a moment as if she expected him to complain. It certainly wasn't the best meal he'd ever eaten in his life, but it was free and he didn't have to cook it, so she wasn't gonna hear a peep from him. Especially while she was holding that wicked-looking frying pan in her hand. He ate another forkful, and she gave him a sharp nod before going back to the kitchen.

After breakfast, which he ate alone, he shuffled out to the front porch and collapsed into a rocking chair. He leaned it back as far as it would go, propped his crossed ankles on the railing, and shoved his hat down over his eyes. The morning was sunny, but not hot, with a nice breeze blowing in now and then. Perfect napping weather. The only sound in the yard was the twitter of birds and the occasional shuffle of the horses and goats Mercy kept. Pure heaven.

Until the scrape of a chair, rustle of skirts, and faint scent of charred apple suggested Mercy had sat down beside him.

He held perfectly still, hoping she'd go away if he pretended he hadn't noticed her.

Ignoring a woman had never in all his long days made her go away, so he didn't know why he'd hoped it would work this time. Mercy waited all of two seconds before she poked him in the ribs.

He swatted at her hand but didn't remove his hat from his eyes. She poked him again.

"What?" he growled.

"Are you really not going to help me with Josiah?"

He sighed. Why did women feel the need to harp over the same conversation a million times?

"I *am* helping you. My big scary presence is supposed to keep him cowering under his bed, remember?"

She snorted. "We both know that won't keep him away for long. He's probably coming up with a plan even now. Gathering more men. Something."

"I agreed to go along with the engagement story."

"What if it takes more than that? What if we have to

go through with it?"

This time, Gray did push his hat back enough to peek at her through one eye at that. "Go through with what? You mean...marriage?"

"Well, you can't just stay on as my fiancé forever."

"Didn't plan on it," he grumbled, ignoring the way his stomach was shimmying about at the thought of Mercy being his wife. It was that charred mess she'd called breakfast that was making him break out in a sweat. Nothing more.

"You don't seem the type to plan anything," she said wryly. "But doesn't mean things won't happen anyway."

He sighed. "Damn, woman, if it'll keep you quiet long enough for me to get a nap in, I'll marry you or Josiah or my horse if that's what it takes."

She didn't say anything, and for one shining moment he thought maybe she'd gone away. He wasn't that lucky, though.

"Well, if you aren't planning on providing any help aside from your *presence* on my porch..."

"I told you, I'm retired."

He could have sworn he heard her curse under her breath, and he pinched his lips together to keep from smiling.

"Fine, teach me to shoot, then."

He pushed his hat back again and frowned at her.

"You know, of all the ways I thought I'd spend my retirement, chasin' off people who wanted me to teach them was the last thing that would have ever occurred to me. I'm no teacher. I told you, no teachin', no killin', no protectin'. You said just bein' here would help. Well, I'm here. No fair tryin' to change the deal now."

"Well, excuse me, but it didn't occur to me that this"—she gestured at him slouching in his chair—"was how you normally looked. Or behaved. Your name is only going to go so far. Eventually they are going to see you like this and…well…" She waved in his direction again.

He grunted. "I don't know what you're goin' on about. I don't look so bad."

She raised both eyebrows at that, her gaze raking over him. He glanced down at his rumpled, travel-stained clothing and the small paunch that was starting to form above his waistline. "Okay, maybe I look a little worse for wear. But that's nothin' that a bath and some fresh clothes won't fix."

"You bathe?" she asked, eyes wide.

"Occasionally," he said, scowling at her.

"And do you own any clean clothes?"

"All right, you've made your point. Go away."

She sighed. "Look, Mr. Woodson—Gray—I wasn't aiming to insult you. Frankly, the fact that you agreed to this whole scheme was more than I dared hope, and I really am grateful."

He grunted and gave her a sharp nod.

"However…"

He sighed and laid his head back against the chair again.

"I can shoot well enough to bring down small game, sometimes, and scare off predators. My daddy made sure I knew that much. But I've never shot a man before. Never even held a gun on one. I'd be no match for Josiah and his men. Or even the sheriff. For all his lily-livered ways, he still has the skills that got him the job. Plus, all I have is my shotgun. That's good enough for my purposes, usually, but it won't do me much good if whoever comes gets too close."

Gray grunted again. She had a point.

"But pistols like yours…" She pointed at the guns he still wore strapped to his hips. "Those would be much better if I needed to fight closer range."

He shook his head, though a twinge of what might have been regret poked at him. "Even if I wanted to teach you, and I don't, these guns are much too big for your hands. They wouldn't do you any good."

"Ah, I'm sure they'd do just fine. Look," she said, leaning forward to grab one from its holster.

"What—?" he yelled, right as she yanked it loose and it went off with an earsplitting *bang*. He yelped and jumped out of the chair with a little hop.

She froze. "Oops."

The gun had blasted a hole in the porch near his foot. He stared at her silently for a moment.

"What in the hell do you think you're doing with my gun, woman?" he spat out when he could finally gather his wits about him again.

She looked down at the pistol in her hand, mouth wide open in shock. "I'm sorry. I didn't mean for it to go off. Seems a bit more sensitive than my old shotgun."

"Yeah, because these guns are actually worth a damn. Just what are you doin' going around grabbin' the gun out of a man's holster?"

Her cheeks flashed red, and her eyes quickly darted to an area much more central than his holster—the double meaning in his words registering.

His anger wavered for a second. He liked a woman with a naughty mind on her. But that was *not* the point at that exact moment.

She straightened her spine. "Well, what are you doing sitting around the house with loaded guns on your hip?"

He looked at her, incredulous. "I'm a gunfighter, darlin'. It wouldn't do me much good if they were empty."

"*Retired* gunfighter," she retorted.

He glared at her throwing those words back at him. "Well, since everyone else around me doesn't seem to want to let me retire, I figured better to be safe than sorry."

"Well, like *I* said, I'm sorry," she said, holding the gun out to him between two fingers.

He scowled and yanked it from her grasp then gave the butt of it a little shake in her direction. "You're a menace, that's what you are."

She folded her arms and stuck her stubborn little nose in the air, her lips working like she was chewing on words she couldn't release. Finally, she said, "I didn't realize you could move that fast."

He just blinked at her. "I can move fast enough with the proper motivation."

She grumbled under her breath, "Maybe I should shoot at you more often."

"I heard that."

She blinked up at him innocently, and he scowled. "I guess it's just a good thing my reflexes kicked in or I'd have a hole through my foot right now."

She snorted. "I didn't think you had any reflexes lef—"

"All right," he said, cutting her off. "First you shoot me, then you insult me. I'm startin' to understand why you're not hitched yet."

"Oh," she said with a forced laugh. "You don't want to get me started on all the reasons it's apparent why *you* aren't hitched."

"I never said I wanted to be hitched."

"Well neither did I!"

"Why are we arguing about getting hitched?"

She threw her hands up. "I don't know. You started it!"

"I did no— Ow!" He jumped out of the way of a small goat that was getting ready to headbutt his leg again. "What the devil is that thing?"

Mercy glared at him. "Be nice to Lucille. She's only upset because you're yelling."

He closed his eyes, his head pounding, and sucked in a deep breath through his nose. When he looked at her again, she was watching him with narrowed eyes, like he was a snake getting ready to strike.

She started to argue, but he held up a finger. "Shh."

Her mouth dropped open. "You can't shush me."

"Shh," he said again.

She took a deep breath, no doubt ready to unleash a world of aggravation on him, but he turned his back on her to walk into the house.

"Where are you going?" she asked, making to follow him.

Again, he held up that finger and shook his head at her. "You just…you just *stay*. Right there. And keep the goat with you."

She glared again but dropped onto the rocking chair next to the one he had vacated, her arms crossed firmly over her chest. Lucille nudged Mercy's leg until she reached down to give her a pet and then, with a last look at Gray, turned tail and wandered off across the yard.

Gray marched into the house and looked around. If Mercy was gonna go around grabbing at guns, he needed to find a good spot to hide the damn things. Only there didn't seem to be a suitable spot. He'd never seen a house so clean and uncluttered in his life. He couldn't put them in the couch cushions, or somebody was liable to get their ass shot off. He didn't want to put it under her bed. That was just putting it more within her reach. He pushed open the door to the kitchen and looked around. A large basket that looked like it hadn't been touched in a while sat in one corner, full of odd scraps of material and sewing supplies.

That would do until he found a better spot. He dug to the bottom of the pile and shoved the guns into it.

Infuriating woman. He didn't like not having his guns on his hips. Felt damn-near naked without them. But if he was gonna retire and all, she was right. Wearing loaded guns to breakfast was a bit unnecessary. Might as well start this retirement thing right.

Of course, he'd already made a serious misstep on that front by agreeing to Mercy's proposal. But he could try and lessen the consequences as much as possible. Not getting accidentally shot would go a long way toward that peace and quiet he was chasing so hard.

As he moseyed back out onto the porch, Mercy's gaze narrowed on his empty holsters. She crossed her arms over her ample chest, and his head spun a little. Damn woman had probably given him food poisoning with her cooking. He'd have to keep an eye on her.

# CHAPTER FIVE

Mercy hadn't brought up shooting lessons again, but that didn't mean she'd given up.

Gray may not like it, but he might have to actually do more than nap on her porch to get Josiah to go away. Frankly, she was surprised Josiah hadn't tried something yet. Then again, it had only been a day since Gray had come wandering into their lives. And since Josiah hadn't had the pleasure of watching Gray fall asleep on every surface he sat on for more than five seconds and move like a fly stuck in honey when he did decide to shuffle off somewhere, he was probably still playing it safe. For the moment.

She absolutely had to figure out a better plan soon, because the second Josiah and his men saw her ferocious gunslinger fiancé in action, they'd probably laugh until they peed themselves and then they'd come in and take what they wanted. And she'd be damned if she let anyone take what she'd worked so hard to build. Her orchard brought in enough on its own to pay for what little she needed, and quite a bit more. She had plans for her farm. Plans that did not include Josiah taking over and destroying everything she loved. She wouldn't ever be beholden to any man. And to keep her independence, she needed her farm and orchard intact, under her control.

The familiar scent of charred meat drifted to her on

the slight breeze through her open kitchen window.

"Damn," she muttered, rushing inside to yank the pork chops off the stove.

She sighed. She wasn't really a bad cook. Most of the time. She just got lost in her thoughts sometimes and forgot about whatever was cooking. And lately, she'd had a lot of concerning thoughts in which to get lost.

She opened the oven to remove the biscuits. At least they had turned out decently. She poked at one deep golden-brown lump. Mostly decent. Might be a bit dry, but it would taste just fine.

A snore echoed from the front porch and Mercy rolled her eyes. Gray was obviously not concerned about Josiah, but then he didn't seem much concerned with anything. She, on the other hand, wanted to know what was going on. And she wasn't going to find out by sitting at home waiting for Josiah or the sheriff to mount their next ambush. She'd also feel much better if more people than just Josiah and his men knew about Gray's presence in their town. And on her team, as it were. It was harder to make a man disappear when there were people around to miss him.

So. It seemed a trip to town was necessary. She could use a few supplies, anyway, if she was going to be feeding the man three square meals and then some a day. A new needle and some thread wouldn't be amiss, either. His clothes were definitely the worse for wear, and if she had to be engaged to him, she was going to clean him up a bit.

Mercy bent to have a quick look through her sewing supplies, stopping in surprise when she came across Gray's guns buried in the basket.

She carefully extracted them, frowning as she considered what to do with them. The chambers were full. Who hid loaded guns? It would make much more sense to simply hide the bullets. Now what was she supposed to do with them? Give them back? Probably the sensible thing to do, but where was the fun in that?

She couldn't stop the smile that formed when a thought occurred to her. She went out onto the porch as quietly as possible and tiptoed as close to Gray as she could. Then she raised a gun in the air and fired.

He came out of his chair with a yelp, knocking off his hat and overturning the chair in the process. His hands immediately went to his hips. She tried not to laugh at the utterly confused look on his face, though combined with hair that stuck out in all directions and his stammered half questions, it was a near thing.

"Misplace something?" she asked, holding the guns up, dangerous ends pointed to the side.

He glanced at the weapons, then up at the roof of the porch where a small hole rained dust down on him.

He brushed it out of his hair. "You shot a hole in your roof."

"You can fix it later," she said, handing him his guns. "Supper is ready."

He took the pair and glared at her as she turned to go back inside.

"What happened to a dinner bell?" he called after her.

"Didn't think you'd hear that over your snoring," she said. "Hurry up, it's getting cold."

She went in the house, slapping a hand over her mouth to hide her laughter as his muttered cursing floated behind her.

He followed shortly after, without his guns, and slid into his seat at the table. He stared at the food on his plate with a dubious expression. She narrowed her eyes, and he cleared his throat and picked up the fork and knife.

"Hat," she said.

He glanced up, brows drawn in confusion. "What?"

She sighed. "I think we've established your manners are little better than a barn animal's, and I haven't said anything about your habit of wearing your hat at all times, even in the house. But you could at least remove it at the table."

"I like my hat," he said with a frown.

She kept staring at him until he shook his head and took it off, dropping it onto the table next to him.

"Better?"

She nearly bit her lip off trying to keep from laughing at his thick mane of hair that was somehow both matted to his head on the top but also sticking up in all directions on the sides and back. The man needed a haircut like a fish needed water. Among other things. But she wasn't going to criticize his hair when she'd been the one to insist he uncover it.

"Marginally," she said. She would have preferred he hang it on the rack by the door, but frankly the fact he'd given in and removed it at all surprised her, so she didn't want to push things too far.

He started sawing at the pork chop with a look of deep concentration. After a few moments, he dropped his utensils, picked up the chop with his hands, and tore into it.

"Really?" she said.

He shrugged. "I'll waste away from starvation if I have to hack this thing into bite-size pieces. This is easier." He raised the chop in a little salute and bit into it again.

She shook her head. "Trust you to take the easiest way."

It took him a bit of work to take a healthy bite. He gestured at her with the pork chop. "You're awful opinionated for someone who wants my help so badly."

She smirked at him. "You must bring out the best in me."

"I could just leave, you know."

"You could, but the weather will be turning bad soon and there's not another town for thirty miles in any direction. Unless you want to go back the way you came, of course. I'm guessing you don't, because if you'd wanted to stay there you wouldn't have left in the first place. That doesn't give you much time to find another town that'll take you in for an entire winter. And with your reputation…"

Something flashed in his eyes that made Mercy's heart clench. It was gone in an instant, but a great flood of sympathy for the gunslinger suddenly washed over her. For all his bravado, he was a man who had no one. No home. No family. Nowhere he could go.

She had no doubt that he wouldn't thank her for her thoughts, so she took a hasty sip of water, trying to dislodge the lump in her throat.

"Well," she continued, though her eyes no longer met his. "I think we both know Desolation is your only choice. Since we've already established if you want to stay here, I'm your best option for a roof over your head and food on your table."

"The food's debatable," he grumbled.

She glared at him, and he held his hands up in surrender. "I'm kidding. It's…" He stabbed the black lump on his plate with his fork. "Edible."

Her lips twitched into a smile before she could stop it. "All right, fine. Since we are stuck with each other for the time being, I suggest a compromise."

He raised an eyebrow.

"If you'll try harder to be more…agreeable," she said with a small smile, "I'll try harder to be more…lenient with your shortcomings."

His eyebrow raised higher, but he gave her a half grin that made her stomach flip and held out his hand. "All right. Truce."

She shook his hand and wondered how long she'd be able to keep her side of the bargain.

•••

Seventeen hours. She made it seventeen hours. But if she had to bite her tongue one more time, she was going to bite the damn thing in half.

Gray had grunted his way through breakfast, ignored her suggestion that he accompany her into town, and was now sitting out in her rocking chair on the porch, whittling a stick into nothingness.

In anticipation of their trip, she'd dragged her hip tub into the kitchen and started the laborious process of filling it with warm water. A courtesy she didn't often bother with for herself. But, in the spirit of hospitality and their truce, she'd thought she'd go the extra mile for her "guest." It just hadn't occurred to her he wouldn't want to bathe. It was fairly obvious he didn't indulge in the pastime often, but…still…

She took a deep breath, wincing a bit at the odor coming from his direction, and tried again.

"You know, I would be happy to wash those for you," she said, glancing down at his clothing.

"What for?" he asked.

She stared at him for a moment, not sure how to answer that. Did he really not understand why she might think his clothes were in need of a washing?

"I just thought you might prefer some clean clothing. You don't seem to have brought any spares with you."

He shrugged and continued to whittle the stick in his hand.

She bit her lip, trying to go about this the tactful way, since she'd promised and all. But the man was trying her patience.

"I'm heating some water on the stove for you. I'm afraid I only have a hip bath, but it is preferable to the creek, especially at this time of year."

He didn't look at her, just kept rocking and whittling. "Don't need it."

Her temples began to throb. Could he really not smell himself?

"If that's all you wanted… Go away," he said.

All right. That was it. She'd tried the nice approach, and, in her opinion, he'd broken the truce first. She stood in front of him, hands on her hips, until he looked up at her.

"My head is beginning to pound, and I'm not sure if it's from you aggravating me or from the smell coming off you. You may not notice it, but the rest of us would like to walk around and still use our noses." She waved to encompass herself, Birdie the horse, and the goats who were munching happily on some crabgrass nearby. "Now, I know you're used to being on your own, but for the time being we are stuck with each other, and since I'm housing you and feeding you, the least you can do is bathe occasionally."

"No, thanks," he said and went back to his whittling.

She nodded. "All right, then."

She marched around the side of the house where the rain barrel sat, grabbed the bucket beside it, and filled it with the cold water. Then, before she could change her mind, she took it around the front again and tossed the bucket of water right in his face.

He jumped up with a shout and dropped his stick and knife while sputtering and wiping the water out of his eyes.

"What in the tarnation are you tryin' to do, woman? Drown me?" he shouted, trying to wring the water out of his shirt.

Mercy's heart pounded, whether it was from fear at having just antagonized a known killer, excitement at upping the stakes in their little game, or just plain enjoyment she wasn't sure. Maybe a bit of all three. Whatever it was, she had never felt so alive.

She let out a peal of laughter, which froze him in his

tracks, his gaze pinned to her.

She shrugged. "You wouldn't go to the bath, so I brought the bath to you."

He glared at her, though she was pretty sure she caught a flash of amusement in his eyes. "You are tryin' my last nerve."

"Good, because you've already trampled the hell out of mine."

He shook his head. "I have never heard a woman with a mouth on her like yours."

She folded her arms across her chest. "I sincerely doubt that. Any woman in a five-mile radius of you is probably driven to curse like a drowning sailor. Now, would you prefer to get into the nice warm bath by the kitchen fire or do you want me to get another bucket of rainwater?"

He snorted, his gaze taking in her crossed arms as though measuring her conviction. "I don't know why your ma named you Mercy. There ain't a merciful bone in your body."

Mercy gave him the sweetest smile she could dredge up. "My mother said she was always thankful for the Lord's tender mercies, of which I was the best."

He snorted again, finally lifting his gaze to meet hers, and she held out her hand toward the door and raised her brows, waiting for him to decide.

He glared, his chest heaving while he stood staring at her, probably mulling over various ways in which to kill her. Finally, he slapped his hat against his leg a couple times and then with an exasperated growl, he marched into the house.

Mercy turned to Birdie with an earsplitting grin. "I can't believe that worked."

The horse softly whinnied at her in commiseration — because of course, the poor old girl had been dealing with Gray for a while — and went back to eating.

Mercy grinned again. "Now for the second part of the plan."

She waited a few minutes until the sounds from the kitchen let her know that Gray was in the bath. Then she took a deep breath and marched in.

• • •

Gray sat in the small tub, his knees almost to his chest, and picked up the bar of soap and scrub brush Mercy had left sitting nearby.

Mercy. He ground his teeth. If ever there was an inappropriately named woman, it was her. Only a mother could think otherwise.

The scent of apples tickled his nose, and he brought the bar closer to give it a good sniff. He sighed, his lips crinkling with distaste. No wonder the blasted woman always smelt like apples. As far as he could tell she used it to scent everything including, apparently, her soap. A more unpleasant smell drifted to him from the direction of his armpit, and he grimaced again. Well, she may have had a point about his need for a bath. It *had* been while. Still, he hated to lose an argument.

He got to work scrubbing at his hair and body, not caring how much water he splashed onto the floor. In fact, every drop that hit the floorboards made him grin with satisfaction. She wanted him to bathe so badly? She could clean up the mess. He ignored the guilt that nagged at him at the thought. She'd started it.

He'd just dumped a bucket of water over this head when the sound of footsteps marching in his direction froze him in place. She wouldn't dare. Would she? He wiped the water from his eyes and tried to shove his dripping hair from his face.

She rounded the corner into the kitchen before the thought of what he'd do if she *did* dare had fully formed in his mind. A startled shriek left his lips before he could stop it, and he dropped his hands to his lap, blocking his tender bits from view.

"What the hell are you doing, woman?" he asked.

She had stopped at his decidedly outraged, and not a little feminine, shriek and stood looking at him with a grin pulling at her lips.

"Miss Douglas!" he said, sounding much more like a disapproving schoolmarm than he intended.

Mercy seemed to tear her eyes away with difficulty and a burst of male pride scorched through his chest. He might be getting on in years, and his middle might be a bit softer and more abundant than it had been a few years ago, but he could obviously still command the ladies' attention. He was tempted to drop his hands and let her look her fill.

He changed his mind as she came toward him with a determined smile, and he sank as far under the water as he could. No good could come from that grin.

"Miss Douglas... Mercy... What are you doing?" he asked.

His pounding heart stopped altogether when she stooped over near the edge of the tub. She came up holding his clothing and his jaw dropped. She wouldn't dare!

She crinkled her nose but gathered the entire bundle in her arms, right down to his socks. And his drawers.

"Where you goin' with those?"

"They need a washing." She jerked her head toward a linen towel draped over the chair. "Wrap up in that when you're finished. It's a nice sunny day. Your clothes will be dry in no time. And while you wait, I've laid out some clothes that you can wear."

He sputtered a bit and half rose from the tub to pull his clothes from her grip. Her cheeks pinkened, but she didn't avert her gaze. In fact, it zeroed in on him. He remembered just in time that standing would give her far more of a view than he'd prefer, and he sank back down with a scowl.

She winked at him and then continued out of the kitchen.

Oh. The truce was *over*.

He finished rinsing as quickly as he could. Maybe he'd be able to get to her before she soaked all his clothes. He slipped and skidded out of the tub, wrapping the towel around his body as well as he could as he trotted out of the house.

No such luck. Mercy had marched straight to her laundry bucket and shoved the whole mass of clothing into it, pushing them under the water. Then she grabbed his shirt and a bar of soap—apple-scented, unless his nose deceived him—and got to work with the washboard.

He stopped beside her, waiting for her to acknowledge his presence. She glanced over at him, and her lips immediately started to twitch.

"Your feet are getting muddy," she said, studiously not meeting his gaze.

"You stole my socks."

She shrugged and scrubbed harder at a particularly tough spot on his shirt. "You both needed a bath."

"I did not."

Her eyebrow rose. "Yes, you did."

Yes, he did. But still. "I'm a grown man. I should be able to choose when I wish to bathe," he insisted, though it was hard to maintain an aggressive tone when he was standing nearly naked in her yard. And she couldn't keep her gaze off him, though she worked hard to pretend otherwise. Couldn't hide the blush in those apple cheeks of hers, either. He let his towel drape a little lower around his waist, unable to resist a grin when her eyes followed.

Her gaze snapped back up to his and narrowed when she saw his smile.

She wrung his shirt out so tightly she was probably imagining it was his neck. "You were making the wrong choice. I helped."

Oh, this woman. "Just because it wasn't the choice you wanted me to make doesn't make it the wrong choice."

"I disagree."

He didn't know whether to laugh or strangle her.

"Look—"

She sighed and shook his shirt out with a snap. "Your stench was peeling the paint off my walls. I did what I had to do."

He opened his mouth to argue, but he'd smelled the evidence himself. He grimaced. "Well now I smell…"

"Much better," she said with a grin.

"Like apples," he corrected.

Her brow furrowed. "You don't like apples?"

"Not particularly."

She snorted. "Then you are definitely in the wrong place."

He nodded. "That might be the only thing we agree on."

She laughed softly and his stomach dropped to the bottom of his bare feet. The woman was a witch. That's all there was to it. He'd never been the amenable sort. Never done what he was told. Yet there he stood, naked in her yard, bathed and scented and fixing to go to town to spread the news of their engagement. That *she* had orchestrated. And what was he doing about it? Standing there in nothing but the skin God gave him, hoping she'd laugh one more time because he'd never heard anything so beautiful in his life. And he'd only known her two days.

Lord, he needed help.

"I've laid out some clothes on your bed," she reminded him, hanging his shirt over the line.

"I'd just as soon wait on my own clothes, if it's all the same to you."

She shrugged. "Suit yourself. That'll set a few more tongues wagging than I had in mind, though."

He frowned. "What are you jabberin' about now?"

She sighed. "We are going into town this afternoon. Remember?"

"I recollect you mentioning it, yes. But I never agreed I'd be going."

Her expression didn't change much, but she scrubbed at the pants in her hands hard enough he was surprised they didn't burst into flames.

"I need supplies."

"Then go get them. I don't see any reason why I need to tag along."

She slapped the fabric in her hand against the washboard. "You are supposed to be my fiancé. This whole engagement farce does me no good if no one is aware you exist. Besides, with Josiah and the sheriff being curiously quiet the last couple of days, it would be a good idea to see what they're up to."

"The whole reason I came here was to be in a place where no one knew me. And now you want to go introduce me to the whole town? Sort of defeats the purpose, doesn't it?"

Mercy stopped her furious scrubbing. "I know that was your original plan. But with the sheriff and Josiah and his men already knowing you are here, it's a bit of a moot point. If they've spread the word that you're here, then everyone already knows. And if they haven't…well, then they are probably up to no good. Maybe devising a way to remove you from the situation. If that's the case, then the more people who know you're around the better. Makes it more difficult to make someone disappear if there are people who will miss him."

Gray raised an eyebrow. "I'm touched that you'd miss me—"

Her mouth dropped open. "That's not what I sa—"

"However, I'm more than capable of dealing with anyone Josiah or that weaselly sheriff might send after me."

She resumed her attack on his clothing. "Be that as it may, I think we'd both be a lot safer if I wasn't the only person who knew you were here."

Gray sighed. She had a point. He didn't like it. But he also couldn't argue against it.

"Fine," he ground out. "But don't expect me to act happy to be meetin' everyone."

She rolled her eyes at him. "The thought never occurred to me. Now…" Her gazed roved over him until he had the inexplicable urge to blush. "Unless you want to be the talk of the county—and I'm assuming you don't, since you don't even want to be the talk of the town—I suggest you go put on those clothes I laid out for you. They should fit you well enough until these are dry."

He raised a brow. "And what unfortunate man did they belong to?"

Her jaw tightened. "My father."

His gaze flicked toward the orchard where the grave stood out like a fresh wound. He swallowed hard. He'd known loss himself. Giving him the clothes had probably been a difficult thing for her to do. An act worthy of his respect. "I thank you for the use of them, then."

Her head jerked up, her eyes wide with surprise. Yeah, his response had surprised him as well. Maybe he wasn't a complete ass after all. Who knew?

He didn't dally but quickly put on the clothes she'd left him—and she was right, they did fit surprisingly well, though maybe a bit tight about the middle—and went to find Mercy again. If he had to go parade around town, he'd like to get it over with. He made it out to the yard where she was hitching her horse to a small wagon before he realized he wasn't wearing his guns. If there was a possibility of running into anyone who might have an issue with his company, he'd want those on his hips. Even if he was loath to use them.

He frowned, his hands absently slapping at his thighs. Where had he left the damn things?

"They're in the woodpile," Mercy said, not even turning to look at him as she went about her task.

His frown deepened, and he marched over to the woodpile by the door to extract his guns. Hiding them from her wouldn't do much good if she always knew where they were. He'd have to find a better spot next time.

That is, if he survived the meet and greet in town. It'd been his experience these things rarely went well when he was around.

# CHAPTER SIX

Gray hopped into the wagon and glared at the horse's rump. "Let's get this over with."

Mercy followed him, plopping down so close to him she was almost in his lap. Not that it was by choice. Small bench. Still, she turned to him with a mischievous grin he was hard-pressed not to return. She was sorely testing his resolve to die a surly ol' bastard.

"Ready to set some tongues wagging?" she asked.

He shook his head. The woman was relentless.

The trip to town was much quicker than Gray hoped. Mercy pulled the small wagon to a stop near the front of the general store, and Gray took a moment to glance around the town. Despite having been there for three days it was the first glimpse he was getting of the town proper. The closer view didn't make much improvement on what he'd seen from afar. Still, he had definitely seen worse.

The town sported the usual businesses one might expect. A barbershop stood on one side of the general store and across the street stood the sheriff's office and, presumably, a jail cell or two. Though it was noticeably silent and empty-looking. Interesting. A small building next to the sheriff's seemed to be the local doctor's office, and a short way farther down stood a blacksmith's shop.

A tavern sat beside the barbershop, a surprisingly grand establishment for such a small town. If he wasn't mistaken, the local parlor house most likely took up the second floor of the tavern. At least judging by the several pairs of eyes that peeped at him from behind the lace curtains adorning the windows.

Gray tipped his hat to his invisible watchers. The madams were often the real power in the towns he frequented, so he always made it a point to stay on their good side. Never knew when he'd need to negotiate for some private lodgings or a temporary hideout. For the right amount of coin, he could usually talk himself into a quiet room where he'd be left alone. Options and backup plans were always good. Not that he had much coin, but if—or when, more like—Mercy kicked his sorry backside out her door, he didn't want to burn any bridges he might need.

He jumped down from the carriage and stood on the clapboard sidewalk, looking back over his shoulder at Mercy, who still sat in the wagon, watching him as though she were waiting for something.

"You comin'?" he asked.

She rolled her eyes with a sigh and gathered her skirts in her hand, preparing to get down.

"Mercy!" someone called.

Gray and Mercy both turned toward the newcomer, though her smile was decidedly more welcoming than Gray's frown.

A clean-shaven, tidy man with nary a wrinkle or gray hair came toward them, a grin stretching from ear to ear as he headed right for Mercy.

"Jamison," she said, giving him a little wave.

He reached up for her, and she braced herself on his

shoulders as he lowered her down, rather more slowly than was necessary. Gray scowled, his eyes narrowing when Mercy held onto the man's arms for a moment. Gray rubbed his chest, his frown deepening at the sudden tightness there. Her cheeks blushed in that pretty way they were prone to do, and his stomach clenched as though he'd been hit.

He blew a breath out through his nose. Mercy was supposedly in danger. That was the whole reason for their situation, was it not? It didn't seem prudent for her to go about giggling in random men's arms. Not that he gave three figs on whom she bestowed those smiles. Wasn't none of his business. Though it wouldn't kill her to throw a few more in his direction.

To be fair, he didn't exactly go around trying to coax a smile to her lips very often, either. Still, she was supposed to be his fiancée, and if this were a true pairing, he certainly wouldn't stand by while another man held his fiancée in his arms.

So, he probably ought to do somethin' about that. For appearance's sake.

He sauntered up to them, standing much closer to Mercy than was socially polite, and waited silently for them to acknowledge his presence. It took longer than he liked.

The other man finally glanced up at him in surprise, and Mercy's flushed cheeks deepened into a darker shade of red.

"Oh, yes, sorry," she said, more flustered than he had ever seen her. "Gray, this is Jamison Fairbanks. He's the best physician in fifty miles."

Jamison laughed and held out his hand. "I'm the only physician in fifty miles, but that's kind of you to say, Miss Mercy. Most people around these parts just call me Doc," he said to Gray.

Gray shook his hand with a grunt while he looked the man up and down, not seeing the appeal. Sure, some might find him attractive. He had that square jawline and broad shoulders that women seemed so fond of. And he dressed in a neat suit that screamed of East Coast money and education. What the man was doing this far west, Gray couldn't fathom.

Mercy watched Gray with the air of someone who expected a snake to jump out of a bush, on edge and confused. But then, most people looked at him that way.

"Jamison, this is Mr. Gray—"

"Her fiancé," Gray interjected, his own surprise at what he'd just said mirroring the others'. He didn't know why he'd wanted to make sure the other man knew his relationship to Mercy. Especially since they didn't truly have a relationship. And he had no desire to puzzle it out, either. Too late to pretend it hadn't happened, though.

He cleared his throat, trying to cover the awkward moment. "Gray Woodson."

Gray saw the exact moment his name registered in the other man's mind, but he had to give him credit. Though he paused with a smile that was perhaps more strained than it had been, his demeanor didn't waver.

"Welcome to town, Mr. Woodson."

That was probably the first time anyone had ever said those words to him. And the doc even sounded like he meant it.

Gray swallowed past the lump in his throat. Damn dust. It was always choking him. Then he scowled when he caught the surprised raised eyebrows coming from Mercy's direction.

"I can be polite," he muttered to her, his voice much more gruff than usual.

"Well," Doc said, "it seems congratulations are in order."

"Thank you," Mercy said, even more flustered than she'd been a moment before, if that were possible. "I haven't had a chance to tell many people yet."

"Of course. Well, I'm glad to be one of the first to hear your happy news," he said, though his smile didn't quite reach his eyes. "If you'll excuse me, I'm expecting a patient soon." He tipped his hat to them, his gaze lingering on Mercy. "Good day."

"Jamison, wait," Mercy said, stepping forward to stop him. "Have you seen the sheriff around?" She nodded toward the seemingly deserted sheriff's office.

"No, in fact I was thinking…" He stopped and grinned, nodding in the direction of the store. "Actually, I don't think I'll deprive Martha of the juiciest bit of gossip this town has seen in twenty years. Aside from your own," he said with a wink. "Go on inside. She's probably busting a gut waiting to talk to you."

Mercy's brow furrowed a bit, but she smiled. "All right, thank you."

She watched the doc walk away before glancing back at Gray. "I wonder what all that means?"

Gray shrugged. "Only one way to find out."

. . .

"Are you coming?" Mercy said, pushing the door of the store open.

"Naw." Gray leaned against the post, his gaze focused on the street in front of him. "I'll just wait out here."

Mercy opened her mouth to argue but shut it again with a small shake of her head. She didn't really need him inside. His presence in her company would be enough to get the gossips going, especially with Martha nearly lying on the counter, trying to get a good peek through the window.

When Mercy stepped inside, Martha stood back up and began wiping the candy jars as if she hadn't just been spying on them.

"Good morning, Mercy," Martha said. "What brings you in today?" Her voice was even, if a bit high-pitched, but she was nearly bouncing on the balls of her feet with excitement.

"Oh, I just need a few supplies," Mercy said, pulling out a list and purposely taking her time about it. "Five pounds of flour, a sack of sugar, a new needle, a spool of thread—white, please—"

Martha hastily gathered supplies as Mercy listed them off, her long black braid swinging back and forth as she moved, but as soon as Mercy got to the end of her list, Martha leaned over the counter with a conspiratorial air.

"Did you notice the sheriff's office looking a bit empty?" she asked.

"Come to think of it, I did. Has he gone somewhere?"

"No one knows. If he did, he didn't tell anyone, and that seems rather odd, doesn't it? Considering he's the sheriff and all."

"Odd indeed," said Mercy, glancing out the door at Gray.

"Well, there was a great to-do the other night, I can tell you," Martha said, her eyes shining. A good gossip session was what Martha lived and died for, and really nothing much went on in Desolation, so even the smallest change in routine was cause for excitement.

"The other day," she continued, "the day of your father's funeral... Oh!" She leaned forward to pat Mercy's arm. "I am so very sorry for your loss. I have a little something I fresh-baked yesterday that I've been meaning to bring over to your place but haven't had two spare seconds. So, it's good fortune that brings you in today! I'll be sure to fetch it before you leave."

"Thank you," Mercy said. "That's very kind of you."

"My pleasure," Martha said, beaming. Then she leaned over the counter again, getting back into her tale. "Anyway, that day the sheriff rode out somewhere with that Josiah Banff and some of his men. I thought to myself they were definitely up to no good. And I must've been right, because less than an hour later they came riding back into town, the sheriff white as a sheet and more spooked than I've ever seen him.

"He and Josiah went into his office and must've been arguing fierce, because we could hear their raised voices from here clear down to Madam DuVere's. Though none of us really got a good handle on what exactly they were saying. It sounded as though Josiah was nervous of somebody new coming to town and the sheriff didn't want no part of it anymore.

"I don't know what they were referring to," Martha continued, casting a surreptitious glance out the window at Gray. "Josiah did not take kindly to the sheriff backing out of town, I can tell you that. But you know Josiah when he gets really angry—he doesn't go around shouting. He gets that low voice that's even more scary, so I couldn't rightly hear what he was saying to the sheriff. But the sheriff wasn't having none of it. Kept saying he was done, he was out."

Mercy frowned. "I wonder what they were talking about?" she murmured, though she had a fairly good idea.

Martha's eyes darted back to Gray, but she plowed on. "Then Josiah and his men rode off and I thought that was that, but later—must've been around midnight, I guess—I heard some horses kicking up a fuss and then the sheriff cursing fit to make the preacher's hair stand on end, and I peeked out of my window, which, as you know, overlooks the sheriff's station…"

Mercy nodded acknowledgment but kept her mouth shut, lest she interrupt the flow of information coming from Martha.

"So I peeked out my window, and the sheriff was strapping all kinds of boxes and bundles on that old mule that Mr. Calvert at the smithy keeps. Looked to be everything he owned, excepting furniture and the like."

Mercy's eyes widened. "Perhaps he's just going on a trip?"

Martha shook her head again. "If he is, it's a very long

trip. Plus"—Martha leaned over even more and glanced around to be sure they wouldn't be overheard—"this morning, before most folks are about, I snuck over and peeked through the windows and as far as I can tell the sheriff plum cleaned out. Just up and left without a word to anyone."

"Really?"

Martha nodded slowly. "That's what it looks like."

"Well now, that *is* interesting."

Mercy glanced out the door to where Gray still leaned against the post. Martha's gaze followed hers.

"Now I know it's none of my business," she said, and Mercy bit her lip to keep from smiling. Martha had never met any business that she didn't feel the need to make hers. "But it does seem to be a big coincidence that the sheriff gets spooked by a newcomer right about the same time that your gentleman friend there shows up." She nodded in Gray's direction.

"Hmm, that *is* a coincidence," Mercy said, and Martha playfully swatted at Mercy's arm.

"Well, who is he?" Martha asked.

"The gentleman is, in fact, my fiancé," Mercy said.

Martha shot straight up, and her hands clutched her bosom as she squealed excitedly. "Oh, Mercy, that is just wonderful news! Who is he? Where's he from? What's his name? How did you meet? He's certainly not from around here." She looked him over again, a slight furrow appearing in her brow. "He's not really who I'd ever imagined you with," she said, contemplating him. Then her frown cleared, and she was all smiles again. "But he does have an exciting sort of look about him, if you get my meaning."

Mercy laughed, though a twinge of guilt wormed its way through her at the deception she needed to maintain. "We haven't known each other long, but the situation suits us. His name is Gray Woodson."

Martha stopped mid-squeal, her eyes round as oranges. "Gray Woodson? As in…'Quick Shot' Woodson?"

Mercy nodded slowly, and Martha let out a long breath. "Well, I suppose we know why the sheriff disappeared. That does add a little flavor to it, doesn't it? Are you…is he… I mean, well, I think…" Martha stammered, and Mercy smiled.

"He's retired, looking to settle down in a nice place. But I expect there will be those who might not take kindly to his presence in town. I do hope you'll help me persuade everyone that he will be a welcome addition to our community. He's…"

She stopped and frowned, trying to think of how to phrase what she wanted to say. How in the world could she describe someone who completely flummoxed her at every turn?

"He's not what I expected, either," she finally said.

She didn't know what sort of expression was on her face, but Martha gave her a long, hard look and then a slow smile stretched across her face.

"Well, whatever it is between you, it seems to suit you. I've never seen you look more…alive."

Mercy blinked, surprised. "Thank you," she said.

"So, when is the wedding? Soon, I assume."

Mercy opened her mouth to answer and then realized she had no idea how to respond to that particular query.

"I'm not sure. Not too soon. There's no rush, after all."

Martha's eyes widened in surprise. "Oh. Well. I just thought… Well, never mind. As long as he's not playing the scoundrel and trying to take any liberties," she said with a wink.

Mercy's cheeks flushed, the sudden image of Gray wearing nothing but a thin linen cloth about his hips assailing her.

Just the memory of him standing there, beads of water rolling down his chest, set her heart racing. Heaven help her, but a few more moments like that and she wouldn't be averse to him trying to take a few liberties. If he didn't aggravate her into an early grave first.

"Well, are you going to bring him in to say hello?" Martha said.

Mercy almost laughed. "He's not the most sociable creature, I'm afraid. But I think we will get him warmed up to everyone soon enough."

Martha nodded, helping Mercy pack the rest of her purchases into a basket. "You can count on me. I'll make sure everyone knows they're to give him a chance before drawing any conclusions."

"Thank you. I would appreciate that."

"Oh, your pie! I'll go fetch it while you load up your wagon," she said and hurried off.

Mercy took a deep breath to regain her composure and then went to deposit her purchases in the wagon.

Gray watched as she put everything in the back, though he made no move to help her. Not surprising. Who would hold up the post if he moved?

She finished stowing everything and came to stand

close to him. He glanced up, obviously surprised that she was voluntarily standing within touching distance.

"Martha is coming out," she said to him, low enough only he could hear. They were alone, but she was conscious of more than one pair of eyes on them. "Be nice. She's my friend."

Gray frowned. "Contrary to your obvious belief, I don't go about tryin' to insult innocent women."

Mercy raised an eyebrow. "I don't think you mean to, but…" She waved a hand from his boots to his hat. "This tends to rub people the wrong way, shall we say."

Gray patted his belly absently. "You know, some women find me quite charmin'."

"Hmm. I'll have to take your word on that."

He chuckled, a gravelly sound that caused her breath to catch in her throat, and she got an inkling why others might find him charming. Not that she wanted to admit it to him. Still, she didn't look away as the seconds stretched, and her cheeks started to warm.

"You know, you could take more than my word for it," he murmured as he wrapped an arm around her waist, pulling her close.

"What are you doing?" She planted her hands on his chest, finding it suddenly difficult to draw in a full breath.

"People are watchin'. I'm bein' a fiancé."

"Gray…"

"Yes?" He bent his head just close enough to brush the tip of his nose along her jawline.

"I…" She swallowed hard and tried to remember all the reasons she wanted this man out of her life as fast as possible.

She glanced up and caught a glimpse of Martha hurrying toward the door, her face alight with excitement.

Mercy pushed away from Gray and tried her damnedest to regain some composure. "Martha's coming."

He blew out an exasperated sigh and released her. "Quit devilin' me, woman. I'll be on my best behavior."

Martha came bustling out a moment later, her hands full of a delicious-looking pie. Gray's eyes widened with interest, and Mercy looked to the heavens. That man and food.

"Welcome to Desolation," Martha said, thrusting the pie into his hands.

Mercy had to keep her lips pinched together to keep from laughing at the expression on his face. That insatiable stomach of his was obviously pleased with the pie, but he didn't seem to know what to do with Martha's exuberant welcome.

"Thanks," he grunted. "Much obliged."

"Martha, this looks wonderful," Mercy said, gesturing to the pie. "Thank you so much. Apple?"

Gray gave a quiet groan that made Mercy want to kick him in the shins.

Martha shook her head. "Cherry."

"Cherry?" Gray said, perking up.

He held the pie to his nose for a good sniff. The low moan of pleasure that escaped his throat had Mercy and Martha both staring at him with open mouths. How could such an alluring sound come out of a man who was so...not?

Even worse, with every moan, half grin, and invasion of her personal space that he committed, she saw less and less of the more unappealing aspects of her counter-feit fiancé—and there were a great many of those, to be sure—and she began to see the man beneath it all. The man he must have been before his hard-living life beat him down. The man he might still be for all she knew, if she could get to know the real *him*.

That man…well, he was one who tempted her. Who put dangerous thoughts in her head and had her body tingling from one end to the other as he admired a pie.

And that just wouldn't do.

Mercy took the dessert from him before he could moan again. Or start eating it with his bare hands. Nothing would surprise her at this point. She placed it on the seat of the wagon and turned to make introductions.

"Gray, this is my good friend, Martha Clifford. Martha, Gray Woodson."

"I'm so pleased to make your acquaintance," Martha said.

Gray grunted something unintelligible at her, but it was enough for Martha to beam.

"I'm just so thrilled for you and Mercy. She's just the best girl out there. You couldn't find yourself a better wife if you tried a hundred years."

"Perish the thought," Gray said, in what Mercy was fairly sure was a truly horrified tone of voice.

"We should be going," Mercy said. Gray, true to his word, had been on his best behavior. But she didn't want to push it too far. Besides, he was eyeing the pie in a way that left no doubt he was thinking of nothing but devouring it then and there.

"Oh," Martha said, her disappointment apparent.

"Well, I'm sure I'll be seeing you again very soon. If you need any help with the wedding, you must let me know!"

"The wedding. Yes…" She glanced at Gray, who had turned his attention back to the sheriff's office and seemed to be ignoring them completely. Before she could say anything else, Gray pushed away from the wagon and started across the street.

"Was it something I said?" Martha asked.

Mercy shook her head. "No, of course not. He's just… well, I don't know what he's doing."

But she was going to find out.

# CHAPTER SEVEN

Gray sauntered across the street, pulled by a curiosity that overrode his instinct to stay the hell out of it.

He ignored the two women who trailed along behind him. A quick peek in the window didn't show much except an empty office. A few scattered papers on the floor and the complete absence of any noise made him pretty sure that whoever had been there had gone. And left in a hurry. He twisted the knob.

"What are you doing?" Mercy said behind him, close enough he almost jumped.

"Damn it, woman, I'm going to tie a bell around your neck."

She merely grinned at him until his own lips threatened to pull into a responding smile. He turned back to the window.

"I wanted to see if the sheriff was in," he said, though that wasn't entirely the truth.

"Martha saw him leave in a hurry in the dead of night."

His eyebrows rose. "Is that so?"

Martha nodded. "With most of what he owned, or so it looked like."

"Hmm." He tried the knob again. Locked.

"Maybe we should break the window," Mercy suggested.

Gray almost snorted. Been in his company three days and already she was starting to act like a criminal.

"I can pick the lock," a female voice said behind them.

The two other women with him jumped and turned with muffled shrieks. Gray straightened up and looked at the newcomer, pretending his stomach wasn't in his throat.

Make that newcomers. While he'd been peeking through the window, the doctor, four women, and another man who, if his clothes meant anything, was the town preacher had snuck up on him. Looks like he'd decided to retire just as all his instincts were leaving him. Good thing, given his hearing had clearly gone.

"Where did they all come from?" Gray asked, his brow furrowing.

Mercy looked behind them, her own brows raised in surprise, and then shrugged. "I guess they wanted to see to what we were up to."

Gray blew out a breath, and she shrugged. "Small town," she said. "Hard to get away with much here."

That was an understatement. The buxom redhead who'd boasted of lock-picking skills was dressed in a very expensive emerald-green gown, crowned with a hat covered in black feathers and rhinestones, as she held up a hairpin. With her eyes and mouth painted in bold colors, rouge staining her otherwise flawless complexion, it wasn't difficult to guess at her profession.

Gray stepped aside and gestured at the doorknob. "By all means."

"Should we be doing this in broad daylight all crowd-ed at the front door like this?" Mercy asked in a mock whisper.

Gray glanced down at her. "Since we're doing this

because the sheriff seems to have disappeared, I don't think there's much chance of us getting arrested. Besides, most of the town seems to be standing here with us, so there doesn't seem much point in trying to be sneaky about it."

"Good point," Mercy said.

"Ta da!" the woman in green said, opening the door with a flourish and standing aside so Gray could enter.

"Much obliged," he said.

She gave him a smile that would make most men blush, but Gray studiously ignored her. He'd already gotten himself tangled up with one woman in this town. He certainly didn't need to double his trouble.

He slowly pushed the door open the rest of the way, though he was pretty sure they didn't need to be so quiet. If he was a betting man, and he *was*, he'd put good money on the sheriff having run out of town. But a little caution never killed no one. Well, that wasn't true. But it killed less.

He stopped just inside the door and Mercy bumped into him with a little *oompf*. He reached out to steady her at the same time the doc did, and Gray pinned him with a stare. Whatever the doc saw in his expression had him holding his hands up with a sheepish smile and taking a step back. Gray released Mercy and took a step back himself.

"Sorry," she said. "Didn't know we were stopping."

"This would be much easier if I had a look alone."

She frowned. "But I want to see, too. I've never snuck into someplace I shouldn't be before."

"You're not really doing it now. Sneaking works a lot

better if you're quiet. And not tailed by half the town. In broad daylight."

She rolled her eyes.

"But just in case someone is hidin' out in here…" He held his finger to his lips.

Her eyes widened, either in anger at the reprimand or with the realization that she was being less than stealthy. He wasn't sure which, but if it kept her mouth shut, he was good.

She held her finger to her lips and nodded, then turned to Martha, who was behind her, and repeated the gesture. Martha nodded and showed the doc, who was already showing four other women and the preacher.

Gray looked heavenward and released a sigh that would make Saint Peter himself weep. How in the absolute bowels of hell had he managed to get himself into this mess?

Back to the matter at hand. He took a few more steps into the office. His followers thankfully stayed at the door, with the exception of Mercy, whom he hadn't expected to follow his orders in any case.

The office was deserted. There was nothing on or near the desk except for a few discarded papers. A rack on the wall that must have held the man's rifle was empty. In fact, there wasn't a sign anyone had been in there in days.

"Wow," said Martha, who had braved a few more feet past the door. "He even took the kettle." She pointed to the potbellied stove in the corner, where the kettle had presumably sat. "I don't think he's coming back."

Gray riffled around the desk, then held up the

sheriff's badge he'd found in a drawer. "I'd call that a good guess," he said, before dropping the badge back to the desk. He rubbed his hand on his shirt, his skin crawling at even that much contact with the law.

"Well, now what are we gonna do?" asked his extravagant lock picker. The three women who hovered near her were also dressed well, though not nearly so expensively, which led him to believe that Mercy had been correct. Mrs. DuVere, whom this had to be, obviously ran a more high-class parlor house for such a small town, but certainly not unheard of.

"The sheriff wasn't much," she said, "but he was better than nothing."

"Well, I suppose we'll just need to find a new sheriff," said the preacher.

Mercy must've caught Gray's questioning glance, because she said, "Reverend Samuel Donnelly, this is my fiancé, Gray Woodson. Gray, this is our minister, Reverend Donnelly."

The preacher's pale-red eyebrows rose at the word fiancé, but like the doc, he kept his opinions to himself and merely tipped his hat in Gray's direction. Interesting town. Maybe they all had their own pasts and didn't feel the need to judge anyone else. It was a nice change.

"Welcome to town, Mr. Woodson," he said, only the slight hesitancy with how he said Gray's last name betraying the fact that he probably knew exactly who Gray was.

Mrs. DuVere, however, had no such discretion. "'Quick Shot' Woodson?" she asked, placing her hands on her hips and giving him an appreciative glance up and down. "Well, look at that, girls. We've got a famous gunfighter in our midst."

Gray's eyes narrowed. "I trust that won't be a problem."

She aimed a brilliant smile at him. "None here. Right glad to have you. Might liven this place up a bit."

He couldn't help but smile back, at least halfway.

"Mrs. Hamilton Brewster DuVere," she said by way of introduction. "And my girls, Maria, Pearl, and Hattie."

Each of the women dropped a little curtsy, and Gray tipped his hat to them before turning back to the rest of the group, who all seemed to be looking to him for some direction. How he'd become leader of their odd little pack, he had no idea. And he didn't like it one bit. He frowned and turned to the doc.

"Well, what do we do about all this?" Doc said.

Martha came back into the room, and Gray glanced at her in surprise. He hadn't even noticed she'd disappeared up the outside staircase that led to the upper floor apartment. "There's not much left up there. I don't think he's coming back."

The preacher picked up a "wanted" poster from the floor and laid it back on the desk. "Looks like we need to find a new sheriff."

The faces around him showed varying signs of dismay and discouragement. Gray leaned against the desk. "The man can't have been such a saint as to inspire all this," he said, waving his hand at them.

"Of course not," Mercy said, though her brow remained furrowed.

"But," Martha chimed in, "it took such a long time to

find someone who'd take the job. We didn't have a sheriff at all for years. If something happened, we'd have to take care of it ourselves and even then, we'd have to hold any prisoners until a sheriff from one of the neighboring towns could come collect them. And as you can imagine, that took a fair bit of time. So…no, the sheriff wasn't much, and he certainly had his…*issues*," she said, glancing at Mercy.

"But with him in town, there was at least some semblance of law and order," the preacher filled in. "Even if it wasn't ideal."

Gray scratched at the stubble on his jaw but kept his opinions of law and order to himself.

The doc looked at him appraisingly, for long enough that Gray raised an eyebrow. "What?"

The doc flushed slightly at having been caught staring, and he glanced at the preacher, who gave him a little nod. Oh, this couldn't be good.

"Well, the thought just occurred to me that, with you being new in town and, I presume…from what I've heard…newly retired from your…old profession…"

Gray nearly groaned. Very diplomatic.

The doc cleared his throat and continued. "Seeing as how we need a sheriff, and you certainly have the necessary skills, and, in a way, have the most experience with law enforcement…"

"From the wrong side of it," Gray pointed out.

"True. The point stands, though."

"What point?" Gray asked, knowing damn well what the man was getting at. But he was going to make him say it.

The tips of the doc's ears turned pink, and he glanced

at the preacher, who took a deep breath and stepped forward.

"The fact of the matter is that we need a new sheriff, and you are the most qualified candidate for the job," he said in a rush.

Gray looked from the preacher to the doc to all the rest of the crowd, whose hesitant murmurs of agreement started gaining strength. He wasn't sure if the feeling building in his gut was anger, panic, or sheer perplexment, but whatever it was, he only had one answer to give.

"No."

He shoved away from the desk, marched through the group gathered in front of him, and headed straight for the wagon. Every time someone even opened their mouth, he repeated "No," over and over again. Maybe if he said it enough times, they'd get the message.

It was lucky for Mercy she was right on his heels because he'd had no intention of slowing down. He wanted out of this town as fast as Mercy's old horse could pull him. If he was smart, he'd bundle up Birdie and hightail it from her place as well.

He jumped into the wagon, scooping up the pie, which he thrust at Mercy as she scrambled into the seat next to him. He cracked the reins, and the wagon took off with a jolt, dumping her back into the seat. She glared at him.

"Well, that was rude."

He glanced at her out of the corner of his eye. "I agree. Where do they get off, ambushing a man like that?"

Her forehead crinkled. "What? No. *You* were rude.

Blurting out *no* like that and then running off. Not to mention nearly leaving me behind."

"You were in the wagon before I left, so you were not almost left behind. And they were the ones crossin' the line. All I was doin' was a little snoopin' around, and they had to go tryin' to force a job on a man like that—and a *lawman* job to boot. It's just plum wrong, is what it is. There I was, mindin' my own business, and they gotta—"

"What? Offer you a respectable job with good wages?"

"Who the hell wants to be respectable?"

She opened her mouth to argue more and then just shook her head, rubbing at her temples like her head was fitful cracking.

For once, Gray understood how she felt.

Him? A lawman?

The whole town was more off-kilter than a one-legged dog in a horse race.

If he had any sense, he'd be packed and gone before dark. Well, after he ate the pie, at least.

# CHAPTER EIGHT

Mercy didn't see Gray again until suppertime, and while he came promptly when called in to eat, he sat silently at the table, avoiding her eyes. If he thought that would keep her from speaking to him, he was sorely mistaken—however, she could wait until after they'd both eaten.

"What's that?" he asked when she put the food in front of him.

"Lemon chicken."

"Is it supposed to be black?"

Her eyes narrowed. "Yes. The char gives it better flavor."

Or at least that's what her father had said whenever she'd made it. If she could ever make it without burning it one of these days, she'd be able to compare, though she really did like the char flavor. With this dish, at least.

Gray tucked in, the only sound coming from him an occasional grunt as he gnawed on his supper. Halfway through the meal, a knock sounded at the door, and Gray and Mercy both froze.

"Probably just someone from town," she said, though her hammering heart betrayed her nerves.

She rose to answer the door, but Gray motioned for her to stay behind him.

"Might as well earn my keep," he muttered.

She couldn't argue with that.

She hung back as he pulled open the door and then

jumped when he uttered a sharp curse followed by a "No!" and slammed the door.

"What in the world…"

Gray stomped away, then turned to come back before stomping away again, all the while saying, "No. No. Nope. Not again. I said no, I meant no. Not only no, but hell no." He glanced at Mercy. "Pardon my language," he grudgingly added. Nice sentiment, though she didn't know why he bothered, since his foul language usage in front of her had never seemed to bother him before.

"What is going on?" she asked.

But he was too busy stomping and swearing to answer.

Mercy blew out an exasperated breath and opened the door. A young man stood there, immaculately dressed with nary a wrinkle in his three-piece suit and brocaded vest, his dusty boots the only thing betraying the hours he must have spent in the saddle to get to Desolation. His face beamed with a brilliant smile at the sight of her.

"Hello there," he said, removing his hat, his fingers quickly smoothing over his thick, curly, dark-brown hair until it was as neat as the rest of him. "Might I speak with Mr. Wood—"

Gray pushed past her, held up a finger, and said, "No!" again, before once again slamming the door.

"Oh, for goodness' sake, what is all this about?" she asked.

Gray just glowered some more and said, "Him," jabbing his finger at the door.

She narrowed her eyes and pulled the door open again. The young—and very handsome, she couldn't help noticing—man still stood in the same spot. He gave her a jaunty wave.

"Anyone who irritates Gray to this degree is welcome in my house," she said, standing aside to usher the gentleman in.

Gray sputtered in outrage, but she ignored him.

"Thank you, kindly, Mrs....?"

"Miss," she said, returning his friendly smile. "Mercy Douglas."

"I am very pleased to meet you, Miss Douglas. I'm Jason Sunshine."

Her eyebrows rose at that, but it wasn't the strangest name she'd ever heard. "Sunshine is an unusual last name."

"Oh, yes, ma'am. Not the one I was born with, either, but my mama always said I was her very own ray of sunshine and the name just sort of stuck."

"It does, indeed, fit you," Mercy agreed.

Gray snorted, and she shot him a scathing look before turning a pleasant smile back on Jason.

"So, Mr. Sunshine, what brings you to Desolation?"

Before he could answer, Gray jumped in. "He's been followin' me around like a newborn duck for weeks. Wanting to learn the 'tricks of the trade.'" Mercy raised her brows, but Gray had turned to Jason.

"There aren't any tricks. Shoot faster than the other guy. End of lesson. Now go away."

Jason simply grinned at Gray, who threw his hands up and stormed back to the table, resuming his meal with a great deal of muttering and dish clattering.

Mercy glanced back at Jason, struck again at the fresh

good looks of him. Not that she was on the market, even without her fake engagement to Gray. But she wasn't dead, either. Mr. Sunshine was just pure adorable. He couldn't be more than twenty-two or so…maybe twenty-five, with a chiseled jawline that could cut glass. And despite his supposed choice of professions, he had a cheerful, innocent quality to him that was very appealing. If Gray was a thunderstorm, this man was the bolt of sunshine that broke through the dark clouds.

Handsome as he was, he wasn't as *interesting* as Gray, though she was embarrassed to attach that word to her fiancé, even in her own mind. Gray was a surly bastard, no doubt about it. In fact, he reminded her of an old, mangy dog she'd found when she was a child. The animal had been missing an ear, most of its teeth, and had fur that was so matted it was hard to tell it was a dog at first. But it had turned out to be the sweetest old thing she'd ever met. She glanced at Gray skeptically. Maybe she had to cut away more of the matted layers before she found his sweet center.

He looked up suddenly and met her gaze, and a bolt of heat hit her straight in the gut and she sucked in a little breath. And then Gray turned that smoldering gaze of his at Jason, and he grimaced.

Mercy turned to their guest and smiled. "Mr. Sunshine, there's plenty of food if you'd care to join us."

Gray growled a protest, but Mercy looped her arm around the young man's. "Ignore him."

Jason grinned. "I'd be much appreciative of a good meal, ma'am."

Gray snorted at that. "You haven't tried it yet."

She threw a quick glare his way before ushering Jason to the kitchen. "If you'd care to wash up first, there's a rain barrel on the side of the house and some fresh towels hanging on the line."

Jason gave her a little nod. "Thank you kindly, ma'am. I'll be right back."

She watched him hustle out the door to go wash up before rejoining Gray at the table.

He put down his chicken leg and licked his fingers, sitting back to stare at her.

"What?" she asked.

"You like him."

She raised her eyebrows. "I don't know him."

"You like him," he said again.

She sighed. "Do I like a handsome young man smiling at me? Sure. What woman wouldn't?"

Gray scowled. "He's not that good-looking."

Mercy ignored him and took a bite of her food, chewing a minute before giving up and swallowing the piece nearly whole. "Why won't you teach him?"

"Same reason I won't teach you. I've got no time for teachin'."

"You've got nothing *but* time."

He scowled again. "Fine. I've got no desire for it, then."

"I can't imagine learning to be a gunfighter is all that involved. One afternoon passing along a few tips, and he could be on his way."

Gray grew quiet and stared at his plate long enough Mercy didn't think he'd answer her at all. Finally, he said, "You don't need teachin' to die."

His voice was so rough and pain-filled that she felt it in her own soul. She swallowed hard, trying to force a bite of dry biscuit past the sudden lump in her throat.

Gray grabbed his chicken again and took another bite. "Everyone does it eventually."

She should probably say something profound, something that would help erase that haunted look from his eyes. But there was nothing she could think of that seemed close to adequate.

"Well," she said, one corner of her mouth tilting up. "He seems a nice enough young man. It wouldn't hurt you to have a few more friends in this world. Why don't you at least try to get to know him?"

Gray snorted. "I don't care to know anyone. Most people who know me try to kill me."

"So, you decided on the off chance he doesn't want to kill you that you'll give him a reason to change his mind?"

He froze with his chicken halfway to his mouth, his lips twitching. "Something like that."

Jason returned before she could say anything else, and she fixed him a heaping plate, which he dug into appreciatively. They spoke of minor pleasantries while they ate. Well, she and Jason spoke. Gray had gone back to his glowering grunts and occasional snarls.

"How did you find me?" he finally blurted out.

Jason glanced at him in surprise but took a quick drink of apple cider and wiped his mouth. "It took a bit of doing," he confessed.

Gray nodded. "That's good, I suppose. I'd hate to think it was easy for you."

Jason grinned. "Oh, not at all. I knew you wouldn't go

back east, and north was most likely out of the question as well. I tried south at first. But when I reached the first town and no one had seen you, I knew you must have gone west."

"Maybe I'd just managed to pass through without anyone realizing," Gray said.

Jason shook his head, his grin growing even wider, if that was possible. "You stand out quite a bit more than you think you do."

Mercy nodded her agreement, adding her own smile to Jason's when Gray glowered at her.

"So, I backtracked and went west, and this was the first town I came across. And they've definitely seen you here."

Gray frowned, and Mercy wondered if his face ever got tired from making that expression. Hers hurt if she smiled too much. Surely the reverse must be true as well.

"That was an excellent meal, Miss Mercy. I thank you."

"No need to flatter her, Sunshine. She's got no interest in you."

Jason blinked in surprise, and Mercy stared, completely speechless.

"It isn't flattery if it's true," Jason said. "I meant every word. As for her interest…" His gaze flicked to her. "I could only be so blessed as to draw her admiration."

"We're engaged," Gray blurted out.

Jason's face froze in an expression so comically stunned that Mercy had to clap a hand over her mouth to keep from laughing out loud.

"That's…" The poor man seemed like he didn't know quite what to say. He glanced at Mercy. "Congratulations?"

...

Gray frowned again. Jason's expression was one of someone who thought they should offer condolences, but at least he managed to say the right thing, even if he looked as though someone had just told him Mercy was engaged to marry a two-faced dancing billy goat.

"You seem surprised," Gray said, though even he knew pointing this out was ridiculous. *Everyone* was surprised, including Gray himself.

Jason laughed a little, obviously flustered. "It is a bit surprising, I suppose. You've only been in town a few days, after all. And knowing what I do of you—"

"You don't know me," Gray said, his words low and sharp.

All amusement faded from Jason's face, and he regarded Gray a moment before nodding. "Perhaps not. I apologize. I truly am happy for you. Both of you. Curious, I confess," he said, back to grinning again. "But happy, nonetheless."

Mercy watched Gray, her brow slightly furrowed. He figured she'd explain the situation, but minutes passed, and she still didn't say a word. The woman was gonna drive him to drink. First, he couldn't get her to shut up, and now, when he actually wanted her to natter on, she sat quietly and blinked at him.

He sighed and dropped his biscuit. "It's a...mutual arrangement."

Jason's eyes widened. "Oh?"

Gray waved toward Mercy, having no desire to go

over all the details with the little twit, if he could even remember them all. He let Mercy fill him in on the now-missing sheriff and Josiah and his crew. Though the fact that they hadn't heard anything from that quarter since the day he'd arrived had him wondering if Mercy had exaggerated the situation there. Then again, Gray's reputation *was* a powerful deterrent. If he did say so himself.

Jason listened to Mercy with interest. Too much interest for Gray's liking, though he could hardly complain and tell the man to stop listening when she spoke.

When she finished, Jason let out a slow whistle and grabbed another biscuit.

"Well, now. That is quite a predicament."

Mercy nodded, and Jason glanced at Gray. "And *he* offered to help you out?"

She hid her smile behind her napkin. Gray pushed his plate away from him, hot anger souring the already leaden dinner in his gut.

"What's that supposed to mean?"

Jason held his hands up. "Nothing at all. Just that… well, you're not exactly the most helpful type under normal circumstances."

Gray's eyes narrowed. "Circumstances can change."

"Obviously."

He leaned forward. "You think you could do a better job protecting her? Maybe you'd like to marry her, then?"

"I'd be honored," Jason said with a huge smile. "If you're so against the idea…"

Gray snorted. "She'd eat you for breakfast and spit you back out before lunch. You're still too wet behind the ears, kid."

Mercy glared at him. "Kindly refrain from referring to me as some sort of man-eating monster."

"My apologies," Gray said, "I'm just going off my limited experience."

Her eyes flashed, and Gray's pulse hammered. Damn, she was a lively woman.

"Perhaps your experience would be a little more to your liking if you didn't spend the few waking moments of your day trying to drive me to drink."

She crossed her arms, and it was damn near impossible to keep his gaze from glancing down to take measure of her dress pulled tight across her plump breasts. Of course, her next words yanked his gaze right back to hers.

"Well, at least he's young enough to be capable of keeping a wife happy. Not sure you can say the same. They do call you Quick after all."

She looked him up and down with a dubious expression that would have had him searching for his balls in his younger years.

"Quick *Shot*. As you well know. And I'm perfectly capable of keeping a wife happy, woman, if I cared to take one."

"So you say." She sat back in a huff.

"I do say. He can't have you, anyway. We've already told the town about our engagement. Changing now would cause more issues than I'm sure you want to deal with."

She sighed. "I never suggested changing fiancés."

He frowned. No, she hadn't. Damn Sunshine. For some reason, his mere suggestion that he take Gray's place had gotten him all discombobulated. He didn't like the thought of Jason anywhere near Mercy. Gray was the one with a verbally binding agreement to be her man. Not that he wanted the job. But he certainly didn't want Sunshine waltzing in and replacing him. He pinned Jason with a glare that would have most men pissing in their boots.

Jason, who had been watching them, his head swiveling back and forth like an inebriated owl, just smiled and crammed more biscuit into his mouth.

"Where are your guns?" he asked, motioning to Gray's empty holsters.

He'd stashed the guns again once they'd returned home, to keep them all safe from Mercy, though he'd kept the holsters on. More out of habit than anything. It was bad enough not having the weight of the guns against his hips. The holsters were going to stay where they were for the time being.

Mercy snickered. "They're stashed in the flour drawer."

"Dammit," Gray said, shoving himself out of his chair to go retrieve them. Now he'd have to find a new hiding spot. Not that the flour drawer had been ideal, seeing as how she dipped into it often. He held them up and grimaced. Not to mention the fact that they were now coated with flour and would have to be cleaned.

When he returned, Mercy was explaining why he kept hiding his guns.

"So, you won't teach her either?" Jason asked. "At least now I know it's not something personal against me."

Gray scowled. "No, it's very personal against you."

Jason waved him off and took another gulp of his apple cider.

Gray slumped into his chair and watched him. "Why do you want to be a gunfighter, anyway? It's not some noble profession."

"That depends on your definition of noble," Jason said.

"Your mother sure as hell won't be proud of you for it."

Jason shrugged. "My mother died when I was ten, and frankly, she'd just be happy to see me safe and making a decent living."

"You have an interesting understanding of the words safe and decent." Gray's eyes narrowed. Sunshine was certainly a stubborn bastard. "You got lawmen constantly on your tail."

Jason shook his head. "You've used that one before, but I've been following you for weeks and I haven't seen one lawman after you. And you certainly don't seem overly concerned about running into one. Especially considering your current arrangement," he said with a wink at Mercy.

Gray shrugged. "That's because I never start the fight. You never start the fight, it's self-defense. Not my fault, so there's nothing to charge."

"Interesting," said Jason. "See, I'm learning so much from you already. Imagine what I could learn if you were actually trying to teach me something. Don't start the fight. Got it."

"No, that's not… You can't just…"

Jason and Mercy both watched him with quizzical expressions, and he threw his hands up.

"You two... You just..." He growled in frustration, jumping up so fast, his chair squeaked against the wooden floor, and marched out the door. He needed a break.

He stood on the porch for a moment, surveying the yard. He slapped his hand against his thigh and a cloud of flour puffed up. Damn. His guns. Where was he going to stick them this time?

One of the goats meandered by, gave him a lazy bleat, and continued on her way past the garden. Hmm. The garden. Mercy frequented the garden, of course, but only to pull specific items. It might do for a few days.

He found an out of the way corner and scraped out a foot or so of soft earth with a small spade he'd found nearby. He wrapped the guns in a mostly clean bandana he'd pulled from his pocket. Then he laid them in the hole and buried them.

The dirt falling over the bundle sent a curious pang through him. Almost as though he were presiding over his own burial. Not such a stretch of the imagination, really. Those guns were a part of him. Had saved his life on more than one occasion. Had been his most trusted companions for most of his life. He'd frankly expected to be buried with them. Probably because of them. Instead, he was burying them to avoid them poisoning other people's lives.

An odd thought. But apt. Those guns were his saviors and executioners, all in one.

And those two in the house wanted him to teach them to live as he did? They didn't know what they asked, and he wasn't going to enlighten them.

Not that he really knew how to teach anything. He

hadn't meant to live the life he'd ended up in. He'd always been good with a gun. There'd been an overabundance of rats on the farm where he'd been raised. His grandfather had let him practice shooting them when the cats proved unable to keep the rodent population down, and he'd gotten good. And fast. A skill he hadn't made widely known. Not that there were many to tell.

His skills with the cards, on the other hand, well that he exploited to the best of his exceptional ability. He'd made a decent living of playing cards. And then one day he'd won too large a hand against the wrong man. Gray hadn't even known the man. Or his reputation. He'd certainly had no plans to utilize his skills. Until after the man had gone for his gun and Gray had reacted without thinking. It had been as the man had lain bleeding at Gray's feet that he'd learned he'd killed a notorious gunfighter. The loudmouths who'd spread the story had sealed his fate.

And he'd have no part of sending anyone else to a similar fate. He'd lived far past the time anyone, including himself, had expected. Gray had earned his retirement.

He stood and brushed the dirt from his hands, sucking in a deep breath of cool evening air. Despite all that had gone on since arriving in Desolation, there was still a sense of peace here that he hadn't found anywhere else in his travels. He didn't know what it was about the place. The town was certainly nothing special. The land around him was covered with apple trees, which did nothing to endear it to him. Yet, something about this place called to him. Tempted him to stay.

"Gray! I'm cuttin' the pie if you want some!" Mercy stood silhouetted in the warm light from the house, waving at him to come in.

Gray rubbed his stomach, a faint smile tugging on his lips.

*Pie.*

He'd worry about all the things that might force him to leave this place tomorrow. Because he knew one thing for certain. No way that Josiah character or his men were as easy to scare off as the morally dubious sheriff.

# CHAPTER NINE

Gray scratched at his chest and waved his hand at a buzzing fly. His belly was full of a surprisingly edible breakfast, his feet were propped on the railing of the porch of his small bungalow, and he'd reached that pleasantly dizzy stage of almost-asleep-ness that he so enjoyed.

It had been quiet for nearly a week, aside from Jason's incessant chattering and Mercy's interminable nagging. And having to deal with Jason bunking with him in the bungalow, since Mercy said it was either that or she'd let the kid stay in the main house with her. Which wasn't going to happen.

He'd even managed to ignore them both long enough to transplant a few wild daisies into his window boxes. He'd been quite enjoying caring for the cheery little buds. All in all, it was a damn fine morning.

That alone should have warned him that it was all about to go to shit.

The distant pounding of several horses' hooves rumbled the floorboards beneath his rocking chair, and he squinted up from under his hat. Judging by the dust cloud coming at them, Josiah had rounded up a few new men and had come to call.

He didn't move. Just watched as they rode in. Jason, on the other hand, came running out of the house as though it were on fire. Gray snorted. The enemy wouldn't be frightened off by hysterics. Might as well save the energy for when it was needed.

"Mr. Woodson! They're here!" Jason called to him.

"Great. Get rid of them for me, would ya?"

Gray pulled his hat back over his eyes and tipped his head back on his chair, taking a deep breath. Such a lovely morning for a nap.

Someone shoved his feet off the railing, and Gray sat up with a grunt. Mercy glared down at him, her ancient shotgun in her hands. "You going to help or just sit there?"

"I should have thought that was obvious," he said, leaning back in his chair again so he could prop his feet back up on the railing.

She made a cute little growling sound in the back of her throat that had him chuckling and stomped off, her muttered curses colorful enough to burn his ears.

"Are you really going to sit there and do nothing?" Jason said, gesturing to the rising cloud of dust that was nearly upon them.

Gray sighed and peered at him. "I doubt they're here to do more than blow a little more hot wind. And if they do start some trouble, Mercy is nothing if not capable of defending herself. I should know."

Jason gaped at him. "But…"

In his experience, men rarely came at him in a thundering cloud of dust for a fair fight. They knew he'd win. So whatever Josiah was on about today, he doubted it was going to amount to much of anything. Later, though…well, he'd likely have to deal with some sneakin' and shootin', which meant he needed a nap.

Gray pulled his hat lower. "When we made our deal, she said my presence should be enough to scare them off. Well, I'm present. Now go away."

Jason scattered with a few impressive curses of his own. Good for him. Gray didn't think he'd had it in him.

He must have dozed off for a second, because when shouting started, he came back around with a rattling snore. He pushed his hat back enough so he could see what was going on. That damn nuisance Josiah Banff was sitting like a general in the middle of Mercy's yard, giving her some sort of ultimatum, Gray assumed. His voice was too low to make out everything he was saying, and Gray didn't want to move closer so he could hear better. He could guess what the man was saying well enough. He'd met plenty of men like Josiah. Mercy, spitfire that she was, had no such issue with volume.

"I've told you a hundred times, Josiah Banff, my property is not for sale. And neither am I!"

She hitched the shotgun up on her shoulder a little higher. Good girl.

"You want it, you'll have to pry it from my cold dead hands!" she shouted.

He shook his head. Not so good. Giving your enemy ideas was really not a great strategy.

"Suit yourself. We all have to live with the consequences of our choices, Miss Douglas," Josiah said. "Have a pleasant morning."

The sound of one lone horse riding off triggered a nagging feeling of foreboding in Gray's gut. Men like Josiah rarely stuck around to do their own dirty work. So, if he was the only one leaving…things were about to get messy.

Gray squirmed in his chair. It had nothing to do with the strange and irritating desire that suddenly crawled through him to rush to Mercy's aid. He just needed a cushion for his chair was all. Though, if ever a woman could manage to weasel her way past his carefully laid internal defenses it would probably be her. But she hadn't. And wouldn't. Because becoming embroiled in her life was *not* part of his plan. He just needed a better chair.

Though one could argue he was already embroiled in it, seeing as how they were publicly engaged and all. But that didn't mean he had to put forth any undue effort. He was supposed to sit there and look pretty. Or scary. Or whatever.

He gave a long-suffering sigh. If he knew Mercy, and he was beginning to think he did, that woman was bound to make the situation worse. He was just about to stand up and see if she needed a hand when the first shot was fired.

*Dammit. What does a man have to do to get a nap around here?*

He peeked around the post in his line of vision. Jason duck-walked between fence posts and barrels, hiding, and then popping up again to shoot his gun as he tried to make his way closer to Mercy. Though as far as Gray could tell he wasn't bothering to aim, and he certainly wasn't managing to hit anything. Gray snorted. "Amateur."

"We could use some help, you know!" Jason shouted at him.

Gray waved him off. "You're doin' fine." Besides, from what he could tell, Josiah's men were worse shots than Jason, which likely meant they weren't there to actually harm anyone. Probably more intent on scaring her off her land than anything else, if he had to venture a guess.

"I don't need his help," Mercy argued, before squealing and jumping back behind her post as a shot rang out in her general direction—although if the dirt that flew up was any indication, they'd still missed her by a good twenty feet. Were they closing their eyes when they fired? Missing by that much wasn't going to scare someone as stubborn as Mercy. Surely Josiah had told them to at least make it look good.

"I'm doing just fine." She popped out from behind the post and fired her shotgun in the general direction of the men—also in no danger of hitting anyone anytime soon.

"See? She's doin' just fine," Gray said.

The commotion stopped for a few seconds as Josiah's men must have finally noticed him. He rubbed a hand across his eyes. Maybe they'd keep ignoring him if he kept his mouth shut.

After a minute, they seemed to realize that he had no intentions of joining in the fight because they resumed their attack, keeping their focus on Mercy and Jason. Not a bad decision, since Mercy and Jason were the ones shooting at them.

A bullet grazed the post that Mercy hid behind, and Gray's feet dropped from the railing.

She peered out from behind the post, her face a masterpiece of righteous anger. "You almost hit me!" she shouted, and Gray chuckled. Only Mercy would berate a man trying to shoot her for daring to get too close to actually hitting her. He sighed. She was startin' to grow on him.

She aimed her shotgun and fired. And hit nothing. But she had managed to scare the horse of the man who'd fired on her, and it bucked and reared until it unseated its rider and took off at a dead run, leaving him in the dust. Probably not what she'd been aiming to do, but it had the desired result. Good on her.

Gray tried to settle back again. It had been close, but she'd performed admirably. He didn't need to get involved. He counted six men, plus the one in the dirt, and he sorely hoped they ran out of bullets soon. It would seriously mess with his retirement if he had to start killing people. Gray rubbed at his chest, realizing he'd probably have to leave town if word got round this was where he was hiding out—which it surely would if he laid out four men at once.

Best just keep this a friendly little disagreement for now.

So when one guy started to get a little closer to Mercy than Gray liked, he bent over and selected a nice, large apple from the basket she had left on his porch the day before. She was busy trying to reload her shotgun and hadn't noticed the man had crept closer and was raising his weapon to fire again.

Gray stood and let the apple fly, hitting the man in the shoulder just as he fired, which caused him to jerk and his shot to go wild. Gray grinned and sat down again, though he pocketed a few more apples, just in case.

The man shouted and grabbed at his shoulder, and

Mercy peeked out from behind her post, frowning in confusion. Then she looked at Gray.

"Did you just help me?"

Gray shook his head. "Nope."

She opened her mouth to say something else, but one of the other men got off a shot, and she ducked back behind her post with a squeak.

"Dammit," Gray muttered. So far, she was doing just fine, but Banff's men were being much more persistent than Gray had thought they would. It was growing increasingly obvious they were not there just to scare or intimidate her into complying but might actually be intent on truly harming her. And that was something he just couldn't—

Before he could finish the thought, a stray bullet shattered the window box next to him. The dirt left in the box dribbled out of the now-broken side, dragging his newly planted daisies with it.

"That's it," he said, standing up and brushing off the dirt that had splattered onto him. "I planted those flowers myself!" he shouted to no one in particular.

Dammit, seeing those little flowers thrive under his care had been an almost religious experience for him. And now it was all ruined. No one was going to get away with that. And...maybe Mercy could use a little help. Since he was joining the fight anyway.

He reached for his guns at his hip, belatedly remembering he'd buried them in the garden. Shit. Well, he'd have to do things the old-fashioned way. He sighed. That was so much more effort than he preferred. Ah well. No help for it.

He marched into the fray, swiftly dispatching the first man who rounded on him with a well-placed fist. He shook his hand. Hitting someone in the face hurt a lot more than one would think. He glanced around for some kind of weapon and spied the stool Mercy used while washing clothes.

He grabbed it and held it over his head.

"Don't you dare!" Mercy called out, sticking her head out from behind her post.

He almost rolled his eyes. "Do you want my help or not?" he shouted back to her.

Oops. Josiah's men had noticed his appearance into their skirmish. Two of them mounted their horses and ran off. Cowardly, but smart of them. The one firing at Mercy stayed behind the barrel he was using for protection, though he hardly needed it. Two others, after a slight hesitation, headed his way. They must have noticed he wasn't armed, or they wouldn't have dared. Or so he'd like to think. He shook his head. He was starting to believe in his own legend.

He got a better grip on the stool and raised it again.

"I use that!" Mercy said, coming out from behind her post long enough to get a shot off in the general direction of the men coming toward him. The shot hit the ground at his feet.

"Aim for the other guys!" he shouted, smashing the stool against the ground.

"I am!"

He shook his head. That woman was going to be the death of him.

He picked up two of the stool legs, which were now

adequately sharp weapons, and held them up to show her with a grin. "See, now *I* can use it."

He ducked just before the fist aimed at his face made contact. He swung with one of his stool legs, bashing the man over the back of the head. The man dropped to the ground, facedown, and didn't move.

One down.

"Where's Sunshine?" Gray called out, slowly turning in a circle, trying to keep both of his other assailants in his line of sight.

"Over here!" Jason's strained voice rang out.

Gray risked a glance in the general direction. Jason grappled with another of Josiah's men. One of them held a gun, though Gray couldn't tell which, as whoever didn't have it tried to wrestle it from the one who did.

"Quit playing with that gun and go help Mercy!"

"Working on it!" Jason grunted.

"I don't need help!" Mercy said, her words breaking off in a yelp as another shot splintered the post near her head. "Stop doing that!"

Gray chuckled, wondering if she really expected the man who was shooting at her to listen and mind like a good little schoolboy, or if she just couldn't help being bossy. He'd also been about to argue her whole refusal-of-help argument, but the shot had made his point for him fairly well. Plus, he was a little busy. The mean bald one on his right chose that moment to lunge right as the smelly bearded guy on his left lifted his gun to get off a shot.

Gray threw his last stool leg at Bearded One like a knife, grinning in satisfaction as the sharp end of the wood sunk into the man's wrist, making him drop his gun with a shriek. Bearded One clutched his hand and ran off. Bald One's fist crashed against Gray's jaw before he could celebrate too much.

He staggered. "Ow!" he yelled, holding a hand to his jaw. "That hurt!"

The man stopped, frowning. Gray could almost see the man's confused thoughts of "well, yeah" crossing his face before Gray flung his hand—and the apple he'd stashed in his pocket—with all his might. The apple found its mark right between Bald One's eyes with a satisfying *crunch*. His eyes rolled up in his head, and he joined the first man on the ground.

Gray glanced at them with a satisfied grin. "I took care of my three!" he yelled out. In case Sunshine was keeping count.

"Great," Jason grunted, still wrestling with his one assailant. He finally shoved against the man and brought his knee up, plunging it into the man's groin.

Gray grimaced and bent over, protecting his own tender bits out of reflex.

Jason's opponent crumpled to the ground, curling around his aching nether regions with anguished yips.

Gray had to admit, he was pretty proud of himself. He'd managed to dispatch all three opponents without killing anyone. Defeated his enemy with his retirement record of zero body count intact. Of course, there was still the man shooting at Mercy. Now that Gray could get a good look at him, and the murderous intent on his face, a flash of hot anger spiked through him. Fists and knees were one thing. Warning shots to keep someone pinned in place might have even been tolerable. But shooting at a woman—*his* woman—with the obvious intent to harm her was something else entirely.

Mercy popped out from behind her post and got off one more shot, which must have gotten close enough to spook the ruffian who'd had her pinned, because after a quick look around the courtyard—and a very brief moment of eye contact with Gray as he advanced on him—the man gave a high-pitched whistle to call his horse, mounted, and raced away. The few remaining men—well, the conscious ones—mounted and followed.

Gray couldn't help a disappointed sigh. They'd bring more trouble when they came back. Sometimes killin' had its uses.

# CHAPTER TEN

"What are we going to do with them?" Mercy asked, looking down at the men who were hog-tied at her feet.

"Bring them to the sheriff?" Jason asked.

Mercy shook her head. "He ran off a few nights ago."

"He take one look at ol' Mr. Woodson here and run off with his tail between his legs?" Jason asked, though his tone sounded more jesting than admiring.

"Actually, yes," she said, ignoring Gray's raised eyebrows. She didn't know why she felt the need to defend him, but...well, credit should be given where it was due, and it *had* been Gray's presence that had scared off the sheriff.

"Apparently being stuck between the dangerous Josiah and the murderous Quick Shot Woodson was too much for the sheriff's poor constitution to handle," Mercy said.

Gray watched her with a curious expression, those eyes of his boring into hers.

"Murderous, eh?" Jason glanced at Gray with a grin.

He stopped staring at Mercy and waved Jason off. "Nothin' but stories. I'm perfectly harmless."

"Uh-huh," Jason said, and Mercy laughed.

Gray was many, many things. Harmless was not one of them.

He finished tying up the last man and stood with his hands on his hips, looking down at them, his face drawn with weary lines. "We can at least take them to the jailhouse. They'll be more secure there. I'd just as soon get them off the property."

Mercy put her hand over her heart. "Why, Mr. Woodson. I didn't think you cared so much for my safety." She kept her tone lighthearted, but she truly was touched that he'd want to get the dangerous men off her property as quickly as possible.

He pinned her with another look she couldn't decipher. She'd pay a nice pile of money to know what was going on in that man's head when he looked at her.

"We keep them here, Josiah might come back around lookin' for them. I'm too tired to fight another posse right now. A man can only defeat so many enemies a day."

Ah. Of course. He was worried about *himself*. Not her.

"Hey, I helped," Jason said. "That one's mine." He pointed at the pudgy one who was still curled up like a newborn baby.

"Took your time about it, too."

Mercy bit her lip to keep from grinning at Gray's droll tone. "That's no way to encourage him," Mercy said. She turned to Jason with a brilliant smile. "You did wonderfully, Mr. Sunshine. I'm sure you'd have been able to take on the whole lot, given the chance."

Gray snorted. "We'll let him try next time, shall we?"

Mercy and Jason both opened their mouths to respond, but Gray ignored them. "Go hitch up the wagon, Sunshine."

Jason scampered off, and Mercy shook her head. "A little praise and encouragement goes a long way. He held

his own today. Did better than I did," she said with a
little laugh.

"You did well enough," Gray muttered.

Her eyes widened. "Did you just pay me a compliment?"

He gave the knot he'd been tying one last tug before
standing up. "You managed to point the gun in the right
direction and didn't shoot any of your own men. Hardly
rousing praise but suit yourself."

She shrugged. "That might be the nicest thing you've
ever said to me."

He opened his mouth to argue—or maybe agree…the
man was impossible to read—but Jason rolled up with
the wagon and Gray turned away to help load the men.
She sighed. She was *never* going to understand that man.

They had barely made it a quarter mile from the
house before Jason began peppering Gray with questions over his performance.

"Surely you have at least one piece of advice for how I
can do better next time," Jason said.

"Nope." Gray kept his gaze glued to the horizon,
though his hands tightened on the reins every time Jason
opened his mouth.

She had a tip. *Be more observant.* Even she could see
that Gray was going to snap if Jason kept at him. He
wasn't the most patient on a good day, and it *had* been a
rather eventful morning.

"I mean, I knew you were a legend with a gun, but I
had no idea you could fight like that. You took three
men out on your own, while I barely managed to handle
one."

"You did wonderfully," Mercy said.

Jason blushed a little. "That's very kind of you to say, Miss Mercy, but I wouldn't have lasted another two minutes. And I'm not real proud of how I got the upper hand."

He glanced down at the man he'd bested, who had unclenched a little but still seemed to be suffering from the blow.

"Did you win?" Gray asked.

Jason frowned. "Yes."

"Are you dead?"

"No."

"Do you want to be dead next time?"

Jason's frown deepened. "Of course not."

"Then you do what you need to do to stay alive and quit complainin' about it."

Jason gave him a sheepish smile. "Good advice."

Gray grunted.

Before they had even brought the horses to a full stop in front of the jail, half the town it seemed was there to greet them.

"Doesn't anyone in this place have anything better to do?" Gray muttered, watching the small crowd of Doc, Reverend Donnelly, Martha, and Mrs. DuVere descend as well as a dozen or so others.

Mercy shrugged. "An infamous gunslinger bringing in four hog-tied captives is bound to cause a bit of a stir."

Gray's full lips turned up into a heart-stuttering smile. Maybe it was just because he didn't smile often, but the sight of it never failed to send her stomach swirling.

Jason jumped down and introduced himself to a

flustered Martha while Gray tied up the horses. Mercy clambered down from her seat and nodded at Doc.

"What have you got there?" he asked.

"Some of Josiah Banff's men who came to my place, looking for trouble."

Doc's eyes widened as he peered into the wagon. "Do they need medical attention?"

She shrugged. "Probably."

Gray hauled the first man out. "They're fine." He glanced at Mrs. DuVere. "Is the door still unlocked?"

"Sure thing, honey," she said, hurrying over to open it for him.

He nodded at her and then looked at Jason. "Bring the rest of them."

Gray didn't wait to see if his orders would be obeyed, just turned and marched his prisoner into the jailhouse.

Doc, Reverend Donnelly, and Martha glanced at one another and then the men moved to help Jason unload the rest of Josiah's men. Doc looked over each of them quickly, murmuring with a slight frown creasing his brow, but he didn't say much as they moved them inside. He seemed to disapprove of their injuries, which was noble of him. But the men had been on her land, *shooting at her*, with obvious intent to harm her so their boss could steal her property. Frankly, she thought they'd gotten off easy.

The jail sported two rather new cells, each equipped with a cot. They put the two most grievously hurt on the cots and left the other two to get as comfortable as they could. Mercy stayed out in the front room, watching Gray as he came from the cells and slumped into the chair behind the sheriff's desk. He leaned back and propped his feet on the desk, folding his hands over his stomach.

When everyone else had rejoined them, they all glanced at one another, at a loss for what to do.

"Now what?" Jason asked.

Again, they all glanced at each other, and then, almost as one, they turned to Gray.

It took him a moment to realize they were all looking at him. His eyes darted among them all. "What?"

Instead of one of them stepping forward, they all turned to Mercy. Great. She got to be the bearer of bad news. She sighed. It was obvious what they all wished to say, and she was pretty sure Gray knew exactly what was on their minds. But since he was going to make them actually spell it out...

"I believe the townspeople would like you to reconsider—"

He dropped his feet from the desk. "No."

She pinned him with her best no-nonsense look. "Accepting the position—"

"No." He stood and started for the door, but she stepped into his path.

"Of sheriff."

His eyes narrowed and he leveled a look at her that probably had most men shaking in their boots. Certainly the men in the room with them. She found it kind of cute, though. Like a gruff-looking puppy that growled and snarled when playing tug-of-war with a rope. Somehow, she didn't think he'd appreciate that assessment, but she couldn't help aiming a brilliant smile at him.

She reached out with one hand and rested it on his arm. "Please?"

He held the look for another breath and then the lines around his eyes eased and the tension in his shoulders relaxed.

He turned back to the group of townspeople. "Is that what you all want?"

As one, they nodded.

"Y'all must be three sheets to the wind," he muttered, before sighing and rubbing his face. "Surely there is someone else more qualified that'll step up."

Every single one of them shook their heads.

"Less qualified?" he asked, hopefully. "There must be at least one other person in this town with a pulse who would be willing…"

"I'll do it," Jason said, stepping forward with an eager grin. "I'm not nearly as qualified, of course…"

"You're not qualified at all," Gray said, waving him back to the corner where he'd been watching. "You're so green the idea is laughable."

Faithful to his sunny disposition, the jab didn't seem to bother Sunshine at all. He just grinned good-naturedly. "True, but the only person who does have any sort of qualification is you, and you don't want the job."

Gray looked around the room. Every person there looked back at him, full in the face. "You all realize my only qualifications are that I can shoot, right?"

Doc shrugged. "You've had the most experience with law enforcement."

Gray's eyebrows shot up to his hairline. "Yeah, because I've either tussled with or am wanted by every law enforcement official between here and Chicago."

"Well, that just gives you a leg up," Martha said. "You know how these reprobates might think and what a lawman would do to catch them, or prevent the crime, or keep the peace, or whatever."

"She's got a point," Mrs. DuVere said.

Mercy watched emotions flit across Gray's face, unable to fully imagine what he must be thinking. The more the silence dragged on, though, she knew he was wrestling with something powerful. Could see it in the grinding of his jaw, the way his gaze kept darting from the door to the group gathered in front of him. It was like he knew this decision might mean getting to know people in town more. Something he clearly feared more than a gunfight.

The furrow in his brow deepened further. "Even if I wanted to accept, and I don't…but sayin' I did…isn't there a mayor or town council or somethin' that has to approve?"

"I *am* the mayor," Mrs. DuVere said. "And you're looking at the town council," she said, pointing to Doc and the preacher. "Minus Mr. Grutski, the undertaker. He's busy today."

Mercy watched Gray with growing concern. She didn't think he'd be able to take too many more surprises.

"You're the mayor?" he asked Mrs. DuVere.

She planted her hands on her hips. "Find it odd that a woman, and one who owns the local parlor house, holds such a position?"

"Yes," Gray said without hesitation, despite the obvious warning tone in her voice.

Mrs. DuVere burst out laughing in that booming, full-bellied way she had. Then she shrugged. "Well, we are a bit odd in Desolation, I suppose. It's fairly isolated out here, so we do what suits us best."

"Ah. Like hirin' an outlawed gunfighter to be your sheriff."

She winked at him. "Exactly."

Gray nodded slowly, then kept nodding. Then he held up a finger, grasped Mercy by the arm, and firmly escorted her outside and back across the street to their wagon. But he didn't toss her onto the bench and send the horses running like she expected.

Instead, he stared off into the distance.

"What are you thinking?" Mercy asked, every muscle in her body tense.

If he was spooked enough to leave, she'd be left high and dry without the protection she desperately needed. Because despite her blustering, she did need him. He might downplay his role in defeating Josiah's men earlier, but she'd have been sunk without him, even with Jason there.

Plus, she just really didn't want him to leave. She'd grown used to his broody presence around her house. He wasn't nearly as disagreeable as he liked to pretend. Well, he was disagreeable, but there was a humor and…a goodness to him under all that bluster. She'd miss him if he left.

Gray didn't answer her for a moment, and then finally he took a deep breath. "Are they all really that desperate?"

That startled a chuckle out of her. "Maybe."

Gray's lips twitched, and an answering tug echoed in her heart. "Look," she said. "You've been searching for a place to settle. And you did want to stay here, didn't you?"

He blew out an exasperated breath. "Well, yeah, but dammit, I didn't want to *work*."

She laughed and shook her head. "It's Desolation. Aside from Josiah, who I'll admit is a problem, but one you are dealing with anyway, I don't think you'll be too busy."

He let out a grunt but didn't argue, so she continued.

"You said you wanted to find a town where no one knew who you were. Well, maybe it wouldn't be so bad to be in a place where everyone knows you and accepts you anyway, murky past and all. Even if you have to *work*."

Gray's frown deepened. "But why would they do that?"

Mercy's smile faded, her own unpleasant memories invading her mind. "We all have our own pasts. Everyone comes to Desolation for a reason. Who are we to judge yours?"

He regarded her for a minute, long enough that she wanted to squirm under his gaze. But she held steady, forcing herself to keep her gaze locked with his.

"I suppose it would be nice to have another place to take a nap than just your porch," he said, maintaining a serious face for a second before a half grin peeped through.

Mercy echoed his smile and nudged his shoulder with hers. "It might not be so bad, you know. Maybe you'll like being on the right side of the law for a change."

He snorted. "I wouldn't go that far." He yanked his hat off his head and ran a hand through his thick hair before shoving the hat low across his forehead again. "Come on."

He started back across the street to the jailhouse. Everyone either had their faces pressed to the window or had been watching out the open door. When they saw him coming, they disappeared from sight and were milling around very unconvincingly in the sheriff's office when Gray and Mercy entered.

Gray stood in silence for a moment, and Mercy wondered if he was trying to force himself to speak. He pinned them all with a gaze that had a few of them shifting uncomfortably. "*If* someone were to accept this position, not me necessarily, but *someone*..."

"Yes?" Mrs. DuVere said with a smile.

Mercy bit her lip to keep her own smile from peeking out. He really wasn't great at being subtle.

"He'd have a few demands."

"Requests," Mercy suggested. Gray had the right to ask for a few things, but it never hurt to ask nicely.

He rolled his eyes. "Let's call them requirements."

She nodded. It was nicer than demands, at least.

"I want a deputy that I get to choose. If I have to deal with all this," he said, waving his hand toward the door, and the town, presumably, "then I'm not going to do it alone."

"That's reasonable," Doc said, and everyone nodded.

"Also, as I assume this'll be an all-day ordeal," Gray said with a sigh. "I want meals delivered promptly at noon every day."

"Won't your...wife-to-be...take care of that?" Reverend Donnelly asked, his pale-blue eyes flicking back and forth between the two of them.

Mercy's stomach dropped. Oh. That was her. "Of course," she said, her cheeks flaming.

Gray shook his head with a look of horror, and she had to resist the urge to stick her tongue out at him. "Mercy is busy enough with her own chores. She doesn't need to be runnin' into town to feed me every day."

Nice of him, though Mercy had no doubt he was more worried about the quality of his food, not about inconveniencing her. Not that she blamed him. Maybe she'd come into town around noon every day anyway and see if he'd share with her.

"I can take care of it," Martha said. "I always make far too much for me and my grandparents, anyway."

His eyes lit up like the Fourth of July. "Excellent."

She glowered at him. He didn't have to seem so happy about someone else feeding him. He very studiously ignored her.

"And I want a generous income," Gray said. Everyone nodded, but he held up a finger. "Very generous."

The others' enthusiasm waned a bit, but Mrs. DuVere didn't seem to have any qualms. "Agreed."

He frowned, like he'd expected her to fight harder. "And I want a new kettle," he added, pointing to the now empty potbellied stove in the corner.

"Done," she said, holding out a hand for him to shake.

He looked at it for a second, like he was trying to work up the nerve to grab a snake by the head. Finally, he groaned and shook her hand. "Fine. I'll be the damn sheriff, then."

# CHAPTER ELEVEN

Reverend Donnelly handed him the badge, and Gray stared down at it. What in the ever-loving hell had he just done? Had he really just agreed to be sheriff?

What would happen if word got out? Would they have to change all his wanted posters to include his new title? Then again, it had been a fair amount of time since anyone had put out a mistaken wanted poster on him. After all, his gunfights were always in self-defense.

Still. Gray Woodson, sheriff, was just…odd.

"Oh, one more thing," Reverend Donnelly said. "The apartment above the jailhouse here comes with the job. I assume you'll want to take advantage of that until… well…" He gestured between Gray and Mercy with that look of faint disapproval that church folk always seemed to sport whenever there was the merest suggestion that a little unwedded bliss might be occurring.

Mercy, her cheeks flaming, opened her mouth, but Gray spoke before she could. "No."

Her head jerked up and her gaze flew to his, stunned.

"But…" The reverend seemed at a loss for words, his cheeks flushing the same pale-red as his hair.

"As long as Josiah Banff is out there makin' threats, I'm stayin' with her."

"Yes, but…" the preacher tried again.

"There's no buts about it, preacher. You've all heard Banff threaten her a time or two. Those men in the cells are there because they showed up at her place with guns blazin' and nothin' but bad intentions. So, what would you rather it be, preacher? Would you rather protect *her* or your own sensibilities? Because that's the only thing that's bein' harmed by my being there."

The preacher's mouth opened and closed a few times, but ultimately, he kept his holier-than-thou shit to himself. Good thing, too.

Gray jerked his head in a sharp nod. "Until Banff is dealt with, I'm not leavin' her side. Anyone who has an issue with it can take it up with me."

He pinned each one with a hard look, but no one else had any wish to weigh in on the matter, it seemed. Good. Then his gaze met Mercy's and he froze. Those blue eyes of hers shone extra bright, and she gave him a small, sweet smile that warmed him from one end to the other. There was gratitude in those eyes, but something else, too. Pride. For him.

A funny emotion sloshed around in his gut. No one had ever been proud of him before. He wasn't quite sure what to do with the feeling.

"Maybe we can help with the situation," Martha said, a slight tremor in her voice the only thing that betrayed her nervousness.

Gray tore his gaze from Mercy with more difficulty than he'd like to admit. He started to question Martha, but Mercy reached out and lightly squeezed his arm. The sensation of someone's fingers on his forearm should not be able to stop all other bodily functions, but he seemed to have forgotten how to breathe. How to do anything, really, except stand and stare at that hand and revel in the heat that seemed to seep into and through him from the contact.

"What do you mean, Martha?" Mercy asked.

Martha smiled. "Well, Mrs. DuVere and some of the girls and I were talking, and we know with everything going on, taking care of wedding arrangements is probably the last thing on your mind. And it's just terrible, with everything else that you've gone through lately, to have to postpone your wedding as well. So, well, we took care of everything for you!"

"What?" Mercy asked, her eyes wide with shock.

"We…oh, come see!" Martha said, grasping Mercy's hand and towing her out the door.

Mercy threw a terrified look at him over her shoulder.

"You might as well go along, since it concerns you, too," Mrs. DuVere said, laughing.

Gray would rather step into an erupting volcano than follow those women out the door but also couldn't seem to stop himself. Like barreling toward the edge of a waterfall, knowing full well you're about to go over but unable to do anything about it.

"You"—he pointed to Jason—"stay here and watch them," he said, flicking a finger toward the occupied cells.

"You got it, Sheriff," Jason said, taking a seat behind the desk.

*Sheriff.*

That was never going to sound right to him.

Gray trailed after the women with Doc and the preacher at his heels. Guess this was a town affair.

His curiosity was piqued when the women pulled Mercy into the tavern and up the staircase that led to the

second-floor parlor house. Doc followed them all
without problem, but Gray was amused to see the
obvious discomfort the preacher felt crossing the
threshold.

Gray took a look around once inside and wasn't all
that surprised to find it opulent but incredibly tasteful.
The most successful parlor houses, at least the ones he'd
visited, were usually decked out with all the comforts a
man might want. Desolation might be a small town, but
Mrs. DuVere obviously ran a profitable business. Or
she'd brought enough money with her from wherever
she'd come from to make it seem so. Either way, her establishment, dripping with velvet, damask wall coverings,
crystal lamps, and plush elegance was a welcome sight.

But the women didn't pause, continuing on through
the establishment's front rooms, through a plant-choked
conservatory, and out onto a balcony that overlooked a
tiled back patio.

Where a wedding arch covered in flowers and ribbons
had been set up.

Gray's heart damn near stopped beating.

A narrow aisle had been created with a few chairs on
each side, leading up to the arch. A few cloth-covered
tables sat nearby, and another longer table stood already
stacked with fine china dishes and cups.

Mercy stood looking around at everything, her mouth
open but completely speechless. His sentiment exactly.

"What do you think?" Martha said, her hands clasped
near her chest as she watched Mercy anxiously.

"I...I don't know what to say," she said. She took a few
deep breaths and seemed to pull herself together

somewhat. She grasped her friend's hand. "It's all beautiful, Martha, truly."

Martha's face immediately melted into a relieved vision of excited happiness. "Oh, I'm so glad you love it! See, you can descend from the back stairs here. We thought that might be better than coming out of the tavern, though you can if you think that would be easier. And coming down the stairs here would make such a pretty image."

"It's wonderful," Mercy said. "But...I...you did this for me?"

"Of course! You were saying that you didn't have time to deal with any of this, what with everything going on, and it's just not fair that you two..." Martha glanced at him and grinned. "I've got a cake all made up and the girls and I have been cooking all day."

"You have?" Mercy said, her voice noticeably fainter. "But you didn't even know we'd be coming into town today."

"We had plans to go fetch you both, but you beat us to it!" Martha giggled. "Everything is all ready. All we need is the bride and groom."

Gray's brain seemed to be encased in some sort of fog that refused to let him make sense of exactly what was going on. But from what he could make out...he was about to get married.

. . .

Mercy tried to swallow past her suddenly dry mouth. "Could you excuse us for just a minute?" she asked, her voice much fainter than she'd intended.

She forced a smile and grabbed Gray's arm, towing him behind her back into the house. Thankfully, the parlor house was full of secluded nooks and crannies, and she ushered him into a small, curtained alcove with a plush love seat and pulled him down with her.

"You don't have to do this," she said. "I know actually marrying me wasn't part of the deal."

Gray took a long, slow breath, his face unreadable. "I said I would if it came down to it."

Her stomach fluttered. "Yes, but I don't think either of us thought it ever *would* come down to it. I'm sure you didn't really mean it when you agreed."

"Didn't I?"

The quiet words reverberated in her head, sending her stomach spinning and her lungs struggling to drag in a breath. "You...you'd really marry me?"

"I said I would," he repeated. His eyes remained fixed on hers, but she couldn't begin to imagine what he was thinking. Feeling. Maybe there was nothing at all going on in his mind. Or maybe everything.

She put a hand to her forehead, trying to clear the sudden buzzing echoing in her ears.

"You did," she agreed. "But, if you've changed your mind... I mean, I know this was all supposed to be temporary. Just until Josiah is gone. Doing this..." She could barely force herself to say the word. "Marriage. It's a lot to ask... It'll be real. Permanent. And I know that wasn't part of the deal. So, I'm just saying, I'd understand if you..."

She blew out a breath, and he leaned forward. He

didn't touch her, but even being a few inches nearer made her heart beat hard enough she was sure he could hear it.

"I know most people don't have a very high opinion of me," he said, his voice gruff, a pain behind it that made her want to wrap her arms around him. "But I'm a man of my word. I said I'd help you. Josiah is still out there. So, I'm not done yet. And I said if it came down to it, I'd marry you for real. Well, it looks like it's come down to it."

"And if it all goes horribly wrong and we loathe the sight of each other within a month?"

He shrugged. "Then I hop on that lazy horse of mine, and we ride out of here. You stay a respectable married woman with the freedom to do whatever the hell she wants without everyone in town naggin' her to get a husband."

"And if I ever want to remarry?"

He shrugged again. "Tell people I died. It'll probably be the truth."

Mercy's stomach sank at the thought of anything happening to Gray, but she didn't have time to analyze the feeling to death just yet. First, she needed to figure out if she was getting married or not. She kept coming up with another dozen reasons why this was a bad idea. Though, getting out of it would cause a stir she really didn't want to deal with. Not that that was a reason to get married.

"The only real question is," Gray said, "do *you* agree to this?"

"Me?"

"Yes. You. If you don't want this, it doesn't happen. People will talk, but people will always talk. I don't care about them. You, however, are more than capable of killin' me in my sleep."

She gasped. "I would never."

He chuckled. "Don't be so sure. We don't know each other all that well yet, and I have no doubt that what you do know of me vexes you to no end."

"That's a fair point."

He gave her that crooked grin she couldn't help but return. Vexing, yes. But he could be kind of adorable when he wanted to be.

"All I'm sayin' is marriage lasts a long time even when you go into it willing," he said. "So. If you object, we tell them to mind their own business and go about ours as planned. If you don't object…" He shrugged. "Then I guess we go out there and get hitched."

She blinked at him. "Yes, but I'm sure I'm…" She gestured at herself. "I'm not…"

He cocked an eyebrow. "You're not what?"

She frowned, not sure if he was playing with her and just trying to make her say it or if he really didn't know what she was getting at. She had no illusions that she was a great beauty. No man would walk into a room and notice her first. Or even fifth or sixth. That hadn't bothered her too much in the past. She had her farm, her orchard, her friends. She only rarely noticed the lack of a husband, and it never lasted long. All in all, she'd grown content with her lot in life.

But Gray had traveled. Lived an exciting life. And was still a very handsome man, if a little worse for wear.

She had no doubt he had been with all sorts of beautiful women. They always flocked to dangerous men. And whatever else Gray was, he was definitely dangerous. When he could stay awake, that is.

She took a deep breath and said it all in a rush. "I'm probably not the type of woman you expected you'd marry."

His eyes widened. "Mercy, I'm a gunfighter. I never expected I'd marry at all, or even live long enough for the thought to cross my mind."

Her shoulders sagged. Partly in relief, though there was more than a little disappointment, too. At what, she didn't want to examine too closely. What had she expected him to do? Declare his undying love and admiration? He barely knew her. He was only in this spot because she'd badgered him into it, and he was apparently too honorable (who knew?) to back out. And besides, did she even want him to go waxing poetic? She barely knew him, either, and what she did know was…well, colorful, to say the least.

"Hey," he said, startling her out of her thoughts. He touched her chin, lightly turning her face to look at him more fully. "I know I couldn't have ever expected all this to happen. But if I do have to be saddled with a wife…" That lopsided grin of his took the sting out of his words and sent her stomach careening again. "Well, you aren't such a bad choice."

Mercy laughed. "Aren't you just the flatterer."

His grin widened. "I mean it. You're strong, brave, smart, and stubborn as a mule. That's a compliment, by the way," he added when she gasped. Then he just stared at her for a heartbeat, as though he wasn't sure what to say or wasn't sure if he should say it. Finally, he shook his head. "Your eyes are the exact color of a field of bluebells I passed once. Soft blue but with flecks of gold like when the sun hits 'em. And when you get your dander up, they flash pure fire."

She no longer worried if he'd hear her heart. Because it had just stopped altogether.

He shrugged. "Maybe it won't be so bad. It's been a while since I knew where I'd be lying my head every night."

Mercy's cheeks flushed hot with the sudden realization that as her husband he might have the expectation of laying his head beside hers. Their engagement might have been fake, but this marriage would be very real. And he would be well within his rights to expect it to be real...in every way. And...she wasn't sure she hated that idea.

"Of course, you can't cook worth a damn, but with Martha feeding me lunch, at least I'll be sure of one decent meal every day," he said.

"Oh!" She shoved him and he chuckled, capturing her hand. And then he pressed a kiss to the back of it.

She sucked in a breath. For an inept, laze-about, retired killer, he could certainly be charming when he wanted to be.

"So?" he asked.

She slowly released her breath and stood. "All right, then. Let's go get hitched."

• • •

As soon as she agreed, Gray's stomach dropped into his boots. He hadn't really expected her to say no. She needed him. Josiah was still out there, ready to pounce. Gray now held four of his men and Josiah wasn't going to let that go unanswered. If anything, the threat from Josiah was even worse.

However, he hadn't really expected her to say yes, either. Sure, she still needed his help, but marriage was a damn permanent way to go about getting it. They probably should have had a longer discussion about what each expected after the I do's. He had never expected to find himself married, that was damn sure, but since it was about to happen, he also saw no reason to not take advantage of some of the more entertaining benefits. Might have been a good idea to ask Mercy where she stood on all that before they were legally bound for the rest of their lives.

Aside from that, their situation probably wouldn't change much. He assumed she would allow him to move into the main house. But if not, he would stay in his little bungalow, which was comfortable enough—if he could get rid of Jason—and they would go on as they had been.

Once Josiah was taken care of, they could see where they stood. He could always move into the apartment above the jailhouse if they got on each other's nerves too much.

It struck him again just how little they knew about each other. How had she made it to her age—which come to think of it, he didn't actually know precisely, though he figured she was somewhere in her late twenties or early thirties. But how had a single woman not in the employ of Mrs. DuVere made it to her age without a husband? Women were scarce in the West, especially in towns like Desolation. So, there would have been no shortage of suitors for her hand no matter her looks or disposition.

Not that she was lacking in either of those areas, despite her apparent thoughts to the contrary. She might not be what some called a classic beauty, but she carried herself in a way that demanded admiration and attention. She'd certainly captured his from the moment he'd clapped eyes on her, and that was something very few managed to do.

Her temperament could use a little work. Or maybe he just brought out the pigheaded side of her. The woman was certainly used to being in charge. Then again, she was efficient and organized and got the job done, so it wasn't a bad place for her to be. He hated someone telling him what to do, but he couldn't deny the results when she was the one holding the reins. Not that he would ever tell her that.

Well. What's done was done. They'd both agreed. And now…he was about to get married. Dear God, help them both.

As soon as they walked out to join the others, they were surrounded. Mercy was whisked off by the ladies who had immediately started chattering about the perfect dress one of the girls had and a bunch of other lady stuff that his ears immediately shut out. Martha had sent Doc Fairbanks over to her shop to assist her apparently elderly grandparents in finishing with food preparation. The preacher was doing whatever preachers did before the wedding ceremonies. And Jason had been given the task of getting Gray cleaned up and presentable. Poor sod.

Doc had graciously offered the loan of one of his suits, of which he apparently owned several, as well as the use of his home for the ordeal. Jason hauled him into the bedroom and pointed him at the ewer and basin, slapping a bar of soap and a towel in his hand.

"Wash," he said, his tone unusually confident. And bossy.

"I had planned on it," Gray said, glaring at him. He hadn't really planned on it, but after a glance in the mirror above the dresser, he'd grudgingly conceded he could probably use a little sprucing up. He *had* just bathed the other day, though, so he wasn't as bad as he might have been.

Once he was clean enough to please Jason, he pulled on the doc's suit, which fit him better than expected. He finished the last button on the vest and then pulled on the jacket, crossing his arms a few times to get a feel for the fit. It would do.

Jason handed him his new badge, and Gray glared at it with distaste. "Is that really necessary?"

"You *are* the sheriff now."

Gray sighed and pinned it to his vest. "Speaking of which, who is watching our prisoners?"

"Frank," Jason said, looking him over with a frown.

"And who is Frank?"

Jason raised his eyes and his lips twitched. This couldn't be good.

"Well, from what I understand, he's sort of the town drunk."

Gray blinked at him. Slowly. "And that's who you thought would be appropriate to watch the prisoners?"

Jason shrugged. "Not really, but no one else volunteered. Besides, Frank promised he wouldn't drink until after I come back to relieve him, and Doc said he's reliable, mostly, if you catch him early enough in the day. I'll head over after the festivities and stay the night there. Figured you two would want a little privacy."

Gray frowned. "You keep waggling those eyebrows at me, and I'm going to shave them off."

Jason laughed, but he stopped it with the eyebrows. He glanced over Gray again, his amusement fading.

"What?" Gray asked, holding his arms out while Jason surveyed him with a slight frown. Gray looked down at himself. "Doesn't it look all right?"

Jason tapped his finger against his chin. "The suit looks great. We just need to do something about…" He gestured to encompass Gray's face and hair. "All that."

"What do you mean? I'm clean."

"Yes, but it probably wouldn't hurt to run a comb through your hair."

Gray waved him off. "What's the point of that? It'll just be covered up anyway." He slapped his hat on his head, pushing it down tight.

Jason shook his head. "You can't wear your hat during the wedding ceremony."

Gray narrowed his eyes. "I'm wearin' my hat."

Jason sighed. "Fine. But you could at least get a shave."

Gray rubbed a hand over the several days' growth of whiskers on his cheeks. Fine. Sunshine might have a point there, but he hated to give the little twit the satisfaction of admitting it.

"Come on," Jason said. "There's a barbershop just across the street. My treat."

He grinned. Gray groaned. But he followed him across the street without further argument. For himself, he wouldn't bother. But Mercy might appreciate his effort. Not that he normally put any stock in what anyone else thought of him. But…since she seemed to be going through the effort of getting all gussied up herself, it might be kind of nice to surprise her with his own fancification.

He took a deep breath, gave himself a mental slap, and opened the door of the barbershop.

The barber's eyes widened when he entered, but aside from a slight stammer in his voice when he said "welcome," the man didn't cause a fuss.

"Right this way, Mr. Woodson," he said, leading him to a chair. "Sorry. Sheriff."

Gray opened his mouth to protest and then remembered that he was, indeed, the new sheriff. That was going to take some getting used to.

It had been a while since he'd had anyone else shave him. Letting strange men near him with razor blades was a hazard he tended to avoid. Aside from an initial tremor or two, the barber did a quick and admirable job of it. The whole process had actually been kind of nice. Enough so that he agreed to a haircut as well. Since his last haircut had been accomplished with a pair of rusty scissors and without the assistance of another person or a mirror, he was probably due.

Even with the extra services, the whole ordeal was finished rather quickly and had left Gray feeling damn near relaxed. And his appearance…

He froze, not recognizing the man who stared back at him from the mirror. With his hair tamed and the whiskers gone, he could fully see his face for the first time in years. There were more lines there than he remembered. A few more grays mixed in with the darker strands of his hair. But the shadows were gone from under his eyes. His mouth wasn't pinched, and his brow wasn't furrowed in a frown. He actually looked a bit…younger. Even… happier?

The thought brought his frown back. He didn't trust happy. Certainly not after so short a time. Desolation seemed like the answer to all his problems. Isolated, with townspeople friendly enough to welcome him but with enough of their own secrets they didn't judge his. But Gray had been fooled before. Appearances were deceiving. Always. And he'd be wise to remember it.

"Now that's a definite improvement," Sunshine said, his irritating smile back in place. "Except for the scowl. Try and get rid of that before your bride walks down the aisle. Oh," he said, glancing at his pocket watch, "we'd better hurry. It's almost time."

The blood drained from Gray's face. His *bride*. Who would be walking down the aisle toward *him*. Within minutes.

For the first time in a very long time, he rethought his rule against drinking. A shot of something strong sounded very, very good just then.

But Jason didn't give him time for that, and suddenly

Gray found himself out of the barbershop and in the lush, newly festooned back courtyard of the parlor house before he could draw a steady breath. The preacher nodded at him, though there was still a hint of disapproval behind his dark eyes. Gray tugged at the collared shirt that suddenly seemed a hair too tight. Then he turned to Jason. He couldn't do this. What had he been thinking?

Before he could get out a word, though, a fiddle struck up a screeching version of the wedding song, and Jason shoved a daisy in Gray's buttonhole. Then he turned him back to face the aisle—and the absolute vision of loveliness who clutched a bouquet of wildflowers, slowly making her way to him.

Or she *had been* walking down the makeshift aisle. But one look at him standing in front of the preacher and she'd frozen right where she was, about halfway between him and the door behind her.

Gray's breath caught in his throat. What was she doing?

# CHAPTER TWELVE

Mercy's heart pounded so hard, her head swam. Gray had turned away for a second, and then Jason spun him around, and he saw her and…froze.

She did, too, waiting on him before she made another move. He seemed in shock. Terror, maybe? Horror? Maybe she didn't look as he'd expected. She'd felt pretty enough a few moments before. But if he didn't make some sort of movement in the next thirty seconds, she was running back the other direction.

His gaze took her in, from the top of her carefully curled hair crowned with a ring of daisies, down the tightly laced corset of the bustled, baby-blue silk gown Mrs. DuVere had pulled out of her own closet, to the soft leather boots with rows of pearl buttons. And back up again.

His eyes met hers, and she held her breath. A slow smile spread across his full lips and took her breath away completely.

She started walking toward him without even realizing she'd decided to move. He looked good. Really good. The suit he wore fit him like a glove, highlighting angles she hadn't known he'd possessed. He ran a hand through his hair, which had previously brushed his shoulders in jagged, unkempt edges. Now it gleamed like polished mahogany and fell back in waves behind his ears. Which she could clearly see, because the hat that seemed at times permanently affixed to his head was now held tightly in his hands.

His face was the most transformed of all, though. Whatever they had done to him seemed to have washed several years from his countenance. For the first time, he seemed...alive. Vital. She was sure the change was temporary. Give the man a rocking chair and a quiet porch, and she had no doubt he'd be snoring in seconds. But for the moment, her handsome groom stood tall and straight, watching her come toward him with what she swore was pride in his eyes.

When she reached him, he passed his hat to Jason and held out a steady hand to her. She took it with one only slightly less steady.

"You look beautiful," he said, his voice pitched low for her and her alone.

Her breath caught in her throat, and she swallowed hard. "You clean up pretty well yourself."

He ran a hand down the suit. "It's nice, isn't it?" He leaned in closer. "I might just keep it. Don't tell Doc."

She giggled—giggled! She had never made that sound in her life. And then they both turned to Reverend Donnelly.

The reverend thankfully didn't drone on with any preliminaries but got right to the vows. They each repeated the words in surprisingly steady voices. When it came time to receive her wedding ring, Gray reached back for his hat and removed a small gold ring from the band, slipping it onto her finger. She made a mental note to ask him later where it'd come from.

Then, with a voice so warm and smooth, it washed

over her like a fine whiskey, he repeated the preacher's words. "With this ring, I thee wed. With my body, I thee worship."

His hand squeezed hers, and her heart jumped into her throat. Oh, heaven help her, they were really doing this.

The ceremony was a blur after that. She'd barely heard the words the reverend spoke as she instead focused on her hands in Gray's, on his thumbs gently rubbing over her fingers. He held tight to her the whole time, whether as a comfort or to keep her from bolting, she wasn't sure. But she was grateful for them all the same. Then it was over, and they turned again to face the reverend.

"I now pronounce you man and wife," he said with a relieved smile, then nodded at Gray. "You may now kiss your bride."

Gray tugged gently on her hands, gazing down at her as he tugged her nearer, giving her time to back away if she wished.

She wasn't sure what she wished. But she didn't pull away.

He wasn't soft or gentle. Like with most other things he tried to avoid, once committed to action, he dove in with everything he had. His lips molded to hers, one hand coming up to cup her face and bring her even closer as the other gripped the back of her dress in a fist. Her head swam and she wrapped her arms around his waist to anchor herself. The sensation of his full, warm mouth against hers was unlike anything she'd ever experienced. And she *had* been kissed before. And kissed well. But no one had ever sent her spinning with just one touch of their lips. So warm and demanding she'd feel the heat of them long after he pulled away.

Only the cheers of their audience broke them apart. Mercy had forgotten anyone else was there. Her cheeks flashed hotly, but Gray didn't seem at all embarrassed. Of course, he wouldn't be. He curved an arm about her waist and kept her close to him as they walked back down the aisle.

They couldn't leave yet. Not with the feast Martha and her grandparents had prepared. And that was probably a good thing. Part of Mercy—a very happy part of her—would love to hop in their wagon and head straight back to her homestead. But the rest of her needed a few minutes to try and calm the nervous energy that made her want to run in circles around the room the way her cat had when it had gotten in the catnip.

Plus, there was the matter over what to do with Jason. He couldn't stay at her farm forever, though she enjoyed having him around. He offset Gray's moodiness nicely and was always happy to help out with whatever needed doing. And he'd been handy when Josiah's men had shown up—had it just been that morning? All the events of the day descended on her, and she was suddenly and overwhelmingly bone-tired.

Martha pushed Mercy and Gray into seats of honor at the table, and Mercy watched in a daze as food was passed up and down between the guests. By the time they were done, she had a plate loaded with food that she didn't remember choosing, but an untimely growl from the direction of her stomach reminded her what she should be doing with it. And the food did go a long way to restoring her equilibrium.

She stole a glance at Gray as she nibbled on her second leg of chicken. He caught her gaze and winked, raising his glass of lemonade to her in a salute. Bemused, she shook her head, though she couldn't help smiling.

Where had her slovenly, complaining ol' retired gunslinger gone?

She had no doubt the moment the wedding finery came off and the guests had cleared, he'd return to his usual ways. He was who he was. And, as aggravating as he could be, Mercy didn't think she'd mind it much. He certainly livened things up anyway. Well, *livened* was a strong word considering his propensity for falling asleep at the drop of a hat. Interesting, then. He made things interesting.

And then she remembered what else would be happening when the wedding finery came off and choked on her chicken.

Gray thumped her on the back. "You're meant to chew that before swallowin'," he pointed out.

Ah, there was the man she'd gotten to know. "Wiseacre." She wiped her mouth and waved off another attempt to beat the chicken from her throat. "I'll keep that in mind," she rasped out, downing half a glass of lemonade.

The setting sun glinted off her wedding ring and she held it out, admiring the gold band with its delicate engraved pattern of entwined daisies circling around it.

She caught him watching her and blushed. "It's so lovely. Where did you get it on such short notice?"

He took a large gulp of lemonade before he answered her, though even then he didn't meet her eyes. "It was my mother's. I always carry it with me in my hat band. She gave it to me the night she died, said to give it to my wife when I married." He shrugged. "I always figured it'd be buried with me and my hat." He glanced at her with a half grin that did funny things to her belly. "I think she'd be happy to know you've got it."

Mercy's heart swelled until she could scarcely breathe. And when he looked up at her from beneath his lashes, as though he was unsure of her reaction, she just wanted to wrap her arms around him and protect him from whatever, or whoever, had put that look on his face.

"It's beautiful," she managed to say past the lump in her throat. "I'm honored to wear it. I'll keep it safe, I promise."

His small half smile tore at her heart. Then he picked up her hand and pressed a kiss to the finger that wore the ring, and her heart damn near exploded. "It suits you."

She stared at him, trying to blink away the moisture in her eyes—really what was going on? Her emotions were all over the place.

The fiddler who had played their wedding march picked up his instrument again and began to play a jig.

"Bride and groom!" Martha shouted, waving them over to the makeshift dance floor.

Mercy glanced at Gray, who raised a brow and said, "I do *not* dance."

Her response broke off in a peal of surprise when Martha grabbed her hands and pulled her out onto the patio. She tried to keep an eye on Gray as she was pulled and twirled. After a few moments, she was laughing and breathless.

And then a sudden spin brought her face-to-face with Gray, who stood staring down at her with a look that set fire to her body.

"I thought you didn't dance," she managed to say.

His long, slow smile sent her knees quaking. "I don't," he said.

Then he scooped her up in his arms and marched out of the courtyard, accompanied by the whoops and applause of their guests, and a mess of butterflies set loose in her belly as she realized what would happen next.

# CHAPTER THIRTEEN

Gray might have been huffing and puffing, but he made it to the wagon—barely—before he put Mercy down. He couldn't lie; he was a bit proud of himself. It had been a while since he'd hauled anything of any size that far. And dropping his new bride on her rear end an hour after their nuptials would have sent the wrong message, surely. Actually lifting her into the wagon, though, wasn't going to happen, but he did hold out a hand to help her up onto the bench before he followed her up.

"What about Jason?" she asked.

Gray grimaced, annoyed she asked about the other man, though he had no reason to be.

"He's sleepin' at the jailhouse tonight. Keepin' an eye on the prisoners."

"Oh," she said, her cheeks flushing. "We'll be alone, then."

He pulled himself into the wagon and grabbed the reins. It had to be a sign of how flustered she was that she didn't insist on driving the horses as she usually did. He was a bit flustered himself. He was no blushing virgin, but—he looked in horror at his new wife, suddenly realizing she very well might be.

"Have you...are you..." Damn. There really wasn't a delicate way to ask a woman that question.

Mercy glanced at him, her brow creased. "Am I what?"

He took a deep breath. *Just say it, man!*

"Are you a virgin?"

Mercy's mouth dropped open before she tilted her head higher. "No."

Gray's shoulders sagged in relief, and she looked at him, thoroughly confused. "Is that a problem?" she asked him.

"Hell no!" he said so loudly she laughed. He broke into a grin. "Sorry. I just...I wouldn't have any idea what to do with a virgin."

Mercy raised a brow. "I expect the same thing you'd do with someone who wasn't. Just, a little more carefully."

Gray snorted. "Point taken."

She regarded him for a moment and then shook her head. "You truly don't mind?"

"No, I meant it. I'm relieved."

"Well, that's a first," she muttered.

At his questioning glance, she sighed. "The first man I was with was my fiancé. I was sixteen. Young, naïve. In love." She shook her head. "We didn't wait until the wedding night. And then he broke off the engagement. Said he couldn't marry a girl who would give herself away before being wed."

Gray gaped at her, truly astounded. "He was an asshole."

That surprised a sharp laugh out of her. "That he was."

"And since then?" he asked. He didn't want to pry, but knowing exactly how experienced she was would help him out a lot.

She looked out ahead of them, watching the land slip by as they rode. "There was another since then. Not great. But I know what to expect."

Gray grunted. Hardly a rousing recommendation of her past lovers. But at least she wasn't a total novice. At the basics, in any case. He might have his work cut out for him.

Though, this was definitely one time he didn't mind at all.

They pulled into the courtyard of Mercy's house, and Gray hopped down, hurrying around to the other side of the wagon so he could help her. He raised his arms and after a second's hesitation on her part, she put her hands on his shoulders so he could lower her to the ground. Which he did as slowly as possible. For one, he didn't want to drop her. But mostly, he wanted to feel her as she slid down his body to the ground. Wanted her to feel him. And from the glazed look in her eyes by the time her toes touched the ground, she had.

"Welcome home, wife."

She shivered in his arms, though the night wasn't cold. And judging by the heated look in her eyes it had nothing to do with fear. A flash of pure male pride that he could cause that reaction in her with little more than a few words had him swinging her into his arms again so he could carry her into the house.

"What are you doing?" she asked, clinging to his shoulders.

"Carrying the bride over the threshold is a tradition, I believe."

"Yes, but you really don't have to…"

"Mercy."

"What?"

"Just shut up and let me carry you into the house."

She narrowed her eyes, but the corners of her lips were pulling into a smile. And she stopped trying to argue. Probably the fastest she'd ever conceded an argument. He had no notions such a miracle would continue, but he'd enjoy it while it lasted.

It turned out it was more difficult to enter a house with your arms full than he'd thought. She finally reached down and opened the door, giving it a good shove as she did so. He turned sideways so they'd fit through the door and then kicked it closed behind them. And then...he stood there. Holding his wife in his arms in the home that had been hers but was now, permanently, *theirs*.

His heart thudded in his chest, hard enough she could probably feel it beneath her fingertips. But he still didn't put her down.

She glanced at him, brows raised. "I think you can put me down now."

He grinned and held her tighter. "I don't know. I think I kind of like you like this."

She squirmed. "I'm too heavy for you. You'll pull something or strain your muscles."

He shrugged as well as he could with her in his arms. "My muscles could probably do with a little more strain." When her eyes widened, he hastened to add, "A little more. Don't go getting any grand ideas."

"Oh, perish the thought," she said, bringing another smile to his lips.

He carried her a little farther into the house and then gently lowered her to the ground. But he didn't release her. "You looked very beautiful today. These were a nice touch." His finger trailed over the crown of daisies still in her hair. They'd been his favorite flower ever since he was a little boy. His mother had always had them in the house when she could. It was one of the few things he remembered about her. So, to see them in Mercy's hair at their wedding... He gritted his teeth, not wanting to show any of the emotion that clambered at him.

"It was very kind of Mrs. DuVere to loan me such a fine gown," Mercy said, smoothing her hands over the material. "I've never worn anything so beautiful."

Gray's knuckles brushed across her cheek. "You should always be draped in silk and jewels."

Her eyes rose to his in surprise, but he wasn't quite brave enough to meet her gaze. "I probably won't be able to give you everything you deserve," he said, trying to find a way to say what he wanted without coming across too strongly. "But everything I have is yours."

"Gray." Her voice cracked, thick with emotion.

"Don't get too excited," he said. "The sum total of my possessions is two guns and a pain-in-the-ass horse."

Mercy's laugh filled the room, a sound that never failed to make him smile, and he wrapped his arms around her waist and drew her closer. She gasped as he brought their bodies flush against each other.

"Are you sure you still want to be my wife in truth?" he asked, not knowing what answer he wanted to hear the most. If she was wise, she'd say no, because getting deeper involved with him was never a good idea for anyone. But he was honest enough to admit, to himself at least, that he wanted her to say yes. Because he needed her. Desperately.

He held his breath as she trailed her hands up his arms to circle his shoulders. She pressed herself even closer and rose on her tiptoes until her mouth was a breath away from his.

"I said yes when the reverend asked me all those questions, Gray," she said. "I meant it. Make me your wife."

He didn't wait for her to ask again. He captured her lips, his mouth moving over hers with an urgency he could no longer control, as he scooped her into his arms again and walked into her bedroom. But if he'd worried that his exuberance would frighten her, he shouldn't have.

As he lowered her feet back to the ground, she returned his kiss with a passion that both startled and amused him. When he licked at her lips, she immediately opened to him and he delved inside, tasting and exploring every bit of her. Her arms tightened around his neck, trailing up to tangle in his hair. And when a quiet whimper escaped her lips, Gray groaned, crushing her to him, staking a claim with his kiss that had her clutching at him with a passion that spurred his own.

He didn't let up, moving his mouth to trail down the column of her throat. She dragged in a shaky breath, tilting her head to give him better access. And when his hand curved around her buttocks and squeezed, bringing her up against the hard length of him, she gasped and ground herself against him.

"Damn, woman," he groaned into her neck. "You keep that up and I won't last ten seconds."

"Well, we'll just have to work on your stamina," she

said, kissing a burning path across his jawline while her fingers tugged at the bowtie Sunshine had meticulously tied what seemed like days ago.

He snorted and pulled her closer again. "I'll admit there are many things I need to work on. But stamina is not one of them."

She shrugged and pushed his jacket from his shoulders. "All I've got to go on is what I've seen since you've been here and—"

He cut her off with a searing kiss that had her swaying in his arms. When he finally pulled away, they were both breathless, chests heaving. "Judging me on my performance during chores is unfair."

His fingers fumbled at the interminable row of tiny buttons on her bodice. "Hmm," she said, unbuttoning his vest and pushing it off his shoulders. "I don't know. One could consider performing your husbandly duties as a chore."

He snorted. "Sweetheart, any man who counts making love to his wife as a chore isn't worth the ink on the marriage license."

Before she could respond to that, he growled in frustration and pushed away from her.

"Wha—?" she sputtered as he marched from the room.

"Stay there, I'll be right back," he said and walked away.

He marched across the small house straight to the kitchen, where he selected the sharpest knife he could find, and then hurried back to the bedroom. Mercy's eyes widened and she took a step back when he came at her with the knife raised.

"What are you doing?" She raised a hand to ward him off, though he was pleased to see she didn't look afraid. More curious and a bit exasperated.

He pointed at her bodice with the knife tip. "I'm cutting that damn dress off you."

He stepped forward, and she warded him off again, this time with a laugh. "You are not cutting up Mrs. DuVere's gown. She'd never forgive me. Just...give me a minute."

She got to work on the buttons, making much quicker work of them than he had.

"If you're impatient, you could work on these," she said as she settled onto the side of the bed and stuck out a foot clad in a small-heeled boot that was also fastened with a dozen or two buttons.

He hadn't paid much attention to women's fashion other than to admire the way a woman looked while wearing it. But he'd never actively hated women's clothing until that moment. There were so many damn layers, he'd probably age another year before he got them all off.

He had removed one of her boots by the time she'd finished with her bodice. She stood to unfasten her corset, so, for expediency's sake, Gray shoved his head under her skirts to continue working on the second boot.

Mercy let out a tiny shriek. "What are you doing?"

"Getting your other boot off."

Before she could respond, he managed to undo enough buttons to remove the second boot about the same time that her corset hit the ground. It was also about that moment that he realized what an amazing opportunity being beneath her skirts afforded him.

He grinned, glad she couldn't see it, because he had no doubt the expression was filled with a hedonistic delight that might offend her if not downright frighten her. But he was like a starving man being presented with a feast. And he was determined to enjoy every bite.

. . .

Mercy had just dropped her corset and reached behind her to untie her skirt when the feather-light touch of Gray's fingers skimmed across her leg. She gasped.

"What are you doing?"

In response, she felt the garter ties holding up her stockings release. Gray wrapped his hands around her leg and dragged them downward, pushing the stocking down as they went. The sensation of his fingers on her skin was enough to set her heart pounding, and she reached for the bed frame to keep herself steady. But when his lips trailed across her inner thigh as he removed the second stocking, her knees buckled and she plopped onto the bed.

Gray didn't let up. Instead, he pressed closer, forcing her legs wider to accommodate him. She fought between the urge to squeeze them shut or open them completely. One would trap him against the most intimate part of her. But the other would give him full, unfettered access. Either option sent her blood roaring through her in a rush of desire.

He'd managed to remove both stockings, but he didn't emerge. Instead, his hands now inched their way upward.

"What are you doing?" she asked again.

He kissed her leg. "Exploring. Shh."

His breath when he shushed her blew gently against her over-sensitized skin and she jumped, her already strained breath catching in her throat.

"I..." Her voice came out in a squeak and she tried again. "I've gotten the bodice off. You can come out from underneath there now," she said, wanting to stop him from doing whatever he had planned while at the same time her body wanted nothing more than to urge him forward.

"I'll be just a minute," his muffled voice said from beneath her skirts.

"Gray." Her voice shook as he found the edge of her bloomers and pulled them off, and she didn't know if she was pleading with him to stop or to continue, or if she'd uttered his name because it was the only word she could remember just then.

She dragged in a breath, trying to get some much-needed oxygen into her body. "You don't need to do that part. I think I can manage."

It probably would have sounded more convincing if her voice hadn't been so faint.

"But I've already begun," he said, his lips continuing their torturous path along her inner thigh before she could dredge up a coherent thought. "And I really don't mind."

His mouth moved even higher up her thigh until he reached her aching center. Surely, he couldn't mean to—

He pressed a kiss to her core that made her gasp and jerk backward with a startled yelp. He emerged and leaned forward, planting one hand on either side of her hips as she sat on the edge of the bed.

"Trust me," he said, capturing her mouth in another searing kiss that had the room spinning. "Trust me," he murmured again against her lips. He looked at her, waiting for a response, and when she finally nodded, his face lit up like it had when Martha had handed him the cherry pie.

He ducked back beneath her skirts, his mouth retracing its path along her inner thighs. He took his time to get back to her center, only this time he did not pause, just pressed a kiss to her aching core. She sucked in a tremulous breath, her hands fisting in the quilt beneath her. When his tongue darted out to taste her, she lost her wits altogether.

"Gray! Wait, wait, stop." She squirmed against him, though she wasn't sure if she was trying to escape or get closer.

He flipped her skirts up. "What? I'm busy."

She tried to choke back a laugh, but with his hair standing a bit on end and his face red, either from his exertions or the airless confines of the depths of her skirts, she couldn't know. Though she was fairly sure her own face was just as red.

"I know, but you…you can't just…"

His eyes flashed, and he crawled on the bed as she scrambled back. "I can't?"

She shook her head, though her body trembled with anticipation as he loomed over her.

"And why can't I?" he asked, his face going absolutely predatory as he wedged his body between her legs again.

"Because, it's not...decent," she gasped out, writhing against him.

The vibration of his laughter, his hips pressing into her, had her arching off the bed. "Then it's a good thing I'm not a decent man."

And with that, he moved back down beneath her skirts. Who knew her husband was capable of such relentless determination? God bless him.

She wanted to argue more, but everything in her world narrowed down to focus on *him*. That decadent sensation of his tongue that drove her wilder with every caress. She thrashed beneath him, the part of her that was embarrassed quickly overtaken by the growing demand of her body.

She'd been caught in a lightning storm once. The bolts had struck all around and one in particular had struck far too close. Just before it had hit, she'd been filled with an energy that made every inch of her tingle with a power she wasn't sure her body could contain. She was sure she'd be incinerated on the spot.

That moment paled in comparison to the sensations Gray created within her.

Her hips bucked beneath his mouth, trying to draw him in closer as the exquisite pressure built within her with such intensity that it bordered on pain. And when his fingers joined in, she lost all control. Her body took over completely, and she ground herself against him, chasing that crest that was just out of reach. Gray redoubled his efforts and the building wave finally crashed over her, pulsing through her until she threw her head back with a cry that was half laughter and half a sob of pure pleasure.

Gray reemerged from beneath her skirts with a look of such heat that she sucked in a breath.

"Don't ever be embarrassed by somethin' that brings you pleasure," he said, fixing that steely gaze on her. "Understood?"

She nodded, still struggling to pull air into her tortured lungs.

"Good." He pulled her to him, his mouth crashing down on hers. She could taste herself on his tongue, but it just made her movements more frantic. Her hands gripped his shirt, while his fumbled with the ties of her skirt and petticoats.

"You do yours, I'll do mine," she said, too desperate to get her hands on him to wait for him to deal with the rest of her layers of clothing.

He grinned and nodded, quickly removing the rest of his clothing while she rolled away to deal with her skirt and petticoats. Then he stood back, letting her look her fill while his eyes roved over her. She had thought she'd be embarrassed in this moment, but she was so busy devouring the sight of him that she didn't give much thought to what he was seeing. Until she met his gaze. And then any misgivings she might have had were wiped away. Because the only thing in his eyes was heat and hunger and an admiration that she had never seen in any man before.

"My God, woman. You are breathtaking."

Her heart stuttered, and she drew in a tremulous breath. And then let her eyes rake over him. She'd seen bits and pieces of him before. But never the whole picture at once. The edges of him might not have been as hard as they once were, and he definitely didn't have the physique of a ranch hand who spent his days doing hard labor under the hot sun. But his shoulders were broad and strong, and he had a great wide chest that made her want to wrap her arms around him and cuddle in.

And the rest of him... Her eyes went wide at the evidence of exactly how pleased he was with his own view.

"You're quite impressive yourself," she said, her gaze taking in every inch of him.

He gave her that half smile she loved so much and reached out to pull her to him. The touch of his skin against hers sent her head spinning again, and she held on for dear life. He toppled them to the bed, and her startled giggle broke off in a gasp when his hand closed over her breast. When his mouth replaced his hand, closing over one pebbled nipple, her hand tangled in his hair, pulling him closer and keeping them captive.

He chuckled. "Always the bossy one?"

She panted out a laugh. "Complaining?"

"Never," he murmured, turning his attention to the other breast.

His hands and mouth explored every inch of her until she was ready to beg him for mercy. He finally moved over her, and just the brush of his hot length against her thigh had her lifting her hips to bring him closer.

"You're still sure?" he asked, the slight tremor in the arms he planted on either side of her betraying his inner storm.

She gripped his shoulders. "Please."

"You tell me if you need me to stop," he said. "We can take this as slow as you need."

In response, she lifted her hips, and when he moved too slowly, she gripped his surprisingly firm buttocks and urged him forward. She knew this first bit wasn't going to be the most pleasant, and she just wanted to get it over with.

He groaned and then buried himself in one hard thrust. She froze at the immediate discomfort, and he held still, letting her grow accustomed to the fullness that stretched her beyond anything she'd ever felt before.

"Easy, darlin'," he whispered. His voice was strained, but he leaned down and captured her lips, kissing her until she was whimpering beneath him.

He murmured things she barely listened to while his mouth and hands worshipped every inch of her, restoking the flames that had been licking at her since the moment they'd entered the house. Hell, since the moment he'd walked into her life. Even through his grouching and grumbling, every aggravating moment, in the back of her mind she'd wondered what it would be like to be with him like this. Even her most imaginative dreams couldn't compare to the real thing.

After a minute, she couldn't help but move against him, wanting, needing something more. He withdrew and then slowly pushed back in, watching her reaction as he moved. It was uncomfortable, almost too uncomfortable. She hadn't been a virgin, but she hadn't had much experience, and what little there was had been a very long time ago. And had been nothing like what Gray had shown her. She didn't want to stop now, though.

The more they moved together, the more that storm built inside her again. The discomfort from his unfamiliar body blended with the pleasure he drew from her with his lips and hands. God, he was destroying her one piece at a time, breaking down who she had been, who she thought she'd been. There was no escape from him. And she didn't want one. But it still terrified her. She'd never be able to walk away now, not as a whole person.

Her breath grew ragged, and she arched into him, her lips moving feverishly over his. He moved faster, harder, and when his thumb reached between them and found that sweet spot that begged for attention, a strangled cry escaped her throat. Two more strokes, three, and once again that wave of unimaginable pleasure washed over her, setting every nerve ending alight. Her toes curled and she grabbed the sheets in her fists to keep from raking her nails down his back.

He was right behind her, his rhythm faltering. And with a final thrust he followed her into the abyss. He lay there for a moment, his forehead resting on her shoulder as they both dragged in ragged breaths, their hearts thundering together. His weight was heavy on her, but she didn't mind. She kissed his neck, nipping a little, and he tangled his hand in her hair, tilting her face so he could capture her mouth in a slow, lingering kiss that seared her very soul.

He rolled to his side, but he took her with them, their limbs still entwined. Then he pressed another kiss to her lips, so gently she nearly forgot how to breathe.

"Are you all right?" he asked.

She let out a breathless laugh. "All right is not the

word I'd use." His brow furrowed, but before he could ask, she snuggled against him and kissed his chest. "That was…remarkable."

His body relaxed and he smiled up at her. "Well, I do aim to please." At her raised eyebrows, he added, "In here, anyway."

She laughed again. "This might just make up for the more aggravating aspects of your nature."

He gave her that lopsided grin she loved and kissed her again. "I guess I'll just have to make sure we do this on a regular basis then. In the interest of keeping up morale and building my stamina, of course."

"Of course," she said. "And speaking of stamina…"

She waggled her eyebrows at him, and he barked out a laugh.

"The spirit is willin', darlin', but you're going to have to give my body a few minutes to recover."

"Hmm, that's all right. I'll just amuse myself while you rest," she said, trailing her lips down his chest while her hands traveled farther down.

He sucked in a shaky breath. "You're goin' to be the death of me, woman." He wrapped his arms around her and rolled her back beneath him. "But what a way to go."

# CHAPTER FOURTEEN

Mercy watched Gray sleeping, still unable to believe that the man lying next to her was her husband.

Sleep smoothed out the lines in his face, the crinkles around his eyes, the constantly furrowed brow. And with the cleanup job he'd done the day before, he looked several years younger than she had originally thought. Even more so than yesterday. At their wedding.

She still couldn't believe that had happened. She frowned.

"What's that for?" Gray said, startling her. He smiled at her reaction and then smoothed a finger over the crease in her brow. "Last night wasn't that bad, was it?"

Heat rushed to her cheeks, and she ducked her head. "No, last night wasn't bad at all."

"Well, that's a rousing commendation, thank you," he said with a chuckle.

She grinned. "That's not what I meant. Last night was wonderful. Unexpected, but wonderful."

"Agreed." He leaned forward to press a gentle kiss to her lips. "So why do I wake this morning to find you frowning down at me?"

"It just occurred to me that we don't really know much about each other."

He raised an eyebrow. "That *just* occurred to you?"

She laughed. "I know that we haven't known each other long, but…I don't know. We don't even know general things."

"Such as?"

She shrugged. "I don't even know how old you are."

"Does it matter?"

"No. But I *am* curious."

"Fair enough. I'm forty-one. I think."

"You think?"

"It's not somethin' I generally keep track of and anyone who cared enough about me to keep track for me died off a long time ago. But I'm pretty sure."

The ache in her heart at the thought that he had no one who cared to celebrate his birth grew even worse at the offhand way he said it. Like it was a throwaway detail that meant nothing. She bit her lip, though. He wouldn't appreciate her pity.

"And you?"

She hated to admit her age and *hated* that she hated it. She didn't have anything to be ashamed of, though her age certainly put her in the "old maid" category. Even that bothered her less than the fact that everyone else seemed so bothered by it. As if not accomplishing the apparently one thing a woman should do by the time she was twenty was a horrible tragedy. She'd married Gray to keep Josiah at bay. But she wasn't ashamed to admit that she was thrilled it would end all the pitying looks and muttered reassurances from every other woman in town. Except Mrs. DuVere, of course. She could always be counted on to congratulate Mercy on escaping matrimony for so long.

"You don't have to tell me if you don't want to," Gray said, and she realized she'd been quiet for far too long.

"No, I don't mind," she said with a quick smile. "I just turned thirty last month."

He nodded, his brow creased a little, and her heart skipped a beat or two. "Does that disappoint you?" she asked.

He shrugged. "It wouldn't have been a bad thing had you been a little older."

Her eyes widened. "Most men seem to prefer a younger woman."

Gray snorted. "Age doesn't generally bother me one way or the other. You could be fifty years old and act like a child or be a child and act more mature than most adults. But if we were closer in age, maybe I wouldn't seem so ancient to you. I just don't want you to ever feel like you're married to an old man."

Her stomach did another flip. His concern about what she felt about his age was something that surprised her. Well, surprised her that he'd admit it, at least.

"As you said, age is just a number. If I was going to guess your age based on the way you've acted, for instance, I would've had to guess, oh...maybe eighty, eighty-five."

He laughed. A full-bellied, open-throated laugh that had her staring at him in shock. She liked the sound. A lot. It had just never occurred to her he was capable of that kind of mirth.

He laid back, his head cradled on a bent arm. "I suppose I do like my naps."

"That's the understatement of the year."

He chuckled again. "If there's anything else you'd like to know about me, you can ask," he said. "Although I think you know pretty much everything."

"Do I?"

He shrugged. "The important stuff, anyway. You know who I am, you know my background—"

"Not really."

Gray cocked an eyebrow. "No?"

She shook her head, and he told her what was probably the bare bones version of how he'd gotten into his first gunfight because of a hand of cards.

She sat up and looked down at him. "Wait. So, you basically became a notorious gunfighter by accident?"

He considered that for a second and then nodded with a wry grin. "I guess so."

She shook her head. "Only you could start out playing poker and end up on a wanted poster."

"Not true. Happens much more often than you'd think."

She laughed and laid back down. The morning sun glinted off her ring, and she frowned a little. "How did your parents die?"

"Scarlet fever."

"How old were you?"

"Eight? Maybe nine."

His voice didn't change, but the sudden tenseness of his body next to her spoke louder than anything else could have. She reached over and took his hand in hers. For a few moments, they laid there in silence, just being together.

"I don't know much about you, either," he said. "Less even, than you knew about me going into all this, since you'd at least heard of me."

She let go of his hand, retreating to her safe space. The questions had been anticipated. After all, she'd just interrogated him about his life. But somehow knowing the questions were coming and actually hearing them, knowing answers were expected—and owed—was entirely different.

Gray turned on his side and looked down at her. "You told me before that everyone in Desolation has their secrets."

She blew out a long breath, knowing where this was going and wishing she hadn't started it. "Yes."

"You know my secrets," Gray said. "And if I'm to protect you, it might help to know yours."

She didn't react for a second. He had a point. A good one. But she'd gone too many years avoiding talking about anything that had brought her to Desolation until opening up now wasn't easy.

"You can ask me what you'd like," she said. "I will try to answer."

Gray nodded, regarding her for a moment. "Who is buried in the orchard?"

Mercy froze. She didn't think he would start with that question. In fact, it hadn't occurred to her he would even wonder.

"My father. He was a good man but—the last few years, he often gambled to excess. Left me to take care of most things." She tried to swallow past the sudden lump in her throat. He deserved to be told the truth. "Everyone in town knew he was gambling away the money I'd earned working the farm—and I was ashamed. Ashamed of my own father." Her voice broke, yet she held his gaze.

"But I loved him, Gray. Faults and all, I loved him."

He took her hand and rubbed his thumb over her fingers. "How did he die?"

The rage that flashed through her veins made her hands shake, and Gray threaded his fingers through hers, giving them a squeeze.

She took a deep breath and slowly blew it out. "I found him facedown in the creek, his head bleeding. The sheriff said he must have fallen and cracked his skull, knocked himself too senseless to pull his face out of the water. But I know it was Josiah. Dad had crossed that creek a thousand times. He grew up here with a cousin of his, the one who left him the property. He knew every rock in that creek bed. And the timing was far too convenient. There's no way his death was an accident."

Gray brought her hand to his lips, kissing the back of it. "He won't get away with it," he promised.

Her eyes searched his and, after a moment, she nodded, apparently seeing what she needed to see. He only hoped he could follow through for her.

"So that's why you're in Desolation?" he asked. "Inherited a homestead?"

She looked at him and shrugged. "To begin with. But Desolation kind of grows on you," she said with a soft smile. "I liked the people. For the first time in a long time, I had a family again. And I had this place and my orchard. There's even a full river flowing through the property, so plenty of water for the trees. Everything seemed to be going well, but then Dad died and…you know the rest."

Gray's brow furrowed. "Everything except why Josiah

wants this place so badly."

"That, I truly don't know." Mercy sighed. "Then again, he's probably just a greedy landowner who wants to increase his property. It's good land, fertile, full-grown orchard on it that brings in a tidy income. And he does own most of the surrounding property. People have killed for less."

"That's true enough." He gave her hand a little tug, bringing it to his lips so he could press a heated kiss to it. "Thank you for telling me."

Mercy gave him a faint smile, still a bit embarrassed that she had told him so much. She reached out and brushed his hair from his face. "You know, you might like it here if you give it half a chance."

He gave her a slow grin that sent heat pouring through her veins. "There are some parts of it I like immensely." He wrapped an arm around her and pulled her close. Whatever else she was going to say evaporated from her mind the moment his lips touched hers. She'd remember later.

. . .

Gray woke a few hours later and reached out for his wife, only to find her empty pillow. He sat up, frowning, and rubbed his face, trying to wake up. A bit of a commotion seemed to be going on outside, and if he wasn't mistaken, Mercy's voice was in the thick of it. What had that woman gotten herself into now?

He yanked his pants and shirt on and pulled up his suspenders, shoving his feet into his boots as he headed for the front door. Which stood open. He hurried out and then stopped short at the sight that greeted him. Lucille the goat ran by, a bright blue ribbon around her neck, while Martha and Mercy chased after her.

"Don't let her get near the pen!" Mercy called out. "We'll have to bathe her all over again."

"I've got her!" Martha said, diving for the animal. She missed. Valiant effort, though.

They weren't the only ones in the courtyard. Mrs. DuVere and Preacher stood beside a wagon full of empty baskets and several more were trundling up in the distance.

"Mercy," he said, grabbing her arm when she ran past him again.

"Oh! Good mor...ning," she said, faltering at the sight of him standing with his open shirt flapping in the wind.

He started buttoning it, though he couldn't help the prideful smile that touched his lips at the sight of his wife staring at his bare chest. In fact, that look in her eyes made him want to take her hand and haul her back into the house only...

He looked around the courtyard again. "What is going on?"

"Apple picking day," she said with a wide grin.

"Apple picking day? What is that?"

She raised an eyebrow. "Well, when the apples are ripe enough to be harvested, we have to go and—"

He raised a hand, closing his eyes briefly against her smirk. "I know what it is. But why is it happening here, with..." He waved his hand at the growing crowd. "Half the town."

"Ah. Well, the townsfolk who wish to purchase apples come over and pick them themselves. They pay me by the basketful, or trade for them. It saves me from having to harvest them all myself, though I do deliver for some of the older folk who can't come out. And I also sell some of the fare from my garden, the soaps and lotions I make, goat cheese. And occasionally a few livestock, if I need to."

"Lucille?" he asked hopefully.

Mercy glared at him, though she seemed more amused than annoyed. "Lucille is not for sale. But she does like to look pretty for apple picking day."

Gray opened his mouth to respond to that and then decided he didn't have the energy.

"What about breakfast?"

She laughed. "Do you ever think about anything other than your stomach?"

He let his gaze rove over her, giving her a slow, heated smile when her cheeks flushed. "Actually, food was the last thing on my mind when I woke this morning. Except my wife was nowhere to be found."

"Sorry about that," she murmured. "We've had this day set for weeks. Couldn't change it, even though it's…"

"The day after our wedding," he said, capturing her hand.

She blushed again, and he went to pull her closer but caught a glimpse of several of the townspeople watching them and grinning. He dropped her hand, unwilling to put on a show for everyone.

She cleared her throat and brushed a curl out of her face. "Are you going to help?" she asked, gesturing to

Preacher's wagon full of baskets.

Gray frowned. "So…what about breakfast?"

Mercy laughed. "Chores first. Food later."

"What?" he asked, genuinely surprised. "Work before food? I need to keep my strength up."

"I think you'll be fine. And it'll be worth the wait, I promise. Martha has brought all sorts of goodies. Perhaps you could help her while I get everyone organized."

"Help her?"

"Yes. It looks like Lucille has gotten into the mud again. I'm sure she'd appreciate the help."

"You want me to wash a goat?" His raised brow should be a sufficient answer to that request, he hoped.

Mercy planted her hands on her hips. "Well, what other skills do you have that might be of use?"

He folded his arms across his chest. "I've got one skill, and unless you want me to shoot the goat, I don't think that skill is going to help much."

Mercy pinned him with her harshest glare. "You will not shoot my goat."

His lips twitched. "Then feed me, woman. I get cranky when I'm hungry."

She rolled her eyes at him. "Then you must be damn near starving most of your life."

He barked out a laugh that made most of the people in the yard turn to stare at him. Mercy just shook her head and pushed him toward the table where Martha had started setting up goodies. "Go see Martha. She'll feed you."

He caught her around the waist before she could escape. "And where are you going?"

She jerked her thumb over her shoulder. "I'm going to go rescue Mr. Sunshine before Lucille eats his jacket."

Gray glanced over to where Jason was engaged in a wicked episode of tug-of-war with the goat and his suit jacket and chuckled. Then he sighed. "All right. I'll... help," he said, forcing the word from his mouth. He'd had grand plans of lazing about in bed all day with his new wife, but apparently that wasn't going to happen. Maybe if he helped, they could get this whole event over with quicker and he could shoo everyone away all the faster.

"Thank you," Mercy said, rising on her toes to kiss him.

*Hmm.* Perhaps there was an upside to this whole helping thing.

He kissed her again. "Is there anything else you need me to do?" he asked, before he could stop himself.

"Maybe...keep an eye out for Josiah or his men."

The mention of Josiah killed the good mood that had been brewing. "Does he usually attend this...apple picking day?"

Mercy shook her head. "He never has before. Occasionally some of the women from his property will come. For the most part, though, he stays away. But..."

He nodded. "But he's not acting as he usually does."

"Exactly."

Gray took a deep breath. "You go do what you need to do. I'll watch for Josiah."

Her whole body relaxed, like he'd taken a literal weight off her shoulders. "Thank you, Gray." This time she quickly kissed his cheek and spun away before he could draw her back in. She gave him a cheeky smile and wave as she hurried off.

For probably the millionth time, he wondered how he'd gotten into this mess. Well, no help for it now. He was neck deep. So, he'd better do what he'd been brought here for and watch for Josiah.

After he got some food first. He hated killin' on an empty stomach.

# CHAPTER FIFTEEN

Mercy placed a plate of brown scrambled eggs and several lumps of meat that Gray assumed were sausage in front of him with a sigh. It'd been only a day since the apple picking—and Martha's cooking—and Gray almost wanted to suggest they do it all again just so they could have another decent meal.

"They're a little better than yesterday," she insisted.

She'd said the same thing every day since he'd arrived. He'd never been able to ascertain an improvement, but he wasn't going to tell her that. He shrugged and shoved a forkful in his mouth. "It's okay," he said after he swallowed. "I'm actually starting to like them this way."

Or maybe his taste buds had just given up and died. Either way, the taste was growing on him. Or at least not turning his stomach.

She shook her head, but the small smile on her lips sent a happy little buzz through him that both confused and exasperated him. His state of being was being entirely too mixed up with Mercy and her reactions.

She fixed herself a plate and sat beside him, and they ate in comfortable silence. He'd never considered himself the domestic type, and he certainly never fathomed that he would be a husband settled down with a wife and property. Plus the weight of the sheriff's badge on his chest hung heavily. He had most certainly never considered *that* development, either. But for some reason it didn't bother him as much as it should. Oh, he'd still rather pin the badge on Frank the town drunk than wear it himself. But now that he'd given his word to take the job…he didn't hate it as much as he'd anticipated he would.

Maybe it wasn't just the burned eggs he was getting used to…

After breakfast, he settled into his rocking chair on the porch and took a deep breath. Josiah and his men hadn't been seen or heard from since just before their wedding two days ago.

And Gray didn't trust that for an instant.

The man was being too quiet.

Men such as him didn't give up so easily. He had to be plotting something, and the longer it took for him to show his hand, the more antsy Gray got. If something didn't happen soon, Gray might go looking for trouble just so he didn't have to continue to wait for trouble to find him.

Birdie wandered by, munching what he assumed was another apple. He'd have to talk to Mercy about just letting her wander around the property, though the dumb animal seemed happy enough to stay in the courtyard where there was an abundance of water, sweet grass, and apples strewn about. Gray narrowed his eyes at the horse who blew a horsey raspberry at him and continued on her way, the goat—her new best friend—at her heels.

Gray shook his head and settled back. He still didn't quite trust his newfound contentment. Well, minus the sheriff job, though Jason had been taking care of things there for the last two days so the newlyweds could spend some time together. For the rest…he would be happy if things continued on as they were. Nights spent making love to Mercy, mornings spent eating and relaxing on his porch, evenings watching the sunset without having to look over his shoulder for whoever might be lurking there before taking Mercy back to bed… Now *that* he could get used to. That wasn't a bad life. The sheriff's job was another matter, as was Josiah Banff. But they weren't something he was going to think about just then. He closed his eyes and let the sun warm his face, his head pleasantly fuzzy.

He didn't know how much time had passed before a poke in the ribs brought him back around with a snort.

"Hey," Mercy said with a laugh. "You just woke up an hour ago. You can't possibly be napping already."

"You underestimate me," he grumbled.

"Oh, never that," she said with that dazzling smile of hers. "I have a present for you."

"Oh?" he said, perking up. He loved presents.

"Of a sort." She held out his guns, the ones he'd buried in the garden. "I dug them up after breakfast and cleaned them for you."

"I really need to get better at hiding these," he mumbled, reaching out to take them.

Mercy shook her head. "If you're going to be sheriff, you're going to need those. I promise I will not touch them without permission again."

He chuckled and slid them into the holsters that he still wore on his hips. The familiar weight of them against his sides eased an anxiety in him he hadn't realized he'd been feeling. Like it or not, they had been a part of him for a very long time. And while he was beginning to hope they wouldn't be such a necessary feature, he did feel more comfortable with them at his side.

"Thanks," he said, giving her that half grin that always made the heat rush to her cheeks. They didn't disappoint him, flushing a pretty rosy red. Well, if Mercy could bend a little, maybe he could try as well.

He cleared his throat. "Maybe I can teach you a few things. One of these days."

Her smile took his breath away. "That would be nice."

Damn, this woman would be his undoing. And he'd love every second of his downfall. He pulled her onto his lap, making her squeak in surprise, though she didn't protest. Instead, she settled against him, draping her arms about his neck.

"If you wanted me to come closer, you just had to say."

"Where's the fun in that?" He wrapped his arm about her hip to tug her against his chest, and she leaned in to kiss him without any further prompting. The small moan that escaped her when their tongues met sent his head spinning. That was the only excuse he had for not noticing that they were no longer alone.

"Well now, isn't this a pretty scene," Josiah said. "I hate to interrupt."

Mercy gasped and jumped from Gray's lap. Gray stood more slowly, keeping Josiah squared in his gaze while also watching the two men on either side of him. Josiah's eyes narrowed, focusing on Gray's chest.

"I heard we had a new sheriff," he said. "Pity the last one didn't stick around a little longer."

"I'm sure," Gray said. "It's such a hassle when law enforcement actually aims to enforce the law, isn't it?"

Josiah smirked. "And now we have an outlaw for a lawman. Now that's about the most damn ironic thing I have ever seen."

Gray ignored that. "What are you doing here, Josiah?" He tried to shift so that Mercy was behind him without being too obvious about it. Mercy, however, did not cooperate. Typical.

"You've got my men," Josiah said. "I'd like them back."

Yeah, Gray figured it was something like that. "I'm afraid they're a little indisposed right now, awaiting trial in my jail cells."

"You've got no cause to hold them."

Gray's eyes widened. "How do you reckon that? Your men attacked my wife on her property. Right in front of the sheriff, no less," he said, gesturing to himself.

Josiah scowled. "You weren't the sheriff when they did it. *If* they did it, that is. It's just your word against theirs."

"And mine," Mercy said. "And we have another witness as well."

Josiah shrugged. "I don't see how that makes any difference. For all anyone knows, you started it and they were just trying to defend themselves. From what I hear, they're not in very good shape and yet here you are, hale and hearty. Seems to me my men were the ones who were attacked that day."

"Just because they lost the fight doesn't mean they didn't start it."

"That's right," Josiah said, giving Gray a long, hard

look. "I've heard you don't like starting fights."

He said it as though it were some sort of insult, and his men snickered like their boss had just brutally put him in his place. But Gray had heard it all before. Like he was somehow less of a man because he didn't provoke fights. He shrugged, completely indifferent. "Doesn't matter who starts. I always finish 'em."

Josiah's jaw muscles popped in and out as he visibly gritted his teeth. Probably debating the wisdom of riling a sheriff with a gunslinger's credentials. "None of that makes any difference, anyhow," he finally said. "Either way, I want them back. Now."

Gray gave him a cold smile. "We both know I'm not gonna let that happen, Josiah. They attacked us. Unprovoked. Even if it hadn't been *my wife* they were aimin' at, that still would have been a problem. They've been arrested and they will sit in that jail cell until they can be transported to the nearest judge for trial."

Gray's hands had been moving as close to his guns as he could unobtrusively manage while he spoke. Josiah was far too angry to let this go, and he wasn't very subtle with his intentions. His men were already squaring up beside him, not even trying to hide what they were doing. Gray turned his head slightly toward Mercy, though he kept his eyes on Josiah.

"Get behind me," he said as quietly as he could. She sucked in a breath and turned to him, her eyes wide. "Just do it," he said, putting as much urgency in his voice that he could. He did *not* have time to argue with her.

"You'll rot in hell before you take my men anywhere," Josiah said, going for his guns.

"Now!" Gray yelled.

Mercy dove behind him just as three shots rang out. Josiah screamed and Gray took a deep breath, his guns both smoking in his hands. He'd worried for a second that he might be a little rusty. It had been a while since he needed to fall back on his skills, but he was glad to see he worried for nothing.

Josiah's guns lay on the ground, and he cradled one bleeding hand with the other.

"You shot my hand!" Josiah said, his face nearly purple with rage and pain.

His men sat stunned beside him, their horses prancing with terror. Gray's bullets had found their marks. One had gone right through the palm of Josiah's gun hand. The other had shot the hat off the head of one of his men. The third man cursed and wheeled his horse around, galloping off before anyone could say another word. Gray had no idea where Josiah's shot had hit, but it hadn't struck him or Mercy, so he wasn't going to worry about it.

Josiah grabbed the reins of his horse with his uninjured hand, the other cradled against his side, bleeding profusely. "This isn't over, Woodson. I'll have you gone, one way or another, before the month is out."

Gray sighed as Josiah wheeled around. The man whose hat had been shot jumped from his horse, gathered his hat and Josiah's gun, and then followed him out of the courtyard. Mercy laid a shaking hand on his arm, and he holstered his guns, then pulled her into an embrace.

"Are you okay?" he asked.

She buried her face against his chest and nodded. "Are you?"

He rubbed his hands up and down her arms, assuring himself that she really wasn't hurt as much as trying to calm her.

"Oh yeah. That wasn't the first gunfight I've ever been in."

She laughed, and the sound soothed the pounding of his heart a little. No, it was far from his first gunfight. But it was the first one where he'd felt true fear.

He smoothed a few strands of hair from Mercy's upturned face and cupped her jaw, drawing her in for a long, slow kiss. Then another. Then he kissed the tip of her nose and just drew her in, holding her until she stopped trembling. It gave him a few minutes for his own frantically beating heart to calm. If Mercy hadn't dug those damn guns out from the garden... He didn't want to think about what might've happened.

Apparently, there was a downside to all this peace and contentment stuff. Having something to care about meant he had something to lose. He hadn't had anything close to that in a long time, and he didn't know how to feel about his change in circumstances. He didn't like this feeling. The fear. The uncertainty. He'd been able to live his life relatively numb and unencumbered for... decades, really. All these...emotions...the worry...he wasn't sure he was equipped to deal with it all.

Finally, he sighed and gently set Mercy away from him. "I think we better head to town and check on Jason and Josiah's men."

She frowned. "Do you think Josiah might've sent men

into town while he came here?"

"It's a good possibility. It's what I would have done," he said with a shrug. "And if he hasn't yet, he will soon. I want to get those men transferred out of here as soon as possible."

She nodded. "We haven't had to transport prisoners in a very long time, but Jamison and the reverend will know what to do."

Gray didn't like that she so quickly relied on the other men to handle the situation. Totally irrational, he was fully aware. Those men had been in the town for years and knew how things were run. So, of course, they were the ones who would know what to do with the prisoners in the absence of the old sheriff. He tried to shove away the jealousy and kissed her forehead.

"Let's look on the bright side. Maybe Martha will have lunch ready."

Mercy punched his shoulder but laughed, and the sound eased the tension in him.

# CHAPTER SIXTEEN

Gray pulled up the wagon in front of the jailhouse and hopped down, moving to the other side to help Mercy from her seat.

"You're becoming the regular gentleman," she murmured to him as he slowly lowered her.

"Don't say that too loudly," he said with a grimace. "I should probably stop being so chivalrous before you start expecting me to be on my best behavior all the time."

She laughed. "Don't worry. I would never expect such an impossible miracle."

He leaned in closer. "I'll make an exception just this once, bein' that we're technically still newlyweds and all."

He dropped a quick kiss on her lips, and she gave him a soft smile that had him wanting to toss her back in the wagon and hightail it back to their bed.

"Ah, you two are just adorable," Jason said from the doorway.

Gray grimaced. "Remind me to kill him one of these days."

Mercy laughed. "I'm going to go visit Martha. You two play nice."

Gray grunted. "I'm not making any promises."

She laughed again, gave him a little wave, and headed off across the street to the General Store.

"It looks like the honeymoon is going well," Jason said.

Gray ignored him until Mercy was safely inside the store and then decided to ignore the comment altogether. "How are things here?"

Jason shrugged and moved aside so he could go into the building. "Pretty uneventful. The doc came by this morning to check up on them. Everyone should heal up well enough."

Gray grunted. "Can they travel?"

"I believe so."

"Good. Go round up the doc. And the preacher, too, I guess. There was an incident this morning."

Jason's teasing manner disappeared, and he nodded, all seriousness for once. "Is everyone okay?"

"Yes, for the most part. Mercy was a little shaken up, maybe, though she wouldn't admit it. It wasn't like the first time. Josiah wasn't there to just scare her. And he was none too happy I disrupted his plans again. I think we can be expecting company soon. He was muttering something about seeing me gone before the month was out. He might try to make good on his deadline."

Jason blew out a low whistle. "I'll go get the men."

He left immediately, and Gray took the time while he waited for them to show up to explore his new office. The last sheriff hadn't left much behind. If Gray were staying, he'd definitely need to get some more firearms and ammo. And a teakettle, which the town council had apparently not provided yet. Damn what he wouldn't do for a good strong cup of coffee right then. The morning had been interminable. Once he got Josiah's men out of town, he was grabbing his wife and taking her home. And probably not leaving for a month.

Jason was back with the men much sooner than Gray anticipated. Maybe the little twit would be useful after all.

"Jason tells us there was some trouble this morning," Doc said as soon as he entered the building. A man who got down to business. Gray liked it.

He nodded. "Josiah showed up at Mercy's place. I sent him away, minus the use of his gun hand. He was mighty upset that we're holding his men, and I'm sure the loss of his gun hand didn't improve his disposition."

Doc's eyes widened. "You shot his gun hand?"

Gray nodded sharply. Doc, Jason, and the preacher exchanged a glance but thankfully didn't offer comments. Good. Gray couldn't tell if they disapproved or not, and he didn't really care. He'd refrained from killing the man. Against his better judgment. If he showed up threatening Mercy again, his hand would be the least of his problems. Gray wouldn't hold back again, even if it did ruin his retirement record of zero kills.

"What do you want to do?" Jason asked.

"We need to get those men out of here as soon as we can. What do you usually do with prisoners?"

Doc shrugged. "I don't think we've had any before."

Preacher shook his head. "We have, though it's been a while. Before you came," he said to Doc. "Though it's been a good long while since we've needed to transport any elsewhere. Other than Frank, the last sheriff didn't bother much with arresting people."

"Frank? The town drunk?" Gray asked.

Both men smiled and Doc said, "Every now and then he gets a little rowdy. Needs to be thrown in a cell for a few hours to dry out. Honestly, I think he does it when he wants to nap."

Gray snorted. He could understand that logic. "Do we need to send them into Denver?"

Preacher shook his head. "We can. Though, there's a good-size town about thirty miles south. They've got a judge that comes by once a month. I think we could probably take them there."

Gray nodded. "Good. Josiah will most likely be expecting us to head to Denver, so if there's another option, we should take it. With any luck he'll send his men north or west and buy us some time."

"Agreed," Preacher said, and Doc nodded.

"So, which one of you wants to volunteer to take them?" he asked, looking between Doc and Preacher.

"Which one of *us*?" Doc asked.

"I need Sunshine here," Gray said, ignoring the way Jason straightened with pride at that. Pickings were slim, and Jason had proved himself. He might not be much good, but he was willing. He didn't know that for sure about Doc or Preacher. And he didn't want to find out when it was too late that he couldn't count on them. So, Jason stayed. And one of them needed to escort the prisoners. Simple as that.

Preacher shook his head. "We haven't left town since the day we arrived. And won't now. But—" He held up a hand to ward off the argument Gray had been about to make. "There are several reliable men in town that we can count on to get them there. I'll round them up if you'd like."

"That would be helpful," Gray said. He didn't like

leaving it in the hands of men he'd never met, but it wasn't like he knew Doc or Preacher all that well, either. And he couldn't fault them for refusing to leave. They obviously had their reasons.

Preacher nodded. "Give me a few hours. It'll take a few days to get there and back, so they'll need to make arrangements. I'm assuming you'd like them to leave today."

Gray nodded again. "The sooner we get these men out of town the safer Mercy will be."

The other men exchanged glances tinged with more amusement than Gray wanted to acknowledge, so he ignored them.

"We'll probably need a wagon," Doc said. "One of them for sure can't sit a horse, and it might be easier to keep an eye on them if they don't have their own horse, anyway."

"That's no problem," Preacher said. "I have a wagon they can use. I'll get it ready after I round up our men." He headed out on his tasks without waiting for a response. Gray was liking the man more and more.

"Doc," Gray said, "I was told I could hire a deputy."

Doc nodded. "You got someone in mind?"

"Yeah." Gray looked over at Jason, whose eyes widened in surprise.

"Me?" he asked.

"Well, you're already doin' the job. Might as well get paid for it."

Sunshine's face lit up, and he started sputtering his profuse thanks.

Gray held up a hand to stop the deluge. "I need

someone here, and you're all I got. Don't let it go to your head."

Jason nodded, but the pleased grin didn't leave his face. Gray sighed. He was creating a monster.

He looked back at Doc. "Since I'm livin' with my wife out at her place, I'm assuming it's okay if Sunshine continues to use the apartment here."

Doc nodded. "I don't see why that would be a problem."

"Great. Well then." Gray sat in the chair behind the desk and scooched down until he was comfy. It had been a very full morning, and he was more than ready for a little break.

The doc waited for a second, but Gray didn't have anything else to say to him. Everyone had their assigned tasks, and he had no intention of holding their hands while they did them.

"I'll see you later, then," Doc said. "Let me know when Reverend Donnelly comes back with the wagon, and I'll help you get the men loaded."

Gray grunted and propped his feet up on the desk. Jason rubbed a hand behind his neck. "I don't know what to say. I am honored that you trust me with such an important job. I know you say it's because you don't have any other choices but…"

Gray waved him off. "Don't get too emotional about it. Like I said, you're the only one I've known longer than a week, and you're here already doing the job. Saves me the trouble of findin' someone."

Jason flushed but still looked pleased. "Do you mind if I go take a closer look at the rooms upstairs? I haven't done much more than grab a quick nap here and there."

"Do whatever you want," Gray said, tipping his chair back. "Just be quiet about it."

Jason flashed him a grin and headed up to explore his new lodgings.

"Deputies," Gray muttered, pulling his hat down over his eyes.

The preacher returned much sooner than Gray expected, but at least he'd managed to get a short nap in first. Jason hustled downstairs when he heard the wagon pull up and Gray sent him over to fetch the doc.

Doc Fairbanks gave the prisoners one last look over while Gray inspected the men the preacher had gathered to escort them south. They seemed reliable enough and didn't show any nervousness or unnecessary roughness in handling the prisoners as they were loaded into the wagon. That was good. The last thing any of them wanted was too many questions about all the goings on.

The preacher watched Gray assessing the men, his eyebrows raised in question.

Gray gave him a sharp nod. "They'll do. How long did you say the journey should take?"

Preacher rubbed his jaw. "Two days there, two days back so long as the weather holds. Maybe a day or so to get everything situated. Should be back within a week, I would think."

"Good." Gray nodded to each of the men who had volunteered to escort his prisoners. "I'm much obliged to you," he said, his voice coming out gruffer than he meant. He wasn't used to dealing with so many people face-to-face. Or any people, really. He certainly wasn't used to thanking them for their efforts.

First he became a lawman, and now he was being polite. He hardly recognized himself some days. He still wasn't sure if that was a good or bad thing.

. . .

Mercy finished up in the General Store, thanking Martha's grandparents for everything they'd done for the wedding. She would have liked to talk to Martha, but her friend was out delivering an order and hadn't returned yet.

It took a few minutes, but she extricated herself as politely as she could from her conversation with old Mrs. Clifford. She loved the dear lady, but the woman would happily chat until the sun went down if left undeterred, and Mercy still needed to return Mrs. DuVere's dress, which was thankfully still in one piece.

She stepped out onto the sidewalk right as Gray was finishing some sort of meeting with several men from town. She watched him walk into the sheriff station, her mind still struggling to wrap around her change in circumstances. He belonged to her now. She belonged to him. Even more extraordinary, both of them seemed to be enjoying their situation, which was something she, at least—and she'd be willing to bet Gray felt the same way—had never expected.

"Admiring the view?"

Mercy jumped a little and put a hand over her racing heart as Mrs. DuVere grinned at her. There was no point pretending she hadn't been ogling her husband, so she just smiled but didn't say anything until he disappeared.

Then she turned to face Mrs. DuVere. "It's much more enticing than I thought it would be," Mercy admitted.

Mrs. DuVere chuckled. "I assume the last few days have gone well, then?"

Mercy's cheeks flushed, and Mrs. DuVere laughed. "I'll take that as a yes."

"I brought your dress back," Mercy said, rather than answer.

"Oh, thank you, dear. You didn't need to return it so quickly. I assumed you'd be…otherwise occupied for a few more days at least."

Mercy had to stop blushing every time the woman made an innuendo or her cheeks were going to melt off.

"We had to come into town, anyway, so it was no trouble."

Mrs. DuVere looked over her shoulder at the jailhouse. "Our new sheriff checking on his prisoners?"

"Yes. We had a visit from Josiah this morning."

"Oh dear." All amusement disappeared from Mrs. DuVere's face. "Why don't you come in and sit a spell, and you can tell me about it."

Mercy glanced at the jailhouse but didn't see any movement. Gray would probably be occupied there for a little while, so she nodded and followed Mrs. DuVere into her establishment. The madam took the dress from her and gave it to Pearl to put away and then motioned Mercy into an alcove in the parlor.

She glanced around, taking in her surroundings. Mrs. DuVere had ridden into town with experience and money and spared neither when she had set up her place.

"No reason we can't be refined even out in the middle of nowhere," she always said. The house was comfortable and ornate, full of plush furniture, gleaming wood, and warm, rich colors, but opulent enough to suggest high-quality for everything from the food and drink to, well, anything else that might be desired.

After a few minutes, one of the maids brought in a tray with a teapot, delicate china cups and saucers, and a plate of delicious-looking cookies that had been at the wedding two nights before.

Mrs. DuVere poured and handed Mercy a brimming cup with three lumps of sugar—just as she liked it—and then settled back in her chair with her own cup. She took a sip and sighed happily. "Okay. Now that we are settled, tell me all about the wedding night. And don't spare any details."

"I...don't know what there is to tell."

"Oh, come on, now. Judging from the smile on your face and the slightly stiff way you're walking, my guess is the honeymoon has been a success."

Mercy choked on her tea. It wasn't that she was necessarily surprised by what Mrs. DuVere said nor was she that embarrassed that the other woman knew what she had been spending the last few nights—and days—doing. She wasn't even surprised or dismayed by the directness of the question. That was simply Mrs. DuVere's way. They had just never discussed such things before. Truthfully, she had never discussed such things, at least in detail, with anyone before.

Then again, there had never been a reason to discuss such things before.

"It...has been surprising," Mercy said.

"Oh really." Mrs. DuVere selected a cookie and dunked it in her tea. "In what way?"

Mercy crinkled her brow. "I don't know. I guess…well, just watching him around the house. I can't get him out of his chair without a gun and a bucket of water. He'd rather nap than do anything else, except eat maybe, so I guess I just didn't expect him to be so…"

She paused, struggling to find the right word.

"Enthusiastic?" Mrs. DuVere suggested.

Mercy giggled. "Dedicated."

"Well, that sounds promising."

"It was," Mercy said, her body running warm with just the thought of the things they had done between those sheets. And out of them.

"And afterward?" Mrs. DuVere asked.

"What do you mean?"

"Well, my second husband, Leonard, God rest his soul, made love like a tiger and then promptly rolled over, farted, and fell asleep. Every time."

Mercy clapped a hand over her mouth and laughed.

"Martin, my first husband, was more of a cuddler. I'd have to wait for him to fall asleep and then push him away to get any sleep myself."

Mercy considered that for a second. "We cuddle a little, I guess, but mostly we talk."

Mrs. DuVere nodded solemnly. "I knew you'd be perfect together. And he'd be perfect for this town."

The small kernel of hope that had been planted in Mercy's chest when Gray had wandered into her life that first day grew even stronger. For someone who seemed so bound and determined to remain aloof from everyone and everything, he was certainly putting down quite a few roots.

"We didn't have a chance to discuss it before the wedding," Mrs. DuVere said, "but are you planning on having children?"

Mercy looked at her, surprised, and Mrs. DuVere hastened to add, "I know that it's none of my business, but depending on your wishes, ignorance isn't bliss. There are a few things you should know sooner rather than later."

"Oh. I haven't given it much thought. Haven't really needed to before."

Mrs. DuVere gave her a wry smile. "Probably not something you *needed* to give much thought to before. However, now that you're a married woman with a, as you put it, *dedicated* man in your bed, it might be something you want to decide."

"I don't know," Mercy said with a small frown. "Children..." For a moment, a vision of a brown-haired little girl running around her yard, chasing a grumpy, rumpled little boy flashed through her head, and she smiled. "I guess having children might be nice. Someday. Though with things the way they are with Josiah, and with things between Gray and me so new... I suppose if we could wait at least a little while it would be nice. But surely that's not up to us."

Mrs. DuVere nodded sharply. "There are ways to help prevent a little bundle of joy from showing up unexpectedly," she said.

Mercy's eyes widened. She wasn't completely surprised. She'd heard talk of such things from other women occasionally. But always in hushed tones and never in much detail. She had never had reason to seek out any further knowledge on the matter, and her mother hadn't had time to impart any great wisdoms before she passed away. The relatives she'd stayed with over the years had never discussed such things with her, either. And her father certainly hadn't.

Mrs. DuVere explained a few methods for preventing pregnancy and Mercy nodded, listening carefully. She didn't know if it was something she should discuss with Gray or not. She had no idea what his thoughts on children were. Perhaps once Josiah had been handled, they could talk about it. Right that second, though, bringing a child into the world wasn't something she wanted to risk. She wouldn't afford Josiah more leverage by giving him another target to aim for.

"It might already be too late, mind," Mrs. DuVere said.

"What?"

"It only takes once, you know. And from the look of those circles under your eyes, I'm guessing it's already happened more than once."

Mercy blushed again, cursing her tell-tale cheeks for their inability to remain cool and collected.

Mrs. DuVere chuckled. "No worries, love. Just something to keep in mind."

Mercy nodded, her head a swirl of information and what ifs.

Mrs. DuVere, having imparted her dizzying words of wisdom, settled back again with another cookie and nodded toward the door. "Do you think he'll settle in well as sheriff?"

Before Mercy could answer, a sudden crash and a yelp of dismay came from the street, and Mrs. DuVere and Mercy looked at each other, eyes wide.

"Oh dear, I wonder what's happened now," Mrs. DuVere said as they both rose and hurried toward the door.

Frank stumbled into view, having apparently just upended a small cart Martha had been using to transport what looked like Gray's lunch and a few other odds and ends. Mercy caught sight of Gray standing in front of the jailhouse watching the scene and excused herself to Mrs. DuVere.

Gray nodded at her, his lips pulling into an adorable half grin, though he continued to watch Frank as he stumbled over the mess he'd made. Martha's grandmother was giving Frank an earful and hitting him about the head and shoulders with what looked like a loaf of bread.

"Well, sheriff, are you going to do something about that?" she asked, nodding in Frank's direction.

Gray shrugged. "Do what? He's just walking on the street."

"Walking is a rather optimistic term for what he's doing," Mercy said, her lips twitching. "He's drunk."

Gray shrugged again. "Don't see how that's any of my business."

"You're the sheriff now. So, you could say it's your only business."

He snorted. "If you say so."

"Gray, I think you're gonna have to arrest Frank," Mercy said, trying to hold back her laughter.

He frowned. "Why would I want to do that?"

"He's drunk," she pointed out. Again. "And stumbling around the streets in broad daylight."

"No law against that."

"No," Mercy said slowly, like she was trying to explain something to a child. Or to a stubborn adult who enjoyed being obstinate. "Though most towns typically like to keep the drunk and disorderliness to a minimum."

"Well, there's only one of him. That's pretty minimum. In fact, I believe that is the exact definition of minimum."

Mercy gave him the exasperated look that statement deserved. "You know that's not what I mean. He's causing problems."

Gray shrugged again. "Not causing problems for me."

Frank finally noticed Gray watching him and raised the bottle in his hand in salute. "Afternoon, sheriff!"

Gray gave him a little wave.

"Gray."

"Mercy," he said, mimicking her disapproving tone.

Her lips twitched and she fought not to laugh. "You know good and well it doesn't matter if he's causing you problems personally, because you're the sheriff now and your job is to make sure that there are no problems in the town for anybody. And Frank is most definitely causing poor Martha problems."

Gray wrapped an arm around her waist and pulled her against him, leaning down to brush his lips against hers. "You're kind of cute when you're lecturing me."

"Oh," she said, half-heartedly pushing away from him, though inside she was melting into a puddle of twitter-pated goo. She caved pretty quickly, though, when his head dipped down to hers. She rose onto her toes to meet him and pressed her lips to his for a delicious second before dropping back to her heels.

"Do you know that man?" Gray asked with a subtle nod at a tall, thin stranger leaning against a pole across the street.

Mercy glanced over, trying not to make it too obvious, since Gray didn't seem to want to draw attention to the fact that they were watching him.

"No. I've never seen him before." She looked up at Gray with a worried frown. "Do you think he's one of Josiah's?"

"I don't know. But it wouldn't surprise me. I'm sure Josiah has eyes all over this town." He pulled her in for a quick, one-armed hug. "Don't worry," he said, kissing her temple. "We'll keep on our toes."

She nodded, though she couldn't quiet the worry pulsing through her. The man pushed away from the post and walked in the opposite direction down the street, and Mercy released the breath she'd been holding.

"Do you think Josiah will still come for his men?" she asked.

Gray shook his head. "I doubt it. I'm sure his spies are keeping him posted, so he'll know that they were moved by now. And hopefully he's too busy taking care of his hand at the moment. Give our men a good head start."

He kissed her again. But another crash from the direction of the store drew their attention before they could get too involved in what their lips were doing.

"I guess I'm gonna have to arrest Frank," he said, letting her go. Reluctantly. "At least I can give him a safe place to dry out."

"By the way, I'm pretty sure that was your lunch he just dumped into the street," she said.

Gray's eyes widened at that and he huffed, jamming his hat harder on his head before marching off toward Frank, grumbling.

"Okay, *now* I'm definitely going to arrest him."

# CHAPTER SEVENTEEN

Gray walked toward Frank, not quite sure how to go about doing this. He'd never arrested anyone before, and he'd somehow escaped ever being captured himself. The prisoners who were on their way to the judge didn't count, since he hadn't technically arrested them.

He stopped in front of Frank, who was half-heartedly trying to help right the cart that he had toppled again, much to the dismay of Martha as he was doing more damage than good. She swatted at him, and he backed up, tripping over his own feet and landing on his ass in the street.

"Frank," he said.

The man looked up at him, blinking his bloodshot eyes. "Who you?" he said, his words slurred.

Gray pointed to the star on his chest and Frank squinted. "Ah, look at that. We got a new sheriff?"

"Apparently," Gray said.

"Is it time to get arrested?"

Gray nearly smiled. "Happen often, does it?"

"Ah sure. Once or twice a week at least." He stumbled to his feet. "I don't mind, though. The sheriff…the other one, not you," he said, pointing somewhere to the right of Gray, "was kind of an ass, but he usually gives me a nice cup of coffee and lets me sleep a little."

"Huh," Gray said. "Well, I can't offer you coffee…" He was starting to feel like he might be running a hotel instead of a jail. "I don't have a new kettle yet. The last sheriff made off with the old one."

"The sheriff stole the coffeepot? You gonna arrest him, too?"

Gray's lips twitched before he could stop them. "Well, I'd like to, though I suppose I don't rightly know for sure if he stole it exactly. It may have been his."

"Huh. So, no coffee?"

Gray shook his head. "Keep up, Frank, we covered that already."

"Right," Frank said with a wink.

"Actually, Sheriff," Martha said. "I was bringing you this along with your lunch, which I will have to go re-make," she said with a glare at Frank. "But you can take this with you now."

She handed him a shiny new kettle and a small bag of ground coffee.

"Oh, well thank you kindly, Miss Martha."

She smiled, then turned one last glare on Frank before continuing gathering up the mess in the street.

"I'll take the pot," Mercy said, plucking it from Gray's hands before he could object. "You've got your hands full."

They both looked down at Frank, and Gray sighed.

Jason came rushing down the stairs from his new apartment and hurried over to help Martha.

"Sorry, Sheriff. I didn't realize there'd been trouble."

"Not trouble so much as Frank here having a few coordination issues. And don't call me sheriff."

Jason opened his mouth, shut it, and then opened it again. "But you *are* the sheriff."

Gray grimaced at him.

"You know," Jason said with a grin, "if we're going to be colleagues, I should probably call you something more familiar. To reflect our new working relationship."

"No, you shouldn't."

"I think I'll call you Woody."

"You do and I'll shoot you."

"What? It's friendly. Makes you seem more approachable."

"I don't want to seem friendly or more approachable."

Jason grinned again. "I like it. Woody it is."

Gray turned to Mercy. "Please let me kill him."

She just smiled and patted his cheek. "No more killing. For today, anyway, Woody." She walked back to his office, her laughter echoing across the street. Gray sighed and rubbed his hand over his face. He should have turned tail and run the second he'd come across Desolation.

"Fine. You can call me Sheriff."

Jason nodded and then turned back to helping Martha. Gray bit his lip to keep from grumbling. It had probably been ridiculous to fight him on it to begin with. He *was* the sheriff, after all. But he didn't think he was ever going to get used to that.

Jason righted the cart that had been knocked over and scooped up the plate that had held Gray's lunch. "That's a shame," Jason said. "That looked good."

Martha blushed. "There's more on the stove. I'd be happy to bring you some when I bring over the sheriff's."

"Well, that would be real kind of you, thank you, Miss Martha."

Gray looked back and forth between the two, but they weren't paying any attention to him.

"So, you just stay and," Gray waved his hand to encompass the mess in the street, "help her take care of all that."

Jason half nodded in his direction but kept talking to Martha as he handed her things.

"Come on, Frank," Gray said, grabbing the man by the collar of his shirt to get him pointed in the right direction. "I'm afraid I don't have any handcuffs or anything for you. I'll try to have them next time."

"Ah, that's no matter, Sheriff. I don't like them much anyhow."

Gray snorted and held out his hand, gesturing for Frank to walk ahead of him. "You play cards, Frank?"

. . .

Gray settled onto the jailhouse porch and surveyed the town. He had been sheriff, and a married man, for an entire week, which was exactly seven days longer than he'd thought he'd last on both fronts. The sheer fact that he hadn't been run out of town yet was something he still had trouble wrapping his mind around. Nope, these people made him their sheriff and seemed thrilled he agreed to take the job. There had to be something wrong with them. He just hadn't figured it out yet.

All was quiet in town today, for the most part. Some raucous laughter broke out every now and then from somewhere, but it was far enough away that Gray wasn't worried about it. Not that laughter was against the law, of course. But something about it sounded like whoever was behind it was up to no good. More power to them as long as they kept it to themselves. He could always send Sunshine out to investigate if necessary. The kid was turning out to be quite useful.

As for the whole sheriff gig, the most surprising thing about it so far had been how little Gray minded the job. Aggravating at times, sure. But…it wasn't boring. He was getting to know—and he feared, getting to *like*—the townspeople, and for some reason they didn't hate him. He couldn't figure out why. He certainly didn't trust it. No one ever wanted him around for long. Especially because trouble always found him, even when he actively tried to avoid it.

For the moment, however, life was relatively peaceful. Gray had no doubt it wouldn't last. But he could enjoy it while it did. Maybe he'd go arrest Frank today so they could get in a few hands of cards. He was sure to be causing problems somewhere.

First, though, Gray was going to enjoy the pleasant weather, since it wouldn't be around much longer, and take a little nap.

He kicked his chair back to lean against the wall and propped his feet up on the railing. He'd just pulled his hat down over his eyes when that laughter he'd been hearing rounded the corner.

Gray peeked out from under his hat. Three young men, probably no more than eighteen or so, were chasing a goat down the road. The creature had several sticks tied to its ankles with string and was frantically trying to get away from them while the boys chased it, laughing.

Why did that goat look familiar?

Gray was out of his chair and had fired a warning shot in the air before the teenagers had even noticed he was sitting there. Everyone froze, even the goat, and stared at him.

He came toward them and the boys all cast anxious looks at each other.

"Sheriff," one of them stammered. "Is there a problem?"

The goat head-butted him on the leg. Yup. He thought it'd looked familiar.

"Two problems. One, I was trying to take a nap and you boys runnin' around town causin' all this ruckus disturbed me. I'm sure you're disturbin' other people, too," he added, since he was supposed to be lookin' out for everyone's peace, after all, not just his own.

"We're sorry, Sheriff. We didn't mean to be disturbing anyone. Just tryin' to have a bit of fun."

Gray nodded. "Fun is fine, but I expect you to have a little more consideration when you're in town."

They nodded hastily.

"And two." Gray pointed at the goat that was kicking at the string around her legs. "That goat belongs to my wife."

All three faces drained of color. One of the boys turned tail and ran, but Gray pinned the other two with a stare that had them frozen in place.

Before he could tell them to return the goat to Mercy's place, Mercy herself rounded the corner in the wagon and barreled straight for them, her face a mask of outraged maternal righteousness.

"You two!" she said, hopping down from the wagon.

"And where's the other one?"

"Ran off that way," Gray said, jerking his head up the street. She lurched to a halt, her skirt tangled up in the trapping of the wagon. She muttered a curse that had him beaming with pride as she yanked on the material.

To the boys, he said, "You wake me up again, I'm arrestin' you. Spread the word. And stay away from the animals."

"Yes, sir," they both said, their eyes bouncing between him and the furious woman about to brain them with a wooden spoon.

He glanced at Mercy, who had nearly worked herself free and nodded back at them. "You better run."

They took off just as she pulled the material loose and made to chase after them. Gray caught her around the waist, lifting her off her feet.

"Ah, let 'em go, darlin'. They didn't hurt the old thing."

"Gray! Put me down!"

"Well, I would, but then you'd go after them, which would probably end with me havin' to arrest my own wife for murder, and I just don't feel like dealin' with the paperwork that kind of situation probably entails."

She kept struggling against him. "If you don't let me go, you're going to be sorry."

He held her tighter and brought his lips close to her ear. "If you don't stop squirmin', we're both going to be sorry. Because just about everyone in town is going to find out just how much I'm enjoyin' your wriggling."

She immediately stopped. To his dismay. Sure, he didn't exactly want to display just how tight his britches had grown below the waist, but he didn't exactly want her to stop making it worse, either.

She blew out her breath with a huff. "I can't believe you just let them go."

"I can't believe you were going to assault them with that spoon," he said, plucking it out of her hand. "I'd have to arrest you for that, you know."

Her mouth dropped open. "Oh, you'd arrest me, but not them even though they assaulted poor Lucille?"

"On second thought"—Gray glanced down at her hands—"you'd probably look good in the handcuffs."

She glared at him again, but the anger had left her face and he could tell she was fighting a smile. "You aren't putting me in handcuffs."

"Never say never," he said, waggling his eyebrows until she laughed and shook her head.

"I'm surprised you didn't arrest those hooligans for waking you up."

His eyes narrowed. "The thought crossed my mind. But then you showed up, and I had the choice between a bloodbath or a prisoner escape. Letting them go seemed the more prudent choice. They were warned they would be arrested if they did it again."

She snorted. "Did what again? Steal my goat or wake you from your nap?"

"How did you know I was nappin'?"

She chuckled. "Lucky guess. Put me down. I have to help Lucille."

He glanced at the goat chewing on the string wrapped around her legs. "If you must."

He released her, watching as she knelt to untangle the goat.

"You could help, you know."

He folded his arms and leaned back against the railing on the jailhouse porch. "I could, but then I wouldn't be able to stand here watching you."

"You're incorrigible," she said, though her smile took the heat out of the words.

"You like me that way."

She shrugged. "You're growing on me." She finished freeing the goat and scooped her up to load into the wagon.

Gray was going to help her, but she had the goat settled in the back of the wagon before he'd made it over there. He shook his head.

"What?" she asked.

"You don't really need anyone for anything, do you?"

She frowned a little. "You make that sound like it's a bad thing to be able to take care of myself."

"That wasn't my intention. I love how independent you are. Makes my life easier."

She chuckled and shook her head, but after a few moments she glanced back at him. "Everyone needs someone," she said quietly. "Even if they can take care of themselves."

He moved closer, brushed his thumb across her cheek. "And who do you need?"

She stared up at him, and he felt himself falling into those deep blue eyes of hers. He cupped her face, and she opened her mouth to say something. Before she could, though, Jason rode up and dismounted, tying his horse in front of the jailhouse.

Gray sighed. The kid had impeccable timing. He

released his wife and stepped back.

"Was there trouble?" Jason asked, his brow creased in concern.

"Just some youths harassing Lucille," Gray said, jerking his thumb at the goat.

"Ah, not Lucille." Jason went around to the back of the wagon to pet the goat, who bleated at him happily. Was there anyone in town who didn't love the guy? Besides Gray himself?

"Why don't you come out for supper," Mercy said to Jason. "We haven't seen you in a few days."

"Not true," Gray said. "I see him every day."

Mercy shot him an exasperated look, and he held up his hands and turned back to Jason. "Yes. Please come," he said, making the words as forced and monotone as he could.

Jason, true to form, didn't take the bait. "I'd love to. Not much for me to do around here, since we don't have any prisoners that need watching. Unless we picked one up since I've been gone?" he asked Gray.

Gray shook his head. "It's been pretty quiet. How did things go at Mrs. Burkett's? Did you catch the thief?"

Mercy frowned in concern. "Mrs. Burkett had a thief?"

Jason snorted. "Someone was stealing vegetables from her garden. I'm pretty sure she knew exactly who it was, too, before I got there."

"So, you caught him?" Gray asked.

Jason had gone over to his saddle bag and flipped it open. "Yep." He pulled out a large rabbit by its ears.

"Oh," Mercy said, hurrying over to take it.

Gray folded his arms across his chest. "Mrs. Burkett

reported a thief, so we'd come get a rabbit out of her garden?"

Jason shrugged. "Apparently."

"How is that the job of the sheriff?" Gray asked Mercy.

She just smiled and added the rabbit to the back of the wagon with Lucille. "She needed help. You helped her."

Gray opened his mouth to argue and then snapped it shut again and rubbed at his temple, which had begun to throb.

"Why don't you two head on out?" Jason said. "I'll handle things here until supper."

Mercy glanced at Gray, who didn't need to be told twice to leave. He was climbing up to the bench of the wagon almost before Jason had finished talking. Mercy rolled her eyes and tried to untie Gray's horse from the post. Birdie, however, was snoring where she stood and refused to budge.

"She's nappin'," Gray said. "She's not goin' to move until she wants to wake up."

"Sounds familiar," Mercy muttered.

Jason laughed. "I'll bring her along when I come out."

"Thanks. Supper will be in about two hours," she said, climbing up next to Gray. Jason nodded, tipping his hat to them as Gray snapped the reins to get them moving.

"Slow down," she said, laughing. "People will think you can't wait to get out of here."

Gray chuckled. It had been a long time since he wondered, or cared, what anyone else thought of him. And that wasn't changing now. Except with maybe one exception. He glanced at Mercy, who was holding onto her hat with one hand and the bench with the other.

She was laughing but said, "If you don't slow down, you're going to bounce poor Lucille right out of the wagon. And she's already had such a rough day."

Gray sighed. "All right."

He pulled on the reins, slowing the horses to a nice steady trot.

It had only taken a few short weeks to turn him from the most feared gunslinger around to a man who catered to the delicate constitution of a spoiled goat. He couldn't imagine what the end of the month would bring.

# CHAPTER EIGHTEEN

Mercy had managed to stop cooking the meatloaf a few moments before it transformed into a lump of leather, and both men ate without complaint. Well, Jason wouldn't have complained even if she'd served him actual leather, but Gray seemed to enjoy his meal rather than tolerate it, so she deemed everything a success.

After supper, Gray resumed his usual spot on the porch for his post-meal nap. Mercy cleared the dishes, thanking Jason when he brought everything into the kitchen.

"Is there anything I can do to help?" he asked as she began to wash up.

"No thanks, I've got this. Why don't you go out on the porch with Gray? It's such a nice night. Probably won't have too many more of these before the cold weather moves in."

"All right, if you're sure I can't help."

She smiled at him. He was such a sweet man. "I'm sure. Go on out."

He grinned, giving her a little bow, and left her to the dishes.

Once she had everything cleaned up, she joined them. Gray, of course, was snoring in his chair. Jason, though, was polishing one of his guns.

"That's beautiful," she said, pointing to the gleaming metal.

"Thanks. Do you want to try it?" he asked, holding it out to her.

She glanced at Gray. He hadn't moved a muscle, but his snores had softened into deep, regular breaths.

She knew what he would say. But as he wasn't paying attention at the moment…

"Yes, please," she said, carefully taking the gun from him.

"Let's go over there, and we can do some target shooting," he said, pointing toward the fence on the far side of the yard.

He lined up several apples along the fence line and then planted his feet, demonstrating how she should stand. She watched him for a few minutes. He didn't get all the apples, but more than she would have, certainly. Then she stepped up to try.

Her first shot went completely wide and hit a tree several yards away.

"Oh!" she said, frustrated and dismayed.

Jason laughed. "No worries. This is why we are doing this out here and not where we might hit something we don't want to. Try again."

She took a deep breath and aimed again. This time the shot hit the fence, but a good three feet from the apple she'd been aiming at.

"Here," Jason said, stepping closer to her. "Try this."

He lifted her arms, showing her how to hold the gun. "See, if you hold it here, then you can look down through the—"

"Sunshine!"

They both turned at the sound of Gray barreling

down on them.

"Yeah, Sheriff?" Jason asked.

"I thought you were going to call him Woody," Mercy said with a laugh.

Jason grinned. "I decided I wanted to keep breathing."

"Smart choice."

"Move, Sunshine," Gray said, stalking closer.

"Gotcha." Jason immediately moved a healthy distance away from her and waited for Gray to reach them. His massive grin, though, said he knew exactly what Gray's issue was and he loved it.

Gray's face was thunderous as he marched toward them, and Mercy's stomach flipped. Was he…jealous?

He certainly had no reason to be. Jason had been nothing but polite. He'd kept a respectable distance between them, even when he'd been showing her how to hold the gun. He'd been a total gentleman.

Despite that, apparently Gray hadn't liked it. And Mercy hated to admit it, but…well, she'd never had a man jealous over her before. It wasn't something she would have ever thought she'd like. Jealousy was a silly, pointless emotion. Still, she couldn't help that spark of satisfaction that shot through her at the thought that Gray wanted her all to himself.

He didn't stop until he was standing in the place Jason had vacated, and he wrapped his arms around her, moving them back up to where Jason had had them.

"If you wanted to learn to shoot, you just had to ask," he said, his voice that gruff, gravely tone she loved so much.

She raised her brows and glanced back at him.

"You're joking, right? I've asked you to teach me so many times you started burying your guns."

Gray frowned and pointed at the apples. "Concentrate," he said, ignoring her comment.

She rolled her eyes and did what he said. When her arms wavered, he stepped closer, plastering his body to hers and enveloping her in his arms. He wrapped his hands around hers and helped her hold the gun steady.

"Look straight down the barrel," he said, his lips brushing her ear.

She shivered but did as directed.

"Aim a little above where you want to hit. Take a deep breath. Now pull the trigger."

She pulled and the apple on the fence exploded.

"I did it!" She turned, letting him pluck the gun from her hand so she could throw her arms around his neck.

He wrapped one arm around her waist and held out the gun to Jason with the other. She planted an exuberant kiss on him. And then another, more lingering kiss. His hand squeezed her waist as he went in for a third, this time kissing her so thoroughly she wasn't sure if the birdsong she heard was from actual birds or a sudden side effect of his lips.

He broke away long enough to haul in a ragged breath, and she let her lips trail across his jawline to his ear. He groaned and leaned into her.

"Sunshine?" he said, addressing Jason, though he didn't turn his attention from her.

"Yeah, Sheriff?" he asked as he took the gun from Gray.

"Go home."

"You got it, Sheriff," Jason said with an ear-to-ear grin.

He tipped his hat to Mercy, and she didn't care at all that Jason knew exactly why he was being dismissed, because Gray's lips had already found her neck and he had hauled her fully against his hard and very aroused body.

"Is he gone?" Gray asked, his fingers already working at the buttons of her blouse.

She tugged at his shirt and glanced over his shoulder, smiling at the cloud of dust rising behind Jason's horse.

"He's gone."

"Good."

Gray walked her backward until she was flush against a tree. And then he began kissing her in earnest, his mouth hot and slick against hers. He didn't wait until her blouse was fully unbuttoned but reached inside the moment there was space enough for his hand.

"Gray." She sucked in a shaky breath and glanced around. "We're outside."

His other hand started hiking up her skirts. "We are. I don't think Lucille and Birdie will tell anyone."

The goat in question wandered by, gave them a thoroughly disinterested look, and kept going.

"See?" he said.

Mercy opened her mouth to protest again, but his fingers slipped beneath her bloomers and any words she'd been about to say were choked off in a gasp.

"God Almighty, woman," he groaned, pressing a finger into her. "If I'd known how ready you were for me, I'd have kicked Sunshine out hours ago."

She laughed, her hands making quick work of his belt

and the buttons on his pants. "If you had your way, you'd ship him off to Siberia."

"Where's that?" he asked. Then she slipped her hand beneath his waistband and wrapped her fingers around him.

"It's over near—"

"Never mind, I don't care." His mouth crashed down on hers and he drew one of her legs up, wrapping it around his waist. "I can't wait," he said, yanking her skirts up and out of the way.

"Me either," she said, doing what she could to get their clothing out of the way. She'd rip every stitch of it off if she had to, as long as—

He entered her before she could finish the thought and for a second, they both clung to each other, reveling in the feeling of being totally joined.

"Gray." The word came out as more of a plea than his name.

"Hang on, darlin'," he said, and for a second, she thought he wanted her to wait. She was about to protest when he began to move, and she realized he truly meant for her to hang on.

He set a punishing pace, and she clung to him, able to do little more than lean back and *feel* as he thrust hard and deep. She wrapped her hand around the back of his neck and drew him back down to her lips. He groaned and his movements faltered. But she was right there with him. Just one more…and she shattered.

"Gray," she gasped, clutching at his shoulders as he gave a final thrust and stilled.

She let her trembling leg slide back to the ground and

he moved just far enough away so that she could drop her skirts. But he didn't let her away from the tree. He rested his head on her shoulder while they both struggled for air.

When they finally had themselves pulled back together, Gray offered Mercy his arm. He glanced back over his shoulder at the spot they'd just left.

"You know, that orchard might finally be growing on me."

Mercy laughed. "You mean you don't want to burn it down now?"

"Well, not that tree, at least."

She rolled her eyes, but inside, her heart skipped.

The last few days had been so wonderful. But the nagging feeling that their peaceful days were numbered wouldn't leave her. She shivered despite the warm sun and their recent exertions.

Josiah would strike soon. She just hoped they were ready when he did.

# CHAPTER NINETEEN

Gray watched as the blacksmith pulled out the bent pin from the wagon wheel.

"There's your problem, Sheriff," the blacksmith, Thomas Calvert, said. "How did you manage to do that?"

Gray rubbed a hand over the back of his neck. "There may have been a goat incident."

Tom laughed. "One of Miss Mercy's goats?"

Gray nodded. "That Lucille. She chased the chickens into the yard as I was pulling out with the wagon and they spooked the horse. Took me for a bit of a ride around the yard. The wagon went up on two wheels and I heard a crack. I wasn't sure it would hold long enough to get it into town. I'm actually surprised it did."

"So am I," Tom said with a chuckle. "How'd the chickens make out?"

Gray snorted. "They're fine. Minus a few feathers, maybe. And Lucille completely ignored us all after nearly destroying the whole yard. The wagon here got the worst of it."

The smithy tinkered with the wheel for another few minutes while Gray watched, a bit bemused. Never in his wildest imagination did he think he'd be casually discussing the antics of barnyard animals with the town blacksmith. His wife's animals, no less. If he was a drinkin' man, he'd be certain he was in some sort of drunken hallucination.

"Can you fix it?" Gray asked, rubbing a hand over the stubble on his chin.

Tom wiped a handkerchief over his face and stood. "Oh, sure. I've got some spare pins around here that should do the trick."

"Good. If Mercy has to go another day without her wagon, she's going to start making me cart her and those damn bushels of apples all over town. I just don't have the constitution for that kind of exertion," he insisted.

The smithy chuckled. "No worries, Sheriff. We'll get you fixed right—"

The faintest breath of a sound came from the doorway. A foot shuffling through the dirt. An exhale maybe. And the hair on the back of Gray's neck stood up and goosepimples rippled down his arms. He pulled his gun, aiming and firing at the man who'd appeared in the blacksmith's doorway before the man had even pulled his pistol all the way out of his holster. The shot struck the man square in the gut, and he collapsed to the ground, dropping his gun as he clutched at his stomach.

The smithy came to stand next to Gray and looked down at the man with a low whistle. "I didn't even hear him come in. I guess they don't call you 'Quick Shot' for nothing."

Gray grunted. It wasn't something that he'd ever wanted to have to prove again.

Several people hurried over, crowding the large open doorway of the smithy's barn. Gray ignored them all, focusing only on the man on the ground. He'd seen him before. He was the tall, thin man who'd been watching him and Mercy the week before. Gray had had a feeling about him then. He should have listened to it.

Mercy burst in, saw what had happened, and hurried to his side, her face a frenzy of shock and worry. Gray sighed. He'd hoped she'd stay away.

"Are you okay?" she asked him, touching his arm.

"Fine."

She looked down at the man and frowned. "Isn't that…"

Gray nodded. "He's been watching us." He kicked the man's gun away from his hand before he bent down to get a better look at him. He'd shot him in the gut—a killing shot, but one that would allow him to get a few answers first.

"Let me see him," Doc said, bending down to examine the man. He whipped out his handkerchief and tried to apply pressure to the wound, not that it would do much good.

Gray barely spared a glance for the doc. "There's nothing you can do for him."

"I might be able to—"

"You can't fix that," he said, pointing to the man's gut. "And I need some answers."

Doc's face hardened, but Gray ignored him and squatted down near the man's head.

"Who sent you?"

The man smirked at him, and Gray gave him a cold smile that made the man's face pale further than it already had from the blood loss. "We both know you're done for. The only question now is how fast you want to go. You answer my questions, I'll let you bleed out quickly and get it over with. Don't answer me, and I'll let the doc here try and save you. He'd probably have to dig around in that gut for a few minutes for the lead. Disinfect the wound with a bit of alcohol. The smithy over there has some good, strong rotgut that would do nicely. In fact, we'll try so hard to save you it might be days before you finally die."

Gray ignored the doc's outraged hiss. He could save his saint routine for someone who hadn't just tried to assassinate him.

"What's it going to be?" he asked the man.

The man glared at him, his chest heaving as he struggled to drag air into his dying lungs. "Bounty," he managed to say, though with great difficulty.

"There's a bounty on my head?" Gray asked, surprised.

"Hundred dollars," the man croaked.

"Oh, my God," Mercy said, her hand fluttering over her mouth.

Gray snorted. "A hundred dollars? That's it?"

Mercy's mouth dropped open. "What do you mean, is that it? Isn't that enough?"

"No! It's insulting," Gray said. "I wouldn't get out of bed for less than three hundred."

"Well, that's not saying much. You won't get out of bed for—"

The man's breath rattled out of his throat, and the doc sighed and closed the man's eyes. "He's gone."

"Damn," Gray said, standing up. "I didn't get much out of him."

Doc glared at him. "That tends to happen when you shoot people in the stomach."

Gray cocked an eyebrow. "Should I have let him

shoot me? Or maybe Tom here if his shot had gone wide?"

Doc bowed his head and rubbed a hand over the back of his neck. "Of course not. But I don't appreciate you using me as a threat of torture to get your answers."

"Look at him, Doc," Gray said, pointing down at the man. "Be honest with yourself. Could you have saved him?"

Doc stared, his face set in hard angles. "No."

"And trying would have only caused him a helluva lot of pain and suffering."

Doc looked like he really didn't want to agree, but finally he said, "Most likely."

"If it makes you feel any better, I wouldn't have let you try, even if he hadn't answered me," Gray said. "I've seen enough wounds like that in my lifetime to know he only had a few minutes left. But I needed answers and if making a few exaggerated threats will get them for me, then so be it."

Doc's jaw popped as he stared down at the man. Then his shoulders sagged, and he blew out a breath. "My apologies." He took a deep breath. "It just goes against everything I am to not try and help."

"I get that. It's nothin' to apologize for. But I'm not goin' to apologize, either, for doin' what's necessary."

The doc gave him a jerky nod. "Do we know who sent him? Or why?"

Gray shook his head. "He didn't say."

"You don't seem very worried," Mercy said.

"I'm not."

She folded her arms across her chest in a huff. "How

can you not be worried that someone just tried to kill you?"

He shrugged. "I'm a gunfighter. People are usually trying to kill me."

She looked like she was about to argue with him about his blasé attitude, which was kind of touching, but he held a hand up to stop her before she could get started, or they'd be there all day.

"I'm also not too terribly worried because I'm pretty sure we already know who is behind this."

Mercy's forehead furrowed. "Josiah."

Gray nodded. "He's backed down on the public attempts to get your land. We knew he was plotting something; we haven't seen him since the last time he showed up at your place. But you knew he hadn't given up."

Mercy sighed. "I know. I'd hoped his threats were empty. But…" She glanced down at the dead man at their feet. "What do we do with him?" she asked, wrapping an arm around Gray's waist.

He pulled her close and kissed her temple.

Preacher stepped forward. "Doc and I will handle it. We can bury him at the back of the churchyard."

Gray glanced at Doc for confirmation, and when he gave Gray a sharp nod, Gray nodded to both of them. Then he paused, frowning slightly.

"Don't bury him just yet. Wrap him up good and stick him out of the way. I have another idea."

"What idea?" Mercy asked.

"Nothin' you want to know about, I'm sure," Gray said.

Mercy gave him the look that comment deserved.

"You're going to tell me, Gray Woodson, so you might as well just get it over with. And shouldn't we discuss what we're going to do about the rest of this?"

"The rest of what?"

"This," she said, waving her hand to encompass the whole room. "This whole situation."

He frowned. "What's there to discuss?"

She blew out an exasperated breath. "The fact that you want to wrap up a dead man for safe keeping instead of burying him, for starters. And the fact that there appears to be a bounty on your head."

Gray grunted. "For a hundred dollars."

"Stop acting like that's not a big deal," Mercy said, her voice rising. "There are men who will come after you for that."

"Not good ones."

"That's not the point, Gray," she said, throwing her hands up. "There might be more of them out there right now."

Gray shrugged. "If there are, I'll handle them."

Before Mercy could argue with him more—bless the woman, he truly didn't think she could help it—Preacher spoke up.

"It wouldn't be a bad idea to have a quick discussion, Sheriff. Since the issue seems as though it is no longer confined to Mercy and her property. Not all of us are as... experienced in dealing with this type of thing as you are."

Doc and Mrs. DuVere nodded in agreement. Gray sighed. He couldn't fight them all.

"Sunshine," Gray said. He knew the man had to be close by somewhere. He was always underfoot.

Jason hurried over from the corner of the smithy, carrying a large piece of canvas.

"Help them with the body," Gray said. "I'm going to get Mercy home. If everyone insists on a…*discussion*," he said, with as much exasperation as he could, just to make sure everyone knew how he felt on the matter, "we can meet back at the jailhouse in an hour."

Jason nodded, already heading to the small group of men around the body.

Mercy turned to him and crossed her arms. "I'm staying," she said, her tone brooking no argument. He didn't bother trying.

"Fine." He rubbed a hand over his face. "I need a good strong cup of coffee."

"I can help with that," Martha said.

"Why don't we meet at my place?" Mrs. DuVere said. "There's more room."

Gray glanced at the crowd they'd gathered, a bit flummoxed as they all agreed on a meeting place. None of this was necessary. The bounty hunters were his problem. It was his head they were after. He'd deal with it. Though it didn't seem he really had a say.

Within a few minutes, he was following the women to the parlor house. Not a place he'd ever thought to bring his wife, but, lady's choice. Then again, they'd been married there, so he supposed normal social conventions didn't apply to his marriage. In any sense.

Mrs. DuVere had him settled in her ornate dining room, a large mug of coffee in front of him along with a plate of delectable muffins and cookies. The snacks might almost be worth attending this pointless meeting.

The rest of the men were back just as he'd gotten started on his second cup of coffee. After a quick wash up in the kitchen—Mrs. DuVere's orders—the town council, plus Mercy and Gray, were seated around the table with their beverage and food of choice and ready to get down to business. Since he still had no idea what that was, he was at a bit of a loss when they all turned to him, waiting for him to say something.

"What?"

Mercy shook her head though her lips were twitching. "What do you think we should do about this situation?"

He frowned. "As I said before, I don't think there's anything *to* do. If we even have a situation, as you call it, which I'm not convinced of. I'm not even all that convinced anyone else will be coming."

"Of course more will come," Mercy said, her eyes wide with surprise.

"Why do you think they won't be?" Doc asked.

"For a hundred dollars?" Gray snorted. "Not worth the trouble for anyone worth their salt—nor the risk of near certain death by me."

"That doesn't mean that a few might not give it a try," Preacher said.

Gray shrugged. "Possibly. If they do, they'll be just as easily dispatched."

"Gray," Mercy said, covering his hand with her own. "You can't be so indifferent about this. This is your life we're talking about."

He squeezed her hand. "I'm aware of that, Mercy. More than you are. As you say, this is *my* life we're talking about. And dealing with this type of thing has been my life for quite a while. I've done okay until now."

Her browed furrowed, but she didn't argue more.

"No one is debating your experience or expertise," Doc said. "You wouldn't be sitting here if you weren't good at what you do. But there's also the consideration of what this means for the town."

Gray frowned. "Meaning?"

Preacher leaned forward, his hands curled around his cup, though he'd had yet to take a sip. "This man didn't come for you on your own land. He came into town. Walked right into the blacksmith's shop. If you weren't so good at what you do, as Doc says, the outcome might have been much different. And you might not have been the only one affected."

Gray's frown deepened and he sat back. They weren't wrong. Had he been a second slower…had the gunman aimed wrong or had Tom gotten in the way…it might not have been Gray or his assailant lying bleeding out in the dirt but Tom.

He was used to his life being in danger. It was just the way things were. But his presence had never put anyone else in danger before. It didn't sit well with him. Not at all. The question was what to do about it.

He glanced at Mercy, a ball of ice forming in his gut at the thought of the probable best solution. A step he didn't want to take.

"I don't think anything needs to be, or even can be, done right this moment," Mrs. DuVere said. "There are too many unknowns right now. We don't know if this man was hired for this specific job or if this was a bounty that was spread around. We don't know if he found you on his own or if he was told where you were."

"True," Preacher said. "If he found you on his own, there's no reason to assume anyone else will."

"Yes, but if he was told…" Martha said.

Mercy nodded. "Then that would mean someone knows where Gray is. And that person might send more men here."

Gray shrugged. "We know who sent him. Josiah Banff."

They were all quiet for a second until Doc sighed. "I would say that's the most likely scenario. But we can't know for sure. I presume you have other possible enemies out there who might want you dead?"

Gray didn't have to think too long before he nodded. People wanting him dead was a given. Though no one had resorted to paying for it to be done before. And for the life of him, he couldn't think of anyone else who would go to the trouble and expense. Aside from Josiah. But he couldn't rule it out, either.

"Until we do know for sure who is behind this," Doc said, "we won't know if there are more coming. So, the only thing we can really do is stay vigilant."

Preacher nodded. "We do what we've always done in Desolation. We look out for each other. Keep an eye on strangers. Report anything suspicious to the council."

They all nodded in agreement and then talk turned to more social matters.

Gray, however, did not agree with them. There *was* something he could do. He wasn't going to sit around waiting to see if another bounty hunter was waiting to ambush him.

He would confront Josiah directly.

Mercy's gaze bore into him, and he slowly raised his gaze to meet hers. The force of those ice-blue eyes struck him hard enough to take his breath away.

She leaned closer, so only he could hear her. "I know what you're thinking. And I forbid it, Gray Woodson. Do you hear me?"

He wrapped his hand around the back of her neck to bring her close enough to brush a kiss against her forehead, then her lips.

"I hear you," he murmured.

But that didn't mean he was going to listen.

# CHAPTER TWENTY

Gray waited until the women excused themselves to deal with matters in the kitchen. Mercy offered to help, as he'd known she would.

The moment she was out of the room, he stood. "Come with me," he said to the men. And God bless them, not one of them hesitated.

When they were on the porch, Gray turned to them. "Where's the body?"

"In the shed behind the church," Preacher said.

Gray nodded and headed in that direction, though he sent Jason to get Birdie from the blacksmith's.

When they reached the shed, Gray had the men help him drag the body out. None of them asked what he intended to do. And none looked surprised when he asked, "Where is Josiah's place?"

"Ride southeast. Josiah's ranch is about six miles out, through the gully and just past the end of Mercy's orchard."

Gray nodded, looking up as Jason walked over to the group with Birdie in tow. Jason glanced down at the body.

"You're taking him to Josiah's?" he asked.

Gray led Birdie closer to the body. "Yes."

The men all exchanged a glance but didn't argue with him. They all knew damn well Josiah was behind it, no matter how much they muttered about other possibilities. So Gray was going to take Josiah's gunman back to him and get some answers. Or at the very least issue a few threats of his own.

Except Birdie was having none of it.

Every time Gray tried to bring her closer to the body, she balked. He finally stood right in front of her and wagged his finger in her face. "Listen here, you spoiled nag, you either hold still and behave or there will be no more apples for you."

She snorted in his face and flipped her head up, knocking off his hat. Disrespectful creature.

"I'll go with you," Preacher said. He'd gone to fetch his own horse during Gray's tussle with Birdie and now brought it over to stand beside the body. "Annie here is used to being around the dead."

Gray didn't know what to make of that quiet statement. Of everyone he'd met in town so far, Preacher was the most closed off, the most private. Of course, in his line of work, he probably dealt with the dead frequently, as he'd been the one presiding over their burials. And their deaths often enough if he attended people during their last moments. Whatever his, or his horse's, experience, Gray was grateful for it. He needed to get the body loaded and gone before Mercy came looking for him.

Jason and Doc started helping him load the body on the back of Preacher's horse.

"That's a proper horse," Gray said to Birdie, pointing at Preacher's mare.

Jason smiled, coming toward them while the other two men finished securing the body. He reached in his pocket and pulled out an apple, which Birdie snatched from his hand before Gray could object.

"Stop spoiling her," he said. "She already won't listen to a word I say."

"Ah, she's a good girl," Jason said, patting her snout.

Preacher mounted his horse and waited for Gray, who nodded at him. But first he turned to Jason.

"Don't let Mercy follow me," he said.

Jason's humor immediately disappeared. They both knew she was going to try.

"I don't care what you have to do," Gray continued. "But she doesn't leave your side. Tie her up if you have to."

Jason nodded. "I'll keep her here. And safe."

Gray nodded, then muttered a curse as the sound of women's voices floated to them from the front of the church. He quickly mounted as Mercy and Mrs. DuVere rounded the corner and came into sight.

"Gray?" Mercy asked.

"Let's go," he said to Preacher.

"Samuel?" Mrs. DuVere said, stepping up to Preacher's horse.

"It'll be okay, Jade," he said, his voice so quiet Gray almost didn't hear him. They exchanged a long look that Gray would have to ponder more at a later time. For the moment, he needed to get out of there before his wife pitched a massive, unholy fit right there in the churchyard.

He gave one last significant nod to Jason and kicked Birdie's flanks.

"Gray, what are you doing?" Mercy asked, hitching up her skirts to run at them.

"Stay with Sunshine," he said as they passed her.

"Gray." She spun on her heels and started after him. "Get back here. You can't go out there alone, with no one but the reverend. He'll kill you, Gray. Gray!"

She tried running after them, but before Mercy got to the fence surrounding the church, Sunshine wrapped an arm around her waist and lifted her off the ground.

"No!" Mercy kicked against Jason, getting him good enough he nearly let go. Doc came over to help him hold her back. "Gray!" she screamed.

The sound tore into his heart, shredding it into pieces. But he didn't stop.

He needed to know what they were up against, and he wasn't going to sit around waiting for someone else to come take a shot at him that he could question. A shot that could kill someone near him. Even Mercy.

Instead of waiting, he was going to find out what Josiah had planned and stop it now. He'd always found it better to ask forgiveness than permission. Though Mercy didn't seem the type to easily forgive. She might be angry at him for the rest of their lives.

But at least she'd be alive. His life meant nothing. But hers...

He gripped the reins tighter and rode southeast, for the first time in his life seeking out a fight.

• • •

Jason and Doc had managed to wrestle Mercy, kicking and screaming, into the church. She'd fought them every step of the way, until the church doors closed, blocking out the sight of the road.

The terror and anger that had fueled her seemed to evaporate, and she slumped to the floor. The men didn't seem to know what to do. They definitely didn't trust her not to go running off after Gray. She couldn't blame them. Every fiber of her being screamed to chase him down and drag him back home. But even through the fear that clouded her mind, she knew doing so would be futile. Gray was every bit as stubborn as she was. More so, maybe.

The fool was going to get himself killed, and there wasn't a damn thing she could do about it.

"Stand down, gentlemen," Mrs. DuVere said. "She's not going to go running off after him. And I promise I won't let her hurt you." They chuckled, though the sound was still a bit uneasy.

"We'll be right outside the door if you need us," Jason said before bowing out, letting Mrs. DuVere take over. She tucked her skirts around her and sat beside Mercy.

They sat in silence for a minute while Mercy mopped up her face and got her breathing under control. She finally took a long, tremulous breath and sat back against one of the pews.

"Sorry about that," she said, more than a little embarrassed at how she'd reacted.

Mrs. DuVere gave her a wry smile. "Men have a tendency to bring out the best in us, don't they?"

Mercy's laugh ended on a little hiccup, and Mrs. DuVere chuckled.

"He'll be fine, you know," she said. "Samuel is with him. People get a little squeamish over killing preachers."

Mercy raised her brows. "Really?"

"Oh, sure. Even the worst of them are afraid of God. And that man of yours isn't exactly defenseless, you know."

Mercy let out a long sigh. "I know. My head knows. I know he could probably take out Josiah and half a dozen of his men before anyone else had even pulled their guns."

"Then what is all this about?" Mrs. DuVere said, waving at her.

"What if there's another dozen men waiting? Gray acts like he's invincible, but he's not."

Mrs. DuVere chuckled. "Ah, give him some credit. Our new sheriff does seem a little too confident for his own good, though even you have to admit, he's got good reason to be. But he's a smart man. And he's obviously good at keeping himself alive or he wouldn't be here at all. He wouldn't go marching into a situation he didn't think he could get himself out of."

"True," Mercy begrudgingly admitted. "Plus, he's just too damn stubborn not to prove me right and get himself killed."

"Well, there you go," Mrs. DuVere said, patting Mercy's hand.

"That doesn't mean I won't worry," she said quietly.

Mrs. DuVere gave her a gentle, knowing smile. "Of course not. That's what you do when you love someone."

Mercy's eyes shot to hers. Love? "But I...I don't think…"

Mrs. DuVere smiled again. "Don't think about it too hard. It'll just make your head ache."

Mercy chuckled and Mrs. DuVere stood, holding out

her hands to help Mercy up. "Come on, you can wait with me for a while. It'll be several hours yet before they get back. No point in both of us being alone and worried when we could be worried together."

Mercy didn't question her about her worry for the preacher. She'd thought she'd seen something between them on more than one occasion. But they had never said anything publicly. Went out of their way, in fact, to avoid being too near each other much of the time. Which meant, whatever was between them, if anything, it wasn't something they wanted to discuss. And that was respected in Desolation. Even if the curiosity was eating her alive.

"All right," she said, getting to her feet. "I could do with a bit of company. Though I want to be home before he gets there. So I can kill him in private."

Mrs. DuVere's laughter rang out. "That's my girl. Come on."

She took Mercy's hand and they walked past Doc and Jason Sunshine coming out of the church. Mercy didn't acknowledge either of them. She probably owed them an apology. She was pretty sure she'd given Jason that swollen lip he was sporting. But at the moment, she was angry and worried, and they had kept her from following her husband. So, until he got back, safe and sound, in one living, breathing piece, she wasn't speaking to either of them.

The men in this town were out of her good graces and would stay that way until she had Gray back.

. . .

Gray and Preacher rode up to Josiah's sprawling ranch house, on the alert for any danger. But though there were several men about the yard and property, working with the horses or on other chores, none seemed to give them more than a curious glance or two. Still, Gray didn't let down his guard.

They rode into the courtyard of the house and pulled their horses to a stop. Two men, a short, lean man with a handlebar mustache and a slightly taller and decidedly more portly man with a scar on his cheek, got out of their porch chairs and came to the steps.

"What are you doing here?" Scarface asked.

"We came to talk to your boss," Gray said. "And give him back the man he's missing."

Scarface and Mustache exchanged a glance but didn't respond to Gray's unsubtle accusation.

"Wait here," Mustache said before turning to go inside.

Gray didn't wait to see if Josiah would see them. He knew he would. Instead, he dismounted and moved to Preacher's horse to untie the body. Preacher dismounted and helped lift it down, then laid it on the barren ground for lack of a better place to put it.

Gray glanced around at the property and started to get an inkling of what might be driving Josiah's attacks. There was a clump of dying cottonwood trees along the sides of a creek beside the house—a creek with barely enough water to flow. Mercy had mentioned her land had plenty of water. And it looked like Josiah's did not.

Many a neighbor had been killed for their water rights. Same story, different villain, he supposed. Well, that wasn't his or Mercy's problem. Not unless Josiah kept making it Gray's problem, and then he'd make him wish he hadn't.

Footsteps clapped on the floorboards and Gray moved back to Birdie's side, ready to ride off quickly if need be. He'd been keeping a side eye on the rest of the men in the yard as well. Most had continued to go about their business. A few were watching the scene unfold a little more closely than Gray would have liked.

Still, he didn't think Josiah would gun them down out in the open like this. Not on his own property. No. Josiah wasn't a man who liked to get his hands dirty. Aside from the anonymous hiring of who knew how many assassins, his threats and previous attacks had all been on Mercy's property. Without witnesses, and without a direct tie to Josiah should there be anyone who saw. Josiah always left before the shooting started. Except the once. A fact he'd be reminded of every time he looked at the scar that would mar his hand.

"Mr. Woodson," Josiah said, "to what do I owe the honor?"

His words were civil enough, but his eyes burned holes in Gray's head.

"We thought you might want your man back," Gray said, nodding at the body at his feet.

Josiah raised a brow. "I wasn't aware I was missing a man."

"No?" Gray bent over and whipped back the covering from the man's face.

Being dead several hours and riding like a sack of flour over a horse's hind end for another had not improved the man's appearance.

Josiah's lips drew up in distaste. "I have never seen that man before in my life. Your handiwork?"

Gray lifted a shoulder in a slight shrug. "It tends to happen when someone walks into my town and attempts to kill me."

Josiah smirked. "I'm sure there must be a long line of men wanting to kill you, Sheriff. You can't possibly mean to lay them all at my door."

"Of course not, Banff. Just the ones who come to town already knowing I'm there."

Josiah's face hardened. "You can't blame me for someone trying to kill a known gunslinger."

"Sure I can. No one in town is particularly interested in telling people where to find me. No one but you."

Josiah lifted his weak chin in the air. "I'm sorry for your troubles, Sheriff. But you have no proof I had anything to do with this attack."

"Don't need any." Gray gave him a cold smile. "And you can stop right now thinking you'll ever get access to Mercy's water rights. Best you find another way, or I'll end this here and now."

"What are you going to do? Gun me down on my own front porch? With all these witnesses?" Josiah said, gesturing at the men who had started to close in. "Even a lawman can't get away with cold-blooded murder. What would that spirited little wife of yours do if she were left all on her own because you were hanged for murder?"

The mention of Mercy made Gray's vision bleed red. Preacher laid a hand on his arm and Gray glanced down at it, confused for a moment. He hadn't even noticed the man getting closer to him. He was letting Josiah get to him, goad him into reacting. That was a good way to get killed. Something that never would have happened before he'd met Mercy, but just the thought of the evil bastard in front of him getting his hands on her…

Gray forced himself to take a deep breath and focused on Josiah, gratified to see the man had paled in the face of Gray's rage.

"I won't bother trying to put the fear of God into you," Gray said, his voice deadly quiet. "If you believed in God, you wouldn't be such a prick."

Josiah straightened, his eyes flashing with anger at the insult.

"But I did come to warn you. Stay out of my town. Stay away from my wife. Call off the bounty and forget you've ever even seen me. Or there will be hell to pay."

Josiah smiled, though his eyes stayed dead and flat. "And you think you're the man to best me?"

Gray returned the smile, his adrenaline surging as Josiah blanched. "Step foot in Desolation again, and you'll find out."

He swung back into his saddle and wheeled about, Preacher right on his heels. He needed to get away from Josiah. If he stayed in that man's presence for one second longer, one of them was going to end up dead.

# CHAPTER TWENTY-ONE

Mercy headed home when the sky began to grow dark. Jason had mounted up and followed her without a word. She hadn't fought him. She was angry, but not stupid. If there were other gunmen out there in the dark, she didn't want to get ambushed on her own. But she hadn't expected him to stay once she was safe in her own house.

She watched him dismount with her eyebrows raised. "I'm home now. You don't need to stay."

His cheeks flushed a little and he played with his hat rim and wouldn't meet her eyes. But he didn't budge from her porch, either. "Sorry, ma'am, but the sheriff said not to leave your side until he returned."

She stared at him, debating the merits of arguing with him. Finally, she sighed and opened the front door, waving him in. "Better come inside, then."

The relief on his face would have made her laugh if she wasn't so angry about the whole situation.

She pulled out some cheese, bread, and apples, and they had a light dinner. She couldn't dredge up the energy to actually attempt to cook anything. Afterward, they sat quietly in the front room. Jason chose a chair that had its back to the wall and was positioned so he could watch both her and the front door. It was the chair Gray usually chose. Mercy hadn't realized until that moment that he'd always chosen the most strategic seat. She wondered if he did it on purpose or if it was just natural to him.

Jason didn't try to draw her into conversation, for which she was grateful. He was a good man who didn't deserve her harsh tongue. But she couldn't really promise that she wouldn't snap at him again with her nerves so on edge. Better to just sit in silence.

After a while, though, she couldn't take sitting with nothing but her own thoughts rattling around in her head. There was something she was curious about.

"Why do you want to be a gunfighter, Mr. Sunshine?"

He gave her a gentle smile. "Have you ever seen the way people react to the sheriff when he walks into the room? Or watched the way he carries himself when he walks down the street? Even when interrogating a man he'd just shot for trying to shoot him, he didn't flinch."

Mercy nodded, smiling faintly. "I think I know what you mean."

Jason nodded. "He told me once, the way people react to him…it isn't respect, it's fear."

"And you want people to fear you?"

He held her gaze. "I'd rather have their respect. But I'll settle for the type of reputation that will make folks think twice about me when I walk into a room. Better their fear than mine."

Mercy gave him a sad smile. There was clearly more to this story, but now wasn't the time to push him for answers. "I'm sorry I pried."

Jason shrugged. "I don't mind. You can—"

The sound of hoofbeats entering the courtyard floated in through the open window. Only one set, as far as Mercy could tell.

Jason was immediately on his feet, his gun in his hand. "It's probably the sheriff," he said, but he waved her back to the other side of the hearth where she'd have some cover if it were someone else. Jason flattened himself against the wall by the door, ready to launch himself at whoever entered.

"Dammit, Birdie, that was my foot you almost stepped on."

The tension in the room immediately evaporated, and Jason and Mercy exchanged relieved looks.

Jason opened the door, though he took care to keep his body behind the wall as he peeked out. Smart. Gray was definitely out there, but that didn't mean there wasn't someone else out there, too.

Whatever Jason saw must have reassured him, because he opened the door wider and stepped out. Mercy could hear them speaking, but she couldn't quite make out what they were saying. Her heart started pounding again. Now that the initial rush of relief had faded, her anger was returning. He'd ridden away, into danger, without a word to her about it first. Told his men, *her friends*, to keep her from following. Left her to worry herself sick for hours.

She knew she was working herself into a lather, but she didn't care. She and Gray were going to have it out, or she was going to explode.

A few minutes later, Jason rode off and Gray pushed open the door. He'd barely gotten two feet inside when she launched herself at him, fists swinging. She pummeled his chest.

"I can't believe you just rode off like that! How dare you?"

She couldn't stem the half-hysterical tide of words and barely noticed the tears streaming down her face. The fear and anger and uncertainty crashed over her in a wave that threatened to pull her under.

Gray caught her wrists and walked her backward enough that he could kick the door closed.

"Mercy," he said, but she didn't let him get another word out.

"You scared the hell out of me!" she screamed.

Then she launched herself into his arms, kissing him like her life depended on it. And may all the saints be praised, he kissed her back, meeting her urgency with his own.

He wrapped his arms around her, lifting her so he could spin them around and push her up against the door. He broke away, his chest heaving, and his hand came up to grip her face, pushing her head back against the door. He rested his forehead against hers as both of them fought for breath. Her hands moved over him, frantically checking to make sure he wasn't hurt, though she knew he wasn't.

"I'm sorry," he murmured.

"Don't you ever do that again, you hear me?"

She pulled off his jacket and yanked at his shirt, desperate to feel his skin against hers.

He shook his head, hiking up her skirts as she ripped his belt from its loops.

"I'm never going to be okay with you riding into danger."

"I know. But I'm not always going to have a choice."

"Then I'll go with you."

"Not if it'll put *you* in danger, you won't."

"I don't care." She shoved his pants down around his hips.

She wouldn't beg him to stay. Ever. She'd known that someday he'd probably ride out of her life. And she'd tried to convince herself she'd be okay with that. But that didn't mean she had to sit idly by while he rode off alone to fight her battles for her, either.

His fingers found her and all thoughts of anything else fled her mind.

"I *do* care," he said.

He entered her with one hard thrust and she gasped, wrapping her leg around his waist. They were both too wound up, too overwhelmed with all the pent-up emotions of the last several hours to take it slow. He pounded into her, and she held onto him for dear life while the wave inside her grew, intensifying, and finally crashing over her so hard she cried out.

Gray followed her a moment later, thrusting once more before his head dropped to her shoulder as he dragged in one ragged breath after another.

He finally set her down and helped her straighten her clothes before righting his.

She couldn't meet his eyes. She'd never been so…out of control before. It seemed to be happening more and more lately. And all due to Gray.

He'd come into her world and turned it upside down, and she couldn't seem to catch her breath from one day to the next.

"Mercy," he said, his deep voice gentle. And hesitant.

He cupped her cheeks, turning her face up to his, and

she forced herself to meet his gaze.

"You still mad at me?" he asked, and she laughed.

"Yes. I should make you go sleep with Birdie in the barn."

He chuckled. "She's mad at me, too. I haven't made her ride so much in a long time."

The reminder of where he'd been that day sobered Mercy, and she stepped away from him.

"What happened?"

"Let me grab something to eat and—" He held up a hand, stopping Mercy from the argument she'd been just about to make. She crossed her arms but didn't say anything.

"Let me grab something to eat, and I'll tell you everything. Not that there's much to tell."

Mercy sighed, but she went to get him some food. *Not much to tell.* He'd ridden out to her enemy's ranch, the man who most likely had put a bounty on Gray's head, with a dead body strapped to his horse, and he said there's nothing to tell.

The man was enough to give anyone apoplexy.

But after he told her of the encounter, she had to concede there really hadn't been much to tell. Though she about choked at the thought of him just riding into that viper's nest with every gun trained on him.

"So, are you still sure Josiah is the one behind this bounty?" she asked.

Gray took a sip of water and nodded. "There's no one else who would go to the trouble. Or the expense. There're cheaper ways to kill someone."

She cocked an eyebrow at him, and he gave her a half grin.

"I mean it. I think if anyone were coming after me because of any past squabble or out of some desire to build a name by killing me, they'd come after me themselves. I can't think of anyone, aside from Josiah, who would benefit from paying someone else to get rid of me." He cocked his head to the side. "At least now we know what the man is after. His creek has run dry, and his ranch is sufferin'. He wants your orchard's water."

Mercy sighed and leaned back in her chair. "So, where does that leave us? Looking over our shoulders for the rest of our lives?"

Gray shrugged. "Pretty much how I live my life anyway."

Mercy frowned. "But you're in Desolation now. You're the sheriff. Married." Hopefully one of these days she'd be able to say that without blushing, but today was not that day. Blast it all. She sighed again. "Things are different for you now."

Gray's brow furrowed, and she wanted to reach across the table and smooth the lines from his face. "Apparently not."

"Well, we can't just continue on like this indefinitely."

"We won't," he said, pushing himself up from his chair.

"What do you mean?" she asked, following as he went around the house, dousing the lamps and checking the locks on the doors and windows.

"Nothing lasts forever," he said as he went into their room and sat on the bed to tug off his boots. "Either he runs out of money, men, or patience trying to kill me and calls it off. Or he succeeds." The rest of his clothing followed, and he sat back against the headboard, bare as the day he was born and not caring a whit.

She slowly divested herself of her skirt and blouse, going even more slowly when she saw him watching.

"You don't sound very worried about the situation," she said, dropping her last shred of clothing to the ground.

He took her hand and drew her closer. "I'm not. Nothing I can control either way. Why worry about it?"

He pulled her onto his lap, her legs straddling his. She sucked in a breath and draped her arms over his shoulders, settling herself over him.

"Because it's your life we're talking about." She kissed him gently. "It's worth worrying about."

He gripped her hips and thrust up as she sank down.

"We'll have to agree to disagree on that," he murmured before he captured her mouth with his.

She wanted to argue more, but his grip on her tightened, urging her to move, and she decided to let it go for the moment. But not forever.

She was going to make him realize his life was worth something if it was the last thing she did.

• • •

They headed to the jailhouse bright and early. Gray assumed everyone else would be as eager to hear about his trip as Mercy had been. Preacher would probably fill them in, but Gray wanted to be there as well. Though, if he were honest with himself, it had more to do with wanting Mercy safely surrounded by allies than anything else.

For the first time in a very long time, he had someone he cared about. And though he'd never admit this to anyone out loud, he wasn't completely confident in his ability to keep her safe.

Mostly confident. But doubt was beginning to edge in.

In a one-on-one fight, he'd win. And if the man who had come yesterday were any indication of what was out there, he had nothing to worry about. But there was the slightest chance that someone better than him might come along. Not a good chance, of course. But he wasn't willing to risk Mercy's life on it. If being around the other townsfolk helped up his chances of keeping her alive, so be it.

They rode together on Birdie, much to the horse's dismay, since the wagon was still being repaired. Birdie had tried to nip at his leg but had nudged Mercy affectionately. Though the nag still refused to move until Mercy produced a sugar cube from her pocket. All the spoiling was not improving the horse's already questionable disposition.

Jason came out to greet them as Gray tied up Birdie at the post.

"Anything?" Gray asked, not needing to elaborate further. He'd given his deputy strict instructions to stay vigilant, and from the looks of the bags under his eyes, he'd taken the task to heart.

Jason shook his head. "All's quiet so far, Sheriff."

Gray nodded. "Head upstairs and get some shut-eye." Jason looked like he was about to protest, but Gray beat him to it. "You'll be useless to me if you're too tired to see straight. I can handle things down here for a few hours. It *is* my job."

Jason gave him a tired half grin. "All right, I'll head up now," he said, tipping his hat to Mercy.

She nodded at him and then followed Gray into the jailhouse while Jason clambered up the outside stairs to his apartment.

Gray slumped into his chair with a groan while Mercy fiddled with the coffeepot, set some of that magical brew to percolating. God, he was going to need a gallon of it to stay awake. Between the would-be assassin, the trip to Josiah's, not to mention the encounter itself, and Mercy alternately berating and fucking him all night, he needed a vacation. A really long, permanent vacation. Oh hey, maybe he should retire. Retirement sounded good.

He snorted at his own joke, and Mercy looked up, her brows raised in question. He shook his head and then held out his hand, pulling her onto his lap when she took it.

"You look tired," she said, smoothing her hands over his face.

He turned his face so he could kiss her palm. "Hmm, that's because my nag of a wife kept me up all night."

She gasped in mock outrage and tried to push away from him, but he chuckled and held on tight.

"I didn't say I minded," he pointed out.

"Uh-huh," she said. "I'll remember that the next time *you* get the urge to stay up all night."

"I'll let you in on a little secret." He rested his chin on her shoulder so he could whisper in her ear. "I *always* have the urge to stay up all night with you."

She giggled and kissed him, pressing against him

when he deepened the kiss. He pulled away before he was too tempted to toss her onto the desk and have his wicked way with her. Of course, he'd been tempted to do that since the moment they'd walked in the door, but he stopped the kiss before the urge overrode his common sense. Barely.

"Maybe we can stay up all night again tonight," she murmured to him, nipping at his ear lobe. Holy hell, the woman was going to be the death of him.

"Absolutely," he said. "But minus the nagging this time."

"Oh!" She slapped at his chest and got off his lap.

He grinned at her, sorry she was no longer cuddling on his lap, but grudgingly willing to make the sacrifice in order to focus on the more pressing matters at hand.

Like taking a nice midmorning nap before the rest of the town council burst in wanting to discuss things to death.

He pulled his hat down over his eyes. And that was as far into his nap as he got.

Martha bustled in not half a minute later with a smile and personality that was far too bright and bubbly for so early in the morning. Not that it was that early, but it was for him. But she came bearing pastries, so he'd forgive her.

"Mercy," she said as she deposited a couple plates of goodies in front of Gray along with a steaming pot of coffee. "Mrs. DuVere and I were just about to have some tea if you'd like to come join us."

Mercy glanced at Gray, her brow furrowed slightly. She obviously didn't want to leave him, but whether it was because she wanted his protection or wanted to keep an eye on him in her own misguided attempt at protecting him, he wasn't sure. He did know, however, that if she was underfoot watching every move he made for the rest of the day, he was going to lose his patience.

"Go along with Martha," he said, giving her a half smile to take the sting from the dismissal. "I'll just be sitting here nappin'. They'll be much better company."

Martha linked her arm through Mercy's. "Come on. Mrs. DuVere's got those tiny cakes that you love so much. And I saw Doc earlier. He was going to stop by this morning to see Gray, so that'll give the menfolk some time to do their talking without us in the way."

"Well, if they're going to be talking about the current situation, I should be here—"

Gray came toward her and grasped her chin in his fingers. "I promise, we won't say anything of consequence until you are here."

She stared up at him, those blue eyes of hers crushing him under their weight. Finally, she sighed. "I'm holding you to that promise, Gray Woodson."

He kissed the tip of her nose. "Yes, ma'am."

Her lips pinched together but more in an effort not to smile, he thought, than in real disapproval. She let Martha tow her out the door, and he sank back into his chair with a sigh, savoring the instant quiet.

And damn it all to hell and back, he hoped the day stayed this way.

# CHAPTER TWENTY-TWO

Martha had Mercy ushered across the street and upstairs into Mrs. DuVere's parlor with a hot cup of tea and a plate of cookies almost before she'd agreed to go.

"So, what happened last night?" Martha asked while Mercy was still catching her breath from being rushed over.

Mercy's cheeks instantly warmed. She knew Martha wasn't referring to what had happened when Gray got home. Or where it happened. Or how many times it happened. But that had been right where her mind had gone. Where her mind had been since the moment she'd woken up, if she were honest. And if Mrs. DuVere's smile meant anything, she knew exactly what Mercy was thinking about, too.

"What happened when the sheriff went out to Josiah's?" Mrs. DuVere added helpfully.

"Ah," Mercy said, setting her cup down. "Not much, I don't think."

Both women looked disappointed, and Mercy filled them in as much as she could, telling them everything that Gray had told her.

Mrs. DuVere sat back, frowning slightly. "That's about all Samuel said as well. I'd hoped maybe Gray had spilled a few more details."

Mercy chewed her lip. "Gray said he threatened him, warned him to put a stop to it. Do you think…?"

Mrs. DuVere shook her head slowly. "No. And neither do you if the look on your face is any indication."

Mercy gave her a faint smile. No one pulled anything over on Jade DuVere.

"Then more men will come?" Martha asked.

"Most likely," Mrs. DuVere said. "So, we'll need to keep vigil—"

A loud crash and shouts from downstairs had them all on their feet and running for the indoor stairs that led to the tavern below.

The scene that greeted them halted Mercy in her tracks. Preacher, Doc, Tom the smithy, and Frank, of all people, were trying to wrestle a man to the ground, but he was putting up one hell of a fight. And he had a gun in his hand, though Preacher's death grip on his wrist seemed to be preventing the man from moving any of his appendages enough to shoot the thing.

"Get the gun!" Preacher yelled to…anyone, probably.

Mercy darted forward and grabbed the gun, but the man wouldn't let go for anything. She yanked at his hand and dragged his flailing arm toward her as the men bore him down to the ground. When he still wouldn't let go, she set her teeth in the fleshy part of his thumb and bit down. Hard.

That worked. He howled and dropped it. Mercy grabbed the gun and stepped back, aiming at the mass of writhing males on the ground, though she kept her finger away from the trigger, since there was no way to hit the bad guy without hitting one of the townsfolk.

The man must have finally decided he was outnumbered because he suddenly went limp. The men on top of him waited a few heartbeats before removing themselves, though Preacher kept firm hold of him until Frank rustled up some rope to tie the man's hands. Then he sat back and sucked in a few lungfuls of air. Mrs. DuVere knelt beside him, pressing a handkerchief to his bleeding lip.

Their new prisoner leaned against a table leg and glared at everyone.

"Who are you?" Doc asked.

The man said nothing but spat in Doc's general direction.

Mercy leveled the gun at him. "Answer the question."

He turned his glare on her. "I don't have to answer nothin'. You ain't the sheriff." He looked around the room, then back to her. "Where is your sheriff? I heard he likes to spend his time in the tavern."

Mercy lowered the gun. "You heard wrong. But I guess we know why you're here."

She glanced at Doc, then Preacher. Both had grim faces but gave her quick nods to show they agreed with her assessment. They'd just caught themselves another would-be assassin.

Preacher wiped at his lip with the handkerchief. "I saw him on my way home last night. He was with another man, making camp just outside of town. Been watching for them ever since."

That brought the man's head with a snap. "You saw us last night?"

Preacher's mouth pulled into a wry half grin. "You had a big enough fire going, anyone passing you from a mile off probably saw you."

The man scowled and looked away, obviously not pleased he hadn't been as stealthy as he'd thought.

Ice ran down Mercy's spine. "Wait, you said you saw two of them?" she asked.

Preacher nodded, his eyes narrowing as he hauled himself to his feet. He, Doc, Mrs. DuVere, even Frank, closed in around the man and Mercy brought the gun back up.

"Where is the man you were with?" she asked.

His eyes widened a bit, but he still managed an impressive sneer. "What man?"

She cocked the gun and moved a step closer though she was careful to stay out of the man's reach. Rope didn't always hold.

"Let me share some information with you," she said, her voice quiet and strained with the effort she was making to keep it from shaking. "The sheriff is my husband. And I have no intention of letting anything happen to him. So, if you don't want to die here today, you'll tell me who you are, who sent you, and where the other man is that you came with. And start with that last one."

The man didn't answer. He just looked up at her, his eyes as cold as a snake's, and smiled.

She didn't wait to try and get more answers out of him. She didn't wait for the others. She just turned and ran for the door.

*Gray.*

• • •

Gray had just lifted the coffeepot to pour himself another cup when the door opened.

"Hey, Sunshine. You want a cup of—"

He caught the glint of sun on a raised gun and heaved the coffeepot as hard as he could. It struck whoever had just come through his door square in the forehead, and the man went down with a squeal that would have made a pig proud. He'd dropped his gun, and Gray kicked it out of the way before grabbing the pitcher of water on his windowsill.

"Hot, hot, hot!" the man screamed, clutching his head.

"Sorry the temperature isn't to your liking," Gray said, tossing the pitcher of water into the man's face.

He sputtered a little, but the howls of pain had stopped so the water must have helped.

Before Gray could say anything else, Mercy hurtled herself through the door, stepping over the man on the ground to throw herself in his arms.

"Hey, darlin'," he said, wrapping an arm around her waist. "What brings you here? Oops, I'll take this," he said, gingerly plucking the gun from her hand and uncocking it before he shoved it in his belt buckle.

"What brings…" She stared at him, utterly nonplussed. "What happened?" she asked instead of answering, nodding down at the man on the ground who was still holding his forehead and whimpering.

"I was just offering Mr….?" He glanced down at the man and waited for him to answer.

"Brown."

"Ah. I was just offering Mr. Brown here some coffee."

Doc, Preacher, Mrs. DuVere, Martha, and Frank had

been right on Mercy's heels and were congregated on the porch, straining to see what was going on.

"You were offering him coffee? With the whole pot?" Mercy asked.

Gray shrugged. "Didn't have time to find a cup."

Mercy half sighed, half laughed and dropped her head to his shoulder.

"What's all this?" Jason's voice said from somewhere out on the porch. "Who's the prisoner?"

"Prisoner?" Gray asked.

Mercy looked back up. "Yes. We caught another gunman over at the tavern. He came with another man…" She looked down at Mr. Brown. "I'm assuming that's him."

"Ah. Well, in that case…"

Gray set Mercy away from him and bent to pick up the man on the ground, except when he got near him the man emitted a high-pitched shriek that had Gray pulling back like he'd just grabbed the wrong dangly bit on a cow and was about to get kicked.

"Okay," he said, drawing the word out while he searched his audience for his deputy. "Sunshine!"

"Here, Sheriff!" Jason said, pushing his way forward.

"Get him up."

Jason hurried to obey as the crowd on the porch parted long enough for Preacher to push through with the other prisoner.

"Ernie!" Gray's coffee friend said.

"Don't say my name, you dolt!" Ernie said.

"Ernie? Would that be Brown as well?" Gray asked. "I detect a certain resemblance, I think."

"He's my brother," the other one said.

"Dammit Claude, keep yer mouth shut!" Ernie yelled.

"Sunshine, why don't you show Ernie here to a cell while we have a chat with Claude."

Jason grinned and grabbed Ernie's other arm so he and Preacher could wrestle him back into a cell.

Mercy had a quick murmured conversation with Martha and Mrs. DuVere before coming back inside the office and closing the door. He didn't bother trying to ask her to leave. She'd just refuse, and he'd end up telling her everything anyway, so she might as well be there.

"Why don't you have a seat?" Gray said. He reached for Claude, who emitted that high-pitched shriek again.

Gray stepped back, wiggling his finger in his ear to get it to quit ringing. Well, all right, then. Mr. Claude Brown apparently had a slight aversion to Gray.

He pushed a chair in his direction and Jason and Doc shoved the man into it with one hand each on his shoulders. Gray sat in his own chair and leaned his elbows on his knees.

"Who sent you here, Mr. Brown?"

Claude just stared at Gray, his eyes so wide the whites were visible.

"Claude?" Gray tried again. "I really don't want to ask again."

The man whimpered, and Gray rubbed a hand over his face and then sighed, sitting back in his chair. He gestured to Jason and Doc.

"Claude," Doc said, "who sent you here?"

Claude shook his head. "No…no one."

"Then why did you come?"

Claude's gaze shot to Gray for a split second and then darted away again, like he was afraid to look too long.

"You came to try and collect on the bounty?" Jason asked.

"Claude, don't say anything!" Ernie's voice filtered in from the back.

A cracking sound followed by a *thud* drew all their attention to the doorway leading to the cells.

Preacher walked out a few moments later, his hardbound Bible held tight to his chest.

"Brother Brown required the word of God," Preacher said. "He'll be pondering on it for a while, I think."

Gray gaped at him, and then broke out in a smile. Well, damn. He hadn't thought the preacher had it in him. He nodded and then turned back to Claude, who was now staring at Preacher with his mouth hanging open.

Preacher hiked his Bible a little higher and pinned Claude with a significant look. "I believe you were asked if you came here to try and collect on the bounty that's on the sheriff's head."

Claude nodded. "Ernie…he said…" His eyes darted frantically between everyone and then settled on Jason, who certainly had the friendliest face. "Ernie said he knew where we could find him and that it would be easy between the two of us."

Gray snorted. Easy? He must be losing his touch.

"No offense, Claude," Gray said, and the man shrank back against his chair like Gray had invaded his space just by saying his name. "But you seem a bit…"

A faint smile touched Claude's lips. "Lily-livered? Yeah. My brother is the one with all the gumption in the family. But he said I had to come, too, that it would be worth it once we collected on the bounty and got the money…" He trailed off, but Gray shook his head with another snort.

"Sorry, Claude. It just seems like a lot of trouble to go through for a hundred dolla—"

"A hundred?" Claude said, perking up and looking around at all of them, confused. "Hell no, I wouldn't have done it for that. Ernie said my share would be two hundred and fifty."

Gray sat back with a low whistle. Mercy moved to stand behind him, her hand stealing up to grip his shoulder. He reached up and held her hand, giving it a comforting squeeze. Which one of them he was trying to comfort, he wasn't sure.

Doc looked down at Claude. "The bounty is up to five hundred dollars?" he asked.

Claude nodded, and Doc and Jason both looked at Gray, their expressions worried. As well they should be. Five hundred dollars was enough to bring out a few gunslingers worth the price of a bullet.

"Sunshine, why don't you escort Mr. Brown here back to his brother. They can be our guests until we can figure out what to do with them," Gray said.

Jason nodded and took Claude back to join Ernie.

Mercy came around so she could meet Gray's eyes. "I guess we know what Josiah's response is to your visit."

Gray nodded. "Damn expensive response."

"If he's the one behind it," Doc said. "I don't have any doubt that he is," he added, before anyone could argue. "But as of yet, we don't have any proof. No one has actually named him, and I doubt he'd be foolish enough to put anything in writing."

Gray frowned, but he couldn't argue. With a lack of hard evidence, they needed someone to crack and confess, or arresting Josiah wouldn't do much good. At least legally.

Jason came back into the main room, and Gray was uncomfortably aware that all eyes were on him, waiting for words of wisdom or a plan of action or...hell, he didn't know. All he did know was that with that large a bounty, more would-be assassins would come. And with bullets flying, Gray wouldn't be the only one in danger. The events of that morning had already proved that. Ernie had gone to the tavern, attacked the men there. And what would have happened if Sunshine had been the one sitting behind the desk when Claude had shown up instead of Gray?

And Mercy...she had been at the tavern.

He cut off that line of thinking. She'd been upstairs with Mrs. DuVere. Not a target. Thinking of her in harm's way made thinking of anything else impossible. And he needed to think.

The town was no longer the peaceful haven Gray had thought it might be. Everyone was already on edge, and it was just going to get worse. And it was his fault. He was the target and the bungling fools who'd come after him so far didn't seem to care who they went through to get to him.

His eyes strayed to Mercy, and he took a deep breath, trying to ignore the panic that was clawing at his gut. The only reason Josiah was after Gray was so he could get to

Mercy. She'd already turned down money and matrimony. Murder was the only way left to get her out of Josiah's way. Once Gray was gone, she'd be his main target again. He couldn't let that happen.

A quick glance at the faces around the room didn't help matters. They'd all already been put in harm's way because of him. He'd need to keep awake, alert. Naptime was certainly a thing of the past. And that pissed him right off.

"What do we do?" Mercy asked.

"We keep alert," Doc said, echoing Gray's thoughts. The others nodded.

Gray stood. "We watch every new face that rides into town."

"More so than usual," Preacher said with a wry smile that broke the tension in the room.

"Check with the man we sent to watch Josiah's, see if he's seen any movement," Gray told Preacher, who nodded and immediately left on his errand.

Mercy rounded on Gray. "You didn't tell me you'd left someone watching Josiah."

Gray shrugged. "I didn't think it was important. It was just a precaution, and not one that I expect will be useful. If Josiah was goin' to make any outward moves, he wouldn't have put a bounty on my head. He'd have just killed me outright. But it doesn't hurt to be thorough."

A slight shudder went through Mercy, and Gray put an arm around her. "Don't worry about me," he murmured to her. "I've gotten pretty good at avoidin' the undertaker over the years." She was the one he was worried about.

She leaned into him, wrapping her arm around his waist. "Yes, but you said yourself that a five-hundred-dollar bounty would—"

He kissed her. And kept on kissing her, ignoring the good-natured ribbing as people filtered out and left them alone.

He couldn't kiss her into silence forever. And she was right to be concerned. Five hundred dollars was more than a year's wages for a lot of men. An impressive amount, to be sure. Gray would be damn proud if his was the only life at stake.

He wrapped his arms tighter about Mercy, her warmth a sharp reminder of why he'd always avoided such entanglements in the past. If you didn't love anyone, you couldn't hurt anyone. And despite all his efforts to the contrary, his feelings for Mercy had evolved into something he couldn't bring himself to name.

Because for all his joking that she would be the death of him, he was very much afraid it would be the other way around.

# CHAPTER TWENTY-THREE

"How's our sheriff holding up?" Mrs. DuVere asked Mercy.

She sighed. "Not well. He acts like everything is fine, but he's not sleeping much and when he does, it's fitful."

"Oh dear," Mrs. DuVere murmured, her brow creased with worry. "We just have to believe he'll get to the bottom of this mess soon enough."

Martha nodded. "Yes, we do."

Mercy didn't need to tell her that if Gray wasn't sleeping, things were bad.

It had been nearly a week since the Brown brothers had been arrested in their horribly bungled attempt to collect the bounty on Gray's head. And while Gray joked about the impressive amount, Mercy could tell it weighed on him. The more days that went by without anything happening or anyone new showing up, the more worried Gray became.

Mercy had asked him one day how they removed the bounty, and he'd just shrugged and said that typically you kill the guy who set it up. She'd discovered then she had a bit of a bloodthirsty streak, as she didn't mind one bit if Josiah met an untimely death. But Gray had shaken his head. They still had no proof Josiah had set up the bounty. Details.

Mercy tried to look at the bright side, hoping that no news was good news. But if there was still a bounty on

Gray's head…well, someone would probably show up at some point to try and claim it.

She'd come into town for more sugar. Jason, who Gray had following her every moment he wasn't with her himself, had polished off the last of the apple pie and ginger cookies she'd made. As Gray seemed able to choke down the ginger cookies better than most things she made, she wanted to bake some more. Hopefully tempt a smile out of him. The only time he seemed himself was at night, in bed. He still made love to her regularly and with great enthusiasm, though something had changed. She wasn't sure what it was, but it was almost as though every time he was with her, he felt like he thought it'd be the last time.

Martha handed her Gray's lunch basket, and Mercy gave them both the best smile she could muster. "Thank you, Martha. I'll see you both later."

They waved as she headed out. She did feel marginally better after talking to the ladies. But she wouldn't feel completely at ease until Josiah was in jail and this damn bounty issue had been handled.

She passed Jason and waved him forward without stopping. "Come on, Mr. Sunshine. Let's go feed the sheriff."

Jason grinned and followed along behind her. Gray's eagle eyes focused on her the moment she stepped off the sidewalk and stayed on her every step she took until she reached him. Had it been anyone else watching her like that, even if it had been him just a few short weeks ago, she'd have stumbled all over the street, uncomfortable with the attention. But she'd gained a confidence she'd never expected to have since their wedding. Watching that fire spark in his eyes when he saw her, knowing what he looked like when he came apart under her hands… It was a heady mixture of control and power that made her hold her head high and want to strut with pride.

Gray's hard face relaxed a fraction, and he half grinned. "You come to feed me?" he asked, nodding down at the basket.

"Yes, though I swear there's no point. You'll just be starving again in thirty minutes."

He patted his stomach. "Gotta keep my strength up." He stepped closer so only she'd be able to hear him. "I've got an insatiable wife who requires my attentions all night long."

Her mouth dropped open, her cheeks immediately flaming, and for a brief second, she considered hitting him over the head with the basket. He must have seen the thought cross her mind because he plucked the basket out of her hands with a laugh.

"Come on," he said, giving her a swift kiss. "I'll share my lunch with you."

She shook her head as she followed him inside, Jason at their heels, but couldn't help the smile that came readily to her lips.

He was incorrigible. But, to her surprise, she loved every second of it. He may have started out a reluctant necessity, but he'd quickly wormed his way into her life, and heart. And now…she didn't know what she'd do without him.

And that terrified her to no end.

...

Gray stepped out onto the jailhouse porch, rubbing his overly full belly and stretching with a groan.

"I don't know how that woman is still single," he said, nodding toward the General Store. "But if it means she'll keep making me lunch, I'm glad of it."

"Oh," Mercy said, lightly swatting him with the now empty basket. "There's more reason to want to marry a woman than just her ability to cook, you know."

"Well, there must be, or I wouldn't have married you," he said with a grin.

She gasped, her eyes flashing, and he laughed, wrapping his arms around her before she could hit him with something harder than the basket.

She struggled briefly but subsided when he nuzzled her neck.

"You're terrible, you know that?" she said, though her voice had taken on that breathy quality that made him want to throw her over his shoulder and haul her straight back to their bedroom for the remainder of the day.

"I know," he murmured, pressing a kiss in the sensitive hollow beneath her ear. "But you love it."

"Hmm," she said, pushing away from him. "Behave."

He put his hands in his pockets to keep from reaching for her again. "How's it going out here, Frank?" he asked the man sitting on the jailhouse steps.

"All's quiet, Sheriff. Haven't seen anyone I didn't recognize."

"Good. Thanks for keeping an eye on things. There's

some food inside for you if you're hungry."

Frank jumped up. "That's mighty kind of you, Sheriff. I'll come right back out when I'm finished."

"Take your time," Gray called after him as Frank hurried inside.

Mercy's eyebrows rose. "You've got Frank helping out?"

Gray shrugged. "Never hurts to have another pair of eyes. He's been surprisingly helpful. I'm thinking of making him another deputy."

Her eyes widened further. "And…was he actually sober?"

Gray snorted. "Yeah. I started pouring coffee down his throat when I'd arrest him. It's no fun playing poker with a man who's too drunk to hold the cards. He's developed a bit of a taste for it. And he seems glad to be of some use." He shrugged again. "I don't think he's kicked the habit entirely, but he seems to be tryin'. Maybe havin' a purpose other than just bein' the town drunk inspired him."

Mercy gave him a soft smile that made his insides go all mushy and caressed his cheek. "You're a good man, you know that?"

He mock-gasped. "You take that back. You'll ruin my reputation."

She laughed and blew him a kiss before turning to head across the street.

His eyes were glued to her. To that smile that made his head spin. To the sun glinting off her hair, highlighting the deeper shades of brown and even a few red that you couldn't see normally. Those blue, blue eyes that would make the sky weep with jealousy.

He reached out and grabbed her hand, half turning her. He didn't want to let her go just yet. She captivated him. Mesmerized him.

It was his only excuse. The only reason he didn't see danger until it was too late.

The man had already pulled his gun. Gray's eyes connected with his just as the shot rang out, echoing in Gray's ears before he could even let go of Mercy to pull his own gun.

Blood sprayed across Gray's chest and Mercy gasped, dropping to the ground at Gray's feet. The man didn't get a chance to shoot again. Gray's bullet hit him square in the chest before he could even center his aim.

But what did it matter? It was already too late.

Gray yelled for help, his stomach dropping to his feet while his heart pounded so hard the world spun about him, making black spots dance at the sides of his vision. People came running from all directions, but Gray ignored them all, his entire being focused on Mercy who lay crumpled at his feet in a pool of blood.

Gray gathered her up and ran for Doc's, who was already on his porch, his door wide, and he ushered them in and through to the back room. Gray laid her on the exam table, his chest heaving.

"I'm not that heavy, am I?" she asked, and Gray's breath punched from his lungs in an explosion that was half relief and half surprise.

He brushed her hair back from her forehead, pressing a kiss to it while he struggled to calm the hell down. He'd never been so terrified in his life as when he'd looked down and seen her lying there in her own blood. Nor more relieved than to hear her voice. See her eyes teasing him.

And never felt more guilty knowing that what had just happened to her was all his fault.

He took a deep, shuddering breath and kissed her head again, then looked up at Doc, who had ripped away her sleeve and was studiously cleaning the wound in her upper arm.

Doc glanced up at him. "Just a graze. A deep one. But she'll be okay."

Gray closed his eyes and counted to five before he opened them again and gave Doc a jerky nod. "Thanks, Doc."

Mercy took his hand and squeezed it. "I'm okay, Gray. It stings like hell," she said, startling a shaky laugh out of him. "But I'll be good."

"Another one?" Doc asked him, glancing at him quickly before turning back to Mercy's wound.

"Yeah." Gray sucked in a breath, nearly choking on the rage that clawed at his throat. "He won't be a problem again."

Doc just nodded and started bandaging Mercy's arm.

She squeezed his hand again. "You can go check on things. I'll be fine here."

He stared down at her, not wanting to leave her side but also wanting to make good and sure the man who'd done this to her didn't have friends.

She nodded at him. "Go on. I'll send our good doctor here over if I need you."

He glanced at Doc, who nodded. He took another

deep breath and leaned down to kiss her. "I'll be right next door."

She gave him a brave smile that shredded his heart into a million pieces. "I'll be fine. Go."

He squeezed her hand one more time and marched back out, trying to get a grip on his emotions before he had to deal with the dead man and what looked like most of the town gathering in front of the jailhouse. Because it wasn't just rage that Mercy had been hurt burning through him. But terror as well. He could face his own death just fine. But not hers.

Frank, Jason, and Preacher had already wrapped the man in some burlap and loaded him into the back of Preacher's wagon. The townspeople milled around, murmuring worriedly, but Gray didn't have the patience to deal with them. He made eye contact with Mrs. DuVere, who gave him a subtle nod and then started rounding people up, inviting them all back to the tavern. God bless that woman.

"Take him over to the churchyard, Frank," Preacher said. "We can bury him at the back, near the big pine tree."

Frank tipped his hat. "Will do, Reverend. I'll get my brothers to help me."

"That would be useful, Frank, thanks."

Frank nodded and slapped the reins, setting the horse in motion.

"Frank's got brothers?" Gray asked, watching him drive off. It wasn't even remotely the most important bit of information he needed right then, but it was what his mind latched onto.

Preacher gave him a small smile, seeming to

understand. "Three actually." He bent and gathered up a small pile of belongings.

"How's Mercy?" Jason asked.

"Doc says she's fine. Just a graze," Gray said, wishing he could feel the same relief Jason obviously did. Aside from the first rush that hit him after Doc had looked at the wound, he couldn't seem to feel anything but a sinking and overwhelming dread.

"There's something here you should see," Preacher said, nodding to the bundle.

Gray nodded and jerked his head toward the jail-house. "Let's go inside."

Jason opened the door for them and sat back on the step. "I'll keep watch, Sheriff."

Gray clapped him on the shoulder, his throat growing tight at the sight of Jason's shaking hands. "Thank you," he said, his voice gruff. "I'll put a fresh pot of coffee on."

Preacher didn't say a word but handed him a sheet of paper. A grainy photo of him graced the page that advertised seven hundred and fifty dollars for the man who showed proof of his death.

"He's raised it again," he said, rubbing a finger over his lips.

Preacher shrugged. "Either that or the Browns don't know how to divide seven hundred and fifty equally."

Gray's lips twitched. Either scenario was likely.

What was more concerning, though, was the presence of the paper. Word of mouth was one thing. It would spread, for sure. But a paper with his likeness on it would spread farther. And certainly aid in his identification.

"They're going to keep comin'," Gray said.

Preacher and Sunshine didn't say anything, and when he looked up at them, they were just standing, watching him. Like they knew what he was going to say and didn't want to help him say it.

"It's not just me that might get hurt," he said quietly.

"It wasn't your fault," Jason said.

Gray's eyes shot to him. "Yes, it was. I saw that man's face before he pulled the trigger. I saw the realization in his eyes that Mercy was a weakness, something that could be used against me. And he won't be the only one to realize it. Hell, I'm not all that sure he was even gunning for me. No one's goin' to beat me in a fair gunfight. Everyone knows it. So maybe they're fightin' dirty. They find out ol' Quick Shot has a wife...no assassin worth his salt is gonna hesitate to use her to get to me. Distract me just long enough to get a shot in. The dead man out there just proved it would work. If he'd had better aim, Mercy would be the one we were burying right now. And it would be my fault, no matter who pulled the trigger."

"I get what you're saying," Preacher said. "But—"

"They're going to keep coming," Gray said again. "And my presence here is putting the whole town in danger."

Jason's head shot up, his eyes widening as if it had never occurred to him Gray might leave.

"And Mercy..." He had to swallow hard past the constriction in his throat. "I only stayed to help her. Bein' here isn't helpin' her anymore."

"Leaving isn't the answer," Preacher said.

Gray shook his head. "It's the only answer."

"You're leaving?" Mercy said.

Gray spun around. Mercy stood in the doorway, her arm bandaged and bound against her chest. And she'd heard every word they'd just said.

*Shit.*

# CHAPTER TWENTY-FOUR

"What do you mean, you're leaving?"

Mercy tried to keep her tone calm, even, despite the panic that clawed its way up her throat and squeezed her heart like a vise.

Gray stared at her for a second and then straightened his back. *Oh*. She sucked in a breath. He was about to spew some nonsense and she wasn't going to have any of it. She barely noticed the other people in the room, looking at each other and then hightailing it out the door as fast as they could. Her attention was all on the man who was about to destroy the fragile world they'd built.

"Mercy," he said, his tone soft like he was talking to a skittish horse.

"Don't Mercy me. I know what's going through your head, Gray Woodson."

He sighed. "I'm not going to stay here and let you die because of me."

Her arm throbbed with the force of the blood pounding through her body, but she ignored it. "Well, aren't you the arrogant one."

His eyes narrowed. "Arrogant?"

"You think everything is about you. I have news for you, since you seem to have forgotten. I was in danger before you ever came here. It's the reason why you stayed, remember?"

"Yes, I remember. And instead of helping the situation,

getting Josiah out of your life, he's now sending people to shoot at me. Only you're the one getting hit."

"And what makes you so sure that was an accident?"

Gray frowned. "What do you mean?"

"I mean, I am the one Josiah wants out of the way. I'm sure you're a complication he'd like to disappear, but he doesn't get what he wants with me alive and fighting him still. For all we know, there's a bounty on my head, too, and me being shot has nothing to do with you. So, your leaving won't do a damn bit of good."

His lips pulled into a faint smile at her cursing, and her heart clenched again. What other man would ever find that endearing? What other man would be okay with her wanting to run her farm and business her way? Would let her handle her own affairs? Would be okay with her domestic shortcomings? Not that it mattered. Even if there were men lining up along the Rockies, they wouldn't be him.

"If he was purposely aiming for you—though I don't think he was—then my leaving still keeps you safer, because you won't have the assassins who are gunning for me to contend with on top of everything else. Jason and Doc and Preacher are here if you truly need help. They are good men who won't accidentally get you killed."

"You are nine kinds of stubborn, you know that, Gray Woodson!"

He snorted. "I'm well aware of that, yeah. Doesn't make me wrong. Josiah was a nuisance before I came. He proposed to you a lot. Tried to buy your property. He didn't try to kill you. The assassins didn't show up until I shot him. That's on me. The bounty is on me. I can't stay here and continue to risk the lives of everyone in this town."

He came toward her, cupped her face. "I can't... won't...continue to risk you."

She wrapped her fingers around his wrists, clung to him. "You're a lazy, opinionated, grumpy, washed-up criminal. By your own admission. You got no business getting all noble and self-sacrificing on me now, damn you."

He shrugged and gave her that half grin that never failed to stop her heart. "People change."

"Not you," she whispered.

He dipped down and pressed a gentle kiss to her lips, then rested his forehead against hers, gripping the back of her neck. "You are the strongest woman I know. You were doing just fine before I got here, and you'll be fine after I leave."

"Gray," she whispered.

He crushed his mouth to hers, kissing her with a desperate urgency that didn't just break her heart but shattered her soul. She'd always sworn she never needed anyone. She'd been left behind too many times to ever rely on anyone else. To ever expect or even hope they'd stay. And she learned a long time ago to just let them go. Because begging them to stay only made it hurt more when they walked away. So, when Gray had wandered into her life, she'd vowed that when he wanted to walk away, as she knew he would someday, she'd let him go. She wouldn't beg.

But as he wrenched his lips from hers and stalked

toward the door, the words she'd forbidden herself to ever use tore from her lips.

"Please." The word ended on a choked sob and she drew in a shuddering breath. "Don't go."

Gray's hand clenched on the doorknob until his knuckles turned white, and for half a heartbeat she thought he might reconsider. Then his gaze met hers and she knew it was over.

"Take care of yourself, Mercy," he said, his words gruff. Final.

And then he was gone.

. . .

Walking out that door had been the hardest thing Gray had ever done. Those words...*please, don't go*...they would echo in his empty heart for the rest of his life. And they'd destroy him over and over every time.

He didn't say a word to anyone as he passed them on the porch. They'd probably heard every word, and he didn't care.

The only person who mattered just then was Mercy.

God. Even thinking her name made his heart ache and bleed.

He rode Birdie back home as fast as she'd take him, and then stood in the courtyard a full five minutes, realizing he now considered this place home.

*Home.*

He'd never had one before. Maybe when he was a small boy, though all he really remembered was moving from place to place. His mama had always tried to make wherever they'd ended up feel like a home. Put up the same white curtains with their little embroidered daisies on them wherever they went. But he didn't remember anything about those places. Except his mama and those daisies.

And then he'd come here. To Desolation. To Mercy. And he'd finally felt like he was home.

Leaving it would be like ripping his heart from his chest and leaving it behind in the dirt.

But he'd do all that and more if it meant keeping Mercy safe.

He forced himself inside and packed up his belongings as fast as he could. He needed to get this over with and get out of town before he changed his mind. Before he let those words that were tearing his soul apart persuade him into staying. Into being a bigger danger for those around him. For her.

He had Birdie's saddlebags loaded up and was on the road moments before the rumble of wagon wheels and a cloud of dust announced the imminent arrival of his wife. A flash of panic whipped at him, and he steered Birdie into the trees. Shame churned through his gut, but he didn't hesitate to lead Birdie farther away from the main road. He couldn't face Mercy again.

If he saw her, heard those words again, he'd never be able to leave. He'd barely been able to force himself out the door the first time, and it nearly cost him everything he was. He wouldn't be able to do it a second time, and for her safety, he needed to leave. He caught a glimpse of the wagon as it drove by. A flash of light brown hair, its burnished highlights glinting in the sun. He rubbed his chest, though nothing he could do would ease the ache there. His fingers brushed against the golden star on his vest...the badge that had once felt so foreign but had started to become a familiar and even gratifying weight.

He'd need to leave it before he left town. He didn't want to take it with him. Didn't want any part of Desolation following him after he left. It would be nothing but a painful reminder of the good life he briefly had. But he couldn't bring himself to just discard it. Besides, it wouldn't hurt to give Sunshine a few last-minute instructions.

Jason was already at the jailhouse when Gray dismounted and tied Birdie to her usual post. His deputy stood leaning against the doorway, his arms crossed over his chest, a look of unfamiliar disapproval on his face.

"Don't you start," Gray said, pushing his way past him.

Jason didn't say anything for a moment, merely watched as Gray went to his desk, removed the star from his chest, and dropped it to the table.

"So, you're really doing it, then," Jason said. "Leaving just like that."

"Yeah. Just like that."

"You're unbelievable," Jason said, derision coating every word.

Gray nearly flinched but squeezed his hands into fists to keep from reacting. "Thanks."

Jason snorted, though more from exasperation than humor. "It wasn't a compliment."

Gray sighed. "I'm aware of that, Sunshine. I just really don't feel like going into all this with you. It's none of your business."

Jason's jaw about dropped. "None of my business? It's every bit of my business, especially since your leaving makes me the new sheriff."

"Congratulations."

"I don't want your congratulations, damn it! I want you to be a man and stay where you're needed. You're the sheriff. You're a husband. How can you just leave?"

"How?" Gray rounded on Jason, making him hastily step back. "Do you think this is easy for me?"

Jason swallowed hard, his eyes wide and anxious, but he didn't back down. "Yeah. I do. Or you wouldn't be doing it. You never wanted any of this in the first place. You've made no secret about that."

"No. I didn't. But that doesn't mean I don't want it now." Gray closed his eyes and sucked in several deep breaths, trying to shove all his emotions back in the dark hole where they belonged. But it was no use. His defenses had been cracked and everything came spilling out.

"All I ever wanted when I came to this place was a nice quiet place where I could hole up and wait to die. Did it ever occur to you to ask why I wanted that so desperately?"

Jason shook his head.

"Of course not." He took a deep breath. "I'm tired, Sunshine. So tired. Do you know how many friends I've watched die? How many men I considered brothers drop dead at my feet because someone was aiming for me and they got in the way? How many women I could have loved running away after the first gunman showed up trying to best me? How many times I've watched someone I care about leave, most times in a pine box?"

Again, Jason shook his head.

"All of them," Gray said quietly, something breaking deep inside of him. "Everyone I've ever cared about. My parents...I barely remember them. And was never with anyone else long enough to get too attached. And then later..." Gray shrugged. "It came with the life. A life I never wanted. I stumbled into a gunfight one day and that was it. I signed my death sentence right then and there. I was a walking dead man. Even alive, I was no better than dead."

Gray swallowed hard, his eyes staring at the ground though he didn't really see it. "I should have let that man kill me that day. My life was over anyway."

He closed his eyes and tried to shake it off. Tried to get back to that place where nothing and no one mattered. But that place didn't exist anymore.

"I should have been dead a dozen times over by now, but I've somehow managed to stay alive. And despite doing my damn-level best to find a nice corner of the world to hole up and die alone in, I've never been able to manage that, either." He tugged his hat lower over his eyes. "And then I find a place called Desolation. A hole in the wall in the middle of nowhere. The perfect tomb. All I had to do was sit there, let my scary name get rid of a problem, and I could die in peace."

Jason gave him a ghost of a smile, and Gray sucked in another deep breath. "But then there was Mercy. And Doc. And Mrs. DuVere. And Preacher. And Frank. And Martha," he said, his voice shaking. He swallowed hard and looked back up at Jason. "And even you, you persistent pain in the ass."

Jason choked out a laugh, and Gray gave him a faint smile before sobering once again. "You all made me *feel* again, damn it." He shook his head. "No, I don't want to leave. But I am *not* going to stay here and let anyone else I care about die because of me."

Jason nodded, his arms still crossed though now it looked more like he was hugging himself. "I get it," he said quietly.

Gray cocked an eyebrow. "Do you?"

"Yeah." A hint of his trademark smile finally peeked back out. "That doesn't mean I like it or agree with it. But I get it."

"That mean you'll shut up about it?"

Jason's grin grew wider, and Gray's chest tightened again. He was going to miss that irritating smile.

"For the moment."

Gray nodded. "I'll take it."

"Everything okay here?"

Gray and Jason both turned toward the voice. Doc stood framed in the doorway. Who knew how much he'd heard.

"The sheriff just stopped by to say goodbye," Jason said.

Doc glanced at Gray, his face unreadable, and Gray braced himself for another berating. Instead, Doc just nodded. "Let's get a drink."

That wasn't what he expected. "I don't drink. And I should get going."

"I know, but waiting a few more minutes won't hurt any. Besides, Birdie is snoring. The whole town knows if she's sleeping, you aren't going anywhere."

Gray rubbed a hand over his face. That damn horse.

Doc chuckled. "Come on. You'll have to wait Birdie out anyway."

Gray opened his mouth to argue more but… For once in his life, he could really use a drink. A real one.

"All right. Let's go."

Mrs. DuVere herself was behind the bar when they entered the tavern.

"Sheriff," she said, with a distinct chill to her voice. "I thought you were headed out of town."

"He decided to stay for a drink," Doc said, clapping him on the shoulder.

"Birdie's asleep," Gray mumbled.

Mrs. DuVere sized him up. "Black coffee?"

"No. Whiskey."

Her eyebrows hit her hairline.

"Make it three," Doc said. "On me."

She got the glasses out and poured, never losing the surprised expression. Gray picked up his glass and sniffed. The fumes alone made his nose burn and eyes water. He'd never understand people's partiality for the stuff. Then again, Frank seemed like a pretty happy guy most of the time. Fuzzy and often completely unaware of what was going on around him, which sounded perfect to Gray just then, come to think of it.

He glanced at Doc who took a small sip of his drink and Jason, who hadn't touched his yet. "Here goes nothin'," he said, and downed half his whiskey in one gulp.

And nearly gagged it back up. He eventually managed

to swallow before exhaling with a pained wheeze. He'd expected strong, but *sweet Mary and Joseph*, his breath alone could probably peel paint now.

Still, as unpleasant an experience as that had been, the world took on an almost immediate fuzzy quality. Very nice. Maybe with enough, he'd go numb entirely. But sipping might be better than just downing the rest of it. He wanted to get drunk. Not strip his throat down to the bone. Doc laughed and slapped him on the back.

"If you'll excuse me, I have to…run an errand," Jason said, pushing his drink toward Gray and giving Doc a look that Gray didn't try to interpret. They could look at each other all they wanted. He just wanted to drink.

Preacher passed Jason on the way out and slid onto his vacated stool. "Mind if I join you?"

Gray turned to him. "You going to yell at me, too?"

"Nope."

"Ask me why I'm still here when I made such a stink about leaving?"

Preacher shrugged. "I saw Birdie sleeping outside. I assumed you were waiting for her to wake up."

Gray pushed Jason's abandoned drink Preacher's way. "Then have a seat."

Preacher raised the glass to him and Doc and took a sip.

Gray gulped another large mouthful of his own and then sighed. There it went. That nice, spinning, fuzzy sensation he'd been hoping would happen.

Maybe if he held very still, he could live in that booze-induced bubble forever. That would be nice. Because the rest of the world just hurt too damn bad.

# CHAPTER TWENTY-FIVE

When Mercy heard the horse ride into the courtyard, she threw open the door, ready to give Gray another earful. Either that or tie him up and hide him in the back room until he got over this ridiculous notion of running away. But it was only Jason. The fight went out of her almost immediately, and she slumped against the doorframe.

Jason dismounted, took one look at her, and nodded. "Just as I thought," he said, pushing his way past her into the house.

"No, please, come in," she said, her voice flat and emotionless. Then her eyes narrowed. "Wait, what do you mean, it's just as you thought?" she asked, shutting the door behind her.

Jason waved a hand at her. "You. This."

She cocked an eyebrow. "You're going to have to elaborate."

He rolled his eyes. "You're just as I expected I'd find you."

"Oh really? And how is that?"

"Just like he is. Pissing mad and absolutely heart-broken."

Mercy's mouth dropped open. "Heartbroken? What are you talking about? Angry, I'll give you that, but I'm not heartbroken. If he wants to leave, he can go right ahead. Even though he promised he would stay to help with Josiah and now he's running away right when things get really bad. He is nothing but a coward or just…lazy. That's what it is, isn't it? He agreed to stay, but only if all he had to do was sit there and let his name do all the work. Then we forced him to be the sheriff, and now he actually has to get off his butt every day and do something good for somebody other than himself."

She knew she was rambling, but she couldn't stop the angry rant that spilled from her. It was too unfair, hurt too bad. And Jason was the unfortunate person it was all going to spill over onto. He stood wordlessly watching her as she paced the room, venting all her fear and anger.

Mercy took a shuddering breath and kept going. "And I know he didn't want to get married, but I told him he didn't have to, and he said he wanted to go through with it and if he didn't mean it then he should've said so. He should've walked away then, but he didn't and now when we need him the most…when I need him the most…" She swallowed hard and forced the rest of it out. "Now he's just going to leave? Well fine. He can leave. I don't want him to stay anyway."

"It's okay to admit you're hurting," Jason said quietly.

Her gaze shot to his and the kind, knowing look in his eyes nearly broke her tenuous hold on her emotions. "Hurting?" Her voice broke on the word, and she cleared her throat, blinking back the tears that threatened to spill.

"Disappointed, disillusioned and…yes, okay heartbroken. Soul sick. For a brief moment, I had the type of life I had never let myself dream of having. Not that I dreamed of being married," she said, waving her hand to dismiss that notion. "In fact, I think I always preferred to never marry. But…" She sighed, some of the fight going out of her. "Having someone there, someone who had my back, no matter what. Someone I could tell everything to. Someone who felt like…home."

She looked back at Jason, his face blurring through her tears. "For just a brief, crushing moment, I thought maybe I'd found that."

Jason reached for her. "Mercy—"

She spun out of his grasp, her anger burning through her with renewed fire. "He had no right to come here and change everything and then just leave. He thinks he can simply turn his back on everything? On me? Well fine. Who needs him? I did fine before he came into my life, and I'll do just fine now that he's gone."

And if there was a Gray-size hole in her heart… Well, she would just have to deal with it.

"It's okay if you're not fine, you know?" Jason said. "Hell, I'm not fine, and I don't even love the man."

Her eyes shot back to his again. She desperately wanted to deny that she loved him but couldn't make her mouth form the words. So she ignored that statement, focused on the rest.

"I'll deal with it. I'm good at dealing with things. I've always had to be the one to deal with things."

Should have known better than to hope she may have found the companion she'd always longed for. "I should have known better. Well"—she shook her head—"I won't let it happen again."

"He's hurting, too, you know," Jason said.

"What?"

"Gray. He's hurting, too. I've never seen him like this

before—and believe me I've been following him for a long time. I've never seen that man show any emotion except annoyance. But this… What he's going through since the moment he walked out your door… He's in hell."

Mercy crossed her arms over her chest and stuck her chin in the air, ignoring the pain throbbing in her injured arm and swallowing past the hard lump that rose in her throat. "Good. I hope he regrets it for every day of his life."

"He will," Jason said. "He already does."

Mercy blew out a frustrated breath and dropped into a chair. "If he feels that badly, then why is he leaving?"

"Because he's a stubborn, cranky, hermit of a man who thinks he's doing the right thing. He doesn't think he has any other choice."

"He's got less brains than a goat," Mercy said.

Jason laughed. "I agree. I tried to tell him that and so did Doc and Preacher. And when he wouldn't listen and insisted on being noble and sacrificing his happiness for the good of the town and the woman he loves—"

Mercy's head jerked up and she stared at Jason in shock. He just smiled at her. "When that didn't work, we marched him across the street to the tavern and got him drunk. Well, hopefully."

Her mouth dropped open even farther at that. "Did you say you got him drunk?"

Jason laughed. "I said hopefully. That was the plan anyway, and he seemed ready and willing. And frankly, I don't think it'll take long, either. As far as I know, he's only had a drink maybe a handful of times in his life. I doubt he can hold much liquor."

"I...I can't believe he would do something like that. He might be lazy, but he's also very keen on keeping sober so his senses and reflexes are sharp when he needs them."

Jason sighed and leaned against the back of the armchair. "He doesn't want to leave you, Mercy. You said you always wanted someone who felt like home. Well, I think it's the same for him. And I think for the first time he finally feels like he's found it. Like he has a place where he belongs. People...one in particular," he said, nodding at her, "who he belongs to."

"Yet, he's still leaving."

Jason shrugged. "Maybe he figures it's better to leave than risk losing everything he loves."

Her eyes widened. "You think he loves me?"

"What I think doesn't matter. Do you love him?"

Mercy didn't answer, too many emotions crashing over her to articulate anything. And the man before her was the wrong person to tell them to anyway.

She pushed out of the chair and stalked to the door.

"Where are you going?" Jason asked.

"My husband is making a mistake," she said.

"Yeah. So what are you going to do about it?" he said, hot on her heels.

Mercy took a long, shuddering breath and grabbed the reins of his horse. "Well, I'm certainly not going to let him leave," she said. "Get me on this horse."

Jason grinned. "Yes, ma'am."

He mounted and hauled her up on the horse behind him. "Hold tight," he said, and she wrapped her one good arm around his waist as he spurred his horse into a gallop. If what they said about Gray being drunk was true, she probably didn't have to worry about him disappearing on her just yet. But she needed to see him. Needed to make sure he knew how she felt and, if truth be told, she kind of wanted to see what Gray drunk looked like. But mostly she wanted to tell him that she loved him and…maybe he would say it in return. And then…who knew. But she couldn't let him leave without telling him.

When they made it into town, Birdie was still tied up in front of the jailhouse, her snores rumbling the windowpanes. Mercy breathed a sigh of relief. Gray wouldn't be going anywhere until that horse woke up. For all his grumbling about her, he loved that old nag.

The moment Jason pulled to a stop, Mercy kicked her leg over and slid down, marching straight into the tavern before Jason could even tie up the horse. The moment she pushed through the door, she drew up short, her eyes going wide. Gray was slumped over the bar, an almost empty glass of whiskey in his hand.

"Gray?" she said, not sure if she should be concerned or give in to the urge to laugh.

He swung around, the last of the whiskey in his glass flying out in a large amber arc through the air.

"Mercy?" He squinted like he was trying to bring her into focus.

She stared, not believing what she was seeing. Granted, she had only known him a short time, but in all those weeks she had never seen him drink anything other than water and coffee, with the occasional lemonade. He wouldn't even drink a mild cider let alone something as debilitating as the whiskey in his hand. He didn't look as bad as Frank usually did—Frank actually looked pretty good at the moment, sitting two stools away and watching Gray with a bemused expression. But…her husband didn't look great. She shook her head and turned to the bartender.

"How many of those has he had?" she asked.

"Just two. The one in his hand would be number three, but I don't think he actually got any of it down."

She shook her head again. Okay, so apparently the man couldn't hold his liquor. At all.

"I'm not drunk," he said, though his words were slightly slurred. He squinted at her again. "What are you doin' here? You should be home, restin'. Iz not safe out here."

He put a hand on the bar to help push himself to his feet, and he managed to stand steady for about half a heartbeat before he began tilting to the left. Doc was immediately there to prop him up and help him back to the stool.

She planted her one good hand on her hip. "What am I doing here? What are *you* doing here? Last I heard, you couldn't wait to get out of town. You must have thrown your belongings in those saddlebags so fast Birdie's head spun and yet here you are having a drink with your buddies."

He made a visible effort to open his eyes wide enough to focus on her. "I was on my way out, but I had to stop at the sheriff's office to leave my badge. An' tell Jason to take care of you."

Her tenuous hold on her anger broke. "It's not Jason's job to take care of me! First of all, I can take care of myself just fine. And second of all, if there *was* anybody else who had the job, it would be *you*. That was what you vowed to do, remember? Stay with me in sickness and in health, for better or worse? Well, this is definitely what I would call worse, and yet at the first sign of trouble, you go running."

"Trouble?" He pushed back to his feet, his eyes clearing a little with the force of emotions running across his face. "This isn't trouble. It's multiple gunmen showing up in town to try and kill me and shoot everyone who happens to stand in the way!"

"So? You're supposed to be the best gunfighter in the west. This is your home, you stubborn mule of a man! So stay and fight for it!"

"I can't, damn you!"

"Why not?" she shouted, almost nose to nose with him.

"Because if something happens to you, I'll never survive!"

She sucked in a breath, too stunned to say another word. His eyes squeezed close, and he breathed deeply through his nose a few times. Then he rubbed his hands over his face and through his hair, and Mercy realized he'd lost his hat somewhere. She wanted to smooth her fingers through the unruly strands, and cup his scruffy, wonderful face. She knotted her fist in her skirts to keep from reaching for him.

"I've never had a place before," he said, so quietly she almost didn't hear him. "Since my parents died...I've never had a place...never had people...someone..." Gray swallowed hard. "Walkin' away might be the hardest thing I'll ever do. But it's easier than watchin' anyone here die. Watchin' *you* die. And being the cause of it."

Mercy lifted her hand to her cheeks, surprised to find that they were wet. "I think you love me, Gray Woodson," she whispered.

Gray smiled at her, slow and sweet, and nodded. "More than I love a nap."

She laughed, though it came out in hiccups and giggles, and buried her face in her hands. He gently pried them off.

"I love you, Mercy Woodson. Despite the fact that you nearly burn down the house every time you cook, and always smell like apples, which I really used to hate, but I think they might be growing on me, and even though you argue with every word out of my mouth—really, you could let a few go every now and then—and you won't stop nagging me about the list of chores you always have lined up for me that we both know I'm never going to do. And you never let me nap in peace, and worse, you keep letting Sunshine in the house even though I've repeatedly forbidden him to step foot—"

She held up a finger. "Gray."

"Yes?" he asked with that lopsided grin she loved so well.

"Shut up and kiss me already."

His grin widened. "Yes, ma'am."

His lips captured hers and he pulled her to him, one arm wrapping around her waist while the other trailed up her neck until he cupped the back of her head. He kissed her until the room began to spin and she had to cling to him to keep on her feet. He didn't let her up for air until someone let out a long whistle and numerous people broke out in cheers and applause.

Mercy broke the kiss and glanced at the audience she hadn't realized had grown to more than sixty people. Their argument must have been louder than she'd thought. Either that or some of her more enterprising friends had run out and pulled people in off the streets for the show, because the tavern was about full to bursting. And every set of eyes was on them.

"Um, maybe we should go somewhere more…private," she said, and their audience issued a near unified gasp of dismay.

"Ah, come on, you two, don't shut us out now," Mrs. DuVere said. "It was just getting good."

Gray snorted and Mercy dropped her head to his chest. He kissed the top of her head and then took her face in his hands, gently turning her to look at him.

"Why did you come here?" he asked.

She took a deep breath. "To tell you that you're making a mistake, and I love you too much to let you leave."

A collective sigh went up around them and her cheeks flamed hot again.

"Well, damn," Gray said and brushed his thumb across her cheek. "I never believed in miracles before but… now I just might." Then he shrugged. "Either that or you haven't the sense God gave a worm, and I'd be well advised to cut tail and run as fast as I can."

"Gray!" she said, playfully slapping his arm.

He chuckled and pulled her in against his side.

"Come on, wife. Let's go home." He led her to the door, still a little wobbly on his legs as they waded through the crowd and stepped outside.

Hope flashed through her, so strong it made her knees weak, and she pulled him to a stop. "So...you're staying then?"

His smile dimmed. "We'll talk about it in the morning," he said, not meeting her eyes.

"Gray..."

Then a shot rang out, echoing so loudly her ears throbbed with the sound.

Gray's arm fell away from her waist, and she stood there. Alone.

# CHAPTER TWENTY-SIX

Fire ripped a path across Gray's head, and the wooden sign above him exploded into a million splinters. The screams and thundering of people's feet as they scattered disoriented him for a second. He shook his head, hissing when the movement sent stabbing pain cascading through his skull.

*Mercy!*

She stood motionless a few feet away, seemingly stunned. Jason, Doc, and Preacher were nearby, ushering people out of the way, getting as many of them back inside the tavern as possible.

"Gray!" Mercy shouted, snapping out of it as she rushed toward him. But there was no time. The gunman who'd shot him sat on his horse in the middle of the road, a cold smile stretching his thin lips as he watched the scene of panic spread out before him.

"Sunshine!" Gray yelled, pushing Mercy into his arms as Jason turned.

"No!" Mercy tried to shove Jason away, but he pulled her to safety behind the thick post that supported the tavern's porch roof.

Gray turned to face the gunman, dragging in deep breaths to try and clear the fog in his head. The adrenaline coursing through him burned off whatever final alcohol still lingered in his system. But that bullet had gotten too close. His head throbbed again, and he pressed a hand to the jagged line of burning pain on his scalp. His hand came away slick with blood.

Way too damn close.

He swayed but managed to keep to his feet. Barely. His hands reached for his guns, but it felt like he was pushing through mud to get to them. Maybe that graze went deeper than he thought. His vision swam, black dots flooding his periphery.

The gunman who'd shot at him dismounted and sauntered closer, living up his moment of besting a legendary gunfighter for all its worth. Irritating for certain, though Gray couldn't really blame him. He was a catch, after all.

"Thanks for making this easy, Old Man," he said, waving at Gray.

At least Gray thought he waved at him. He couldn't quite make his eyes work right. He leaned his shoulder against the post at his right. It would make it harder to pull his gun, but he wasn't all that sure he could pull it anyway. Certainly not fast enough to best a man who already had his gun trained on him. Why hadn't he shot again? Still trying to savor his moment of glory, maybe?

"I aim to please," Gray said, though his voice sounded like it was coming from far away.

"No!" Mercy shouted. She broke free from Jason and rushed to Gray.

"Stop!" the gunman yelled.

Jason skidded to a halt a few feet away from them. Mercy however, placed her body in front of Gray while she clapped a handkerchief to his head.

"Mercy, get back," Gray said.

She ignored him. Because of course she did. She dabbed at his head again and winced, though whether it was from causing him pain or because she was using her injured arm to tend him, he didn't know.

"Don't you ever listen, woman?" he mumbled.

"No," she said with a tremulous smile. "I'd have thought you'd be used to that by now."

His eyes shot to hers as her other hand trailed down to his until she reached the gun in his hand. Her eyes bore into his. She was steady, calm, and his shaking fingers released the weapon. He glanced over to Sunshine who was hopefully the only other one who noticed Mercy hiding the gun in the folds of her skirt. Jason's hand made a subtle move toward his own gun, and Gray let out a long breath. They were both too stubborn for their own good. He loved them for it. But damn.

"I said, get away," the gunman said, keeping his gun trained on Gray and Mercy.

She half turned to him. "Are you really going to shoot a man who doesn't have a fair chance?"

The man snorted. "For seven hundred and fifty dollars and the right to say I killed Quick Shot Woodson? Hell yeah."

She gave him a slow, cold smile that both filled Gray with pride and a hint of fear. "Good," she said. "I wasn't planning on being fair, either."

She and Jason both pulled their guns, and Jason moved until he stood shoulder to shoulder with Gray. The gunman's eyes widened, and he pulled his other gun, keeping one on Gray and Mercy but aiming the other at Jason.

Gray tried to take the gun back from her. He appreciated the thought, but the last thing he wanted was for Mercy to be dueling for his life. But every time he'd tug at her or try to move to pull her arm down, Mercy would swat at him with her other arm, though it must have pained her to do it.

"Blasted woman, give that to me," he muttered.

"No. Now hush," she snapped back without an ounce of bite.

"I don't know what you're trying to do, mister," the gunman said to Jason. "But I ain't got no fight with you. Or with the woman. I'm just here for Woodson."

"Then you do have a fight with me," Jason said.

"And with me."

Gray's mouth dropped open as Doc stepped up beside Jason, pulling his own gun from somewhere to aim at the gunman.

He shrugged at Gray's (and Mercy's and Jason's) obvious surprise. "I keep one around for emergencies. This seems to qualify."

Gray started to laugh, then groaned as the action sent a fresh round of pain shooting through his head.

"You don't have to do this," he murmured to Mercy and his…his friends?

"Yes, we do," Preacher said, coming to stand on Gray's other side, a wicked-looking dagger in his hand.

Barkeep stepped up, wielding his broom, and Gray inched up the post, standing a little straighter, his eyes wide.

The barber stepped up, too, holding his scissors like a knife. He gave Gray a nod and turned to glare at the gunman. Martha planted herself next to Mercy, waving her marble rolling pin. Mrs. DuVere and her girls poured out of the tavern. The girls all held wine bottles by the neck, brandishing them like they couldn't wait to bludgeon someone over the head. Mrs. DuVere marched over and stood beside Preacher, winking at Gray before she leveled her gun at Gray's assailant.

More townspeople joined them, each holding anything that could be used as a weapon, and Gray's chest grew so tight, he rubbed at it. What were all these people doing?

Doc turned a cold smile on the gunman. "Sorry, Mister. But Sheriff Woodson belongs to this town. And we take care of our own."

Gray sucked in a breath, completely…flabbergasted. He didn't know how to react or what to think. Why? Why would they all do this for him?

"See?" Mercy said, for his ears alone. "I told you this was your home."

A noise escaped him that he'd meant to be a laugh but sounded more like a sob. Home?

He looked around at the people gathered by him, gathered with weapons gripped tight to help him, defend him.

For the first time in his life, that tiny spark of hope in his chest that he tried so hard to ignore flared. Maybe… maybe he had finally found the place he belonged. Maybe he could actually live a full life that didn't end prematurely at the end of a gun.

He pushed away from the post and Jason was there to steady him. His head pounded somethin' fierce, but he ignored it. Mercy wrapped an arm around his waist and Martha stepped nearer, ready to flatten anyone who got too close.

The gunman had slowly backed up as more and more people came out to stand by Gray, but he hadn't lowered his gun. He'd have to shoot through more than one person to get to him, but he looked like he might still try.

Just then, Frank came hurtling from the jailhouse, swinging the teakettle with a garbled yell. The gunman spun around but not fast enough, and the teakettle slammed into his arm with a crack. The gunman dropped his weapon, howling in pain.

Gray's eyes widened. Frank looked pretty surprised himself. But he shook it off and stood up straighter, giving Gray a nod.

"I might have to make him a deputy now," Gray muttered.

Mercy smiled. "As I said. You aren't alone anymore."

The townspeople all nodded, and Gray cleared his throat, wiping at the sudden moisture in his eyes. "Must have gotten some dirt in there," he murmured, and Mercy laughed and kissed his cheek.

Doc nodded to the stunned gunfighter who still knelt on the ground, cradling his arm.

"You. Get out."

The man's eyes widened. "You're not going to kill me?"

"Not this time," Preacher said. "You get to deliver a message for us."

The man's face paled, but he jerked his head in a nod.

"Spread the word," Preacher said. "To anyone else

thinking about coming for the sheriff. You tell them even if they manage to get a lucky shot off—and that's a big if—this is Quick Shot Woodson we're talking about. That person will never make it out of town. Let alone collect any bounty. The townspeople will make sure of it. All five hundred and sixty-three of them."

"Soon to be five hundred and sixty-four," Mercy said, putting her hand on her belly.

Doc grinned, Preacher laughed, and Jason beamed like a proud uncle.

Gray stared at Mercy, down at the hand covering his... his child?

The world around him spun again. He opened his mouth to say something, anything. But the black spots took over his vision and everything went dark.

. . .

Mercy gasped when Gray hit the ground, and she dropped to her knees beside him, patting his cheeks.

"Jamison?" she asked, glancing up at Doc, worry coursing through her.

But Doc just laughed. "He'll be fine. I suspect his delicate constitution has more to do with your condition than his. Good luck with that one," he said, though there was a twinkle in his eyes.

"You won't get away with this," the gunman said as Frank yanked him off the ground and dragged him to his horse. "Josiah Banff is a powerful man. He won't let this go."

Preacher stepped forward. "Frank, perhaps you

should escort our new witness here to a jail cell."

The man frowned even as Frank nodded. "Witness? What do you mean, witness?"

Mercy stood and rounded on him. "He means that you just gave up your boss. And if you want any sort of protection from him — and you're going to need it — you'll tell the authorities everything you know about Josiah and this bounty."

If possible, the gunman's face paled even further, and he stuttered a few times but then slumped, letting Frank half walk, half drag him to the jailhouse. Maybe he'd realized speaking against Josiah was his best bet to stay alive. Whatever it was, she didn't dwell on it, because Gray's eyes blinked open and gazed at her with bemused wonder.

She helped him to his feet, and Doc turned to Jason. "Deputy Sheriff, I think it's past time Josiah saw the inside of a jail cell."

All amusement in Jason's eyes died. "Agreed."

"I'll go with you," Preacher said.

Jason nodded and turned to Gray. "We'll head out and arrest him, Sheriff, and that should be the end of all discussions about you leaving again."

"Thank you," Gray said, clearing his throat. "I…" He took a deep breath. "Thank you."

Doc smiled. "You've had our backs since day one."

Gray opened his mouth, probably to refute that claim, but shut it with a grunt when Mercy elbowed him in the ribs.

Doc continued, unaware of Gray's antics. "It's time for Josiah and anyone else who has an inkling to cause trouble to know that from here on out, Desolation will no longer allow its citizens to be terrorized. We take care of our own."

"Here, here!" the crowd cheered.

And this time Mercy didn't try to hold back her happy tears.

She wrapped her arm around her husband's waist and leaned against him.

"Welcome home, my love."

# CHAPTER TWENTY-SEVEN

Mercy held the wad of cotton to Gray's temple while Doc wound some torn linen strips around it to hold everything in place.

She sighed and looked down at him. "You know, if you'd hold still, this would go a lot faster."

"Or you could just not do it at all, and we'd be done already," he grumbled.

Mercy exchanged an exasperated look with the doctor.

"Head wounds tend to be bleeders," the doc explained. Again. "If nothing else, it'll keep your hat from getting bloodstains."

Gray griped some more, but he did stop fidgeting, so that argument must have done the trick. Doc finished wrapping him up and stepped back to admire his handiwork. He gave a sharp nod and then fixed Gray with his steady gaze.

"I'd like you to stay here tonight so I can keep an eye on you. Head wounds can be tricky. Mercy, you are welcome to stay with him," he said, giving her an awkward smile. "There are several cots set up in the next room you are welcome to use."

Mercy nodded, though Gray was still muttering under his breath and pouting.

The doc turned back to him. "If all looks well in the morning, I'll send you on your way home. But you'll need to take it easy for a few days."

That perked Gray right up. He was giving Doc his full, undivided attention now. Mercy pressed her lips together to keep from laughing, a wave of fond amusement washing over her as she stared down at her grouchy old curmudgeon. Nothing made the man happier than a nap. She shook her head.

"It would probably be best to stay in a quiet room, not have too many visitors for a bit. Get lots of rest," Doc continued, with Gray nodding eagerly.

Mercy rolled her eyes. "Be careful, Jamison. Any more instructions like these, and he'll be walking around bashing himself in the head just so he has an excuse to lay about all day."

Gray harrumphed. "I wouldn't need an excuse if I'd just been allowed to retire in peace." He tried to glower at her, but his eyes softened almost immediately. He held out a hand, pulling her in when she took it.

"How are you?" he asked. His eyes strayed to her belly and he reached out, laying a hand on her almost reverently. "Are you sure? About the…"

She cocked an eyebrow, smiling gently. "I'm fine. And yes, I'm sure. Well, relatively sure in any case. My…" She glanced up, belatedly realizing they were having a fairly intimate conversation in front of the doctor, but he had quietly left the room without them noticing.

"My…courses are never late and were due just after our wedding. And there have been signs. I've been tired and a few other things. After chatting with Mrs. Du-Vere…" She smiled again and shrugged, laying her hand lightly on her belly.

A grin pulled at Gray's lips, though it didn't quite

form all the way, and she furrowed her forehead. "Are you…are you pleased?"

He raised startled eyes to hers. "I…" He paused for a second and then barked out a choked laugh. "I guess I just never pictured myself as having youngins. But… yeah…I think… Yes, I'm pleased." He laid his hand over hers. "Are you?"

"Yes. Terrified," she said with a little laugh. "But yes. Though…"

She frowned again, a nagging dread eating at the edges of her happiness.

"What is it?" He pulled her closer so she stood between his legs, half sitting on his lap so he could wrap his arms around her.

"Josiah…"

He pulled her against his chest and rested his head on hers. "He won't bother us anymore. He'll have to cool his heels in our jail cell for a day or two maybe, once Sunshine and Preacher get back with him. But I'll ship him out as soon as we can get some men gathered, along with his gunman. They can explain their actions to the judge down south. And if the assassin wants to keep his neck from the rope, he'll give up Josiah right quick."

She sighed and leaned into him. "I hope so. I just wish it was all settled. It was one thing when it was just me he was threatening. But now there's you…" She drew a gentle finger along the edge of his bandage. "And the baby…"

She was hardly able to get that word out. It seemed so foreign. So unconnected to anything in her life.

She laid her head on his shoulder. "I do feel safer

knowing the whole town is behind you. But…" She let out a shaky breath. "I will just rest easier when he's behind bars. Preferably far away from us."

He pressed a kiss to her temple. "I know. I promise you, I won't let him harm either of you. Even if I have to go back to shooting people during my retirement. If ever someone deserved it, it's him."

Gray's eyebrows suddenly shot up to his hairline. "I just realized that if I have to stay home and take it easy for a few days, I'll be missing my midday meals from Martha."

She gasped. "Oh, you! Just for that, I think I'll feed you apple pie every day."

He blanched in horror. "I'll tattle on you to the doc. That's nothing short of torture, and I'm sure there's some law against treating prisoners inhumanely."

She planted her hands on her hips. "So you're my prisoner now?"

"Your willing prisoner," he said with a wink.

"Ha!" She pushed away from him, but he didn't let her get too far.

"You have to be gentle with me, woman. I'm injured."

He pulled her back in, and she pursed her lips, trying to glare at him. But it was difficult to maintain an air of disapproval when he sat there with a bandaged head, his hair sticking up in all directions, looking at her like he was the most innocent angel to ever step foot on the earth.

She sighed and cupped his face. "What am I going to do with you?"

"I can think of a few things," he said, waggling his eyebrows.

She rolled her eyes. "Your head is still bleeding, and the doctor told you to rest."

He widened his eyes and rubbed his belly. "I meant that you could feed me. I missed my supper. You have such a wicked mind, Mrs. Woodson."

"Um-hmm." She leaned into him. "I'll show you wicked, Mr. Woodson…"

Their lips met, and she sank into him, the knowledge that she'd almost lost him, *twice*, settling around her. She trembled and wrapped her arms about his neck, pouring her whole heart into that kiss. He crushed her to him, and the way his hands roved over her, almost as though he was ensuring she was still whole and healthy in his arms rather than from unbridled passion, made her think he was realizing the same thing.

They'd come too close to losing each other that day.

If the doctor hadn't insisted on them staying in his clinic that night, she'd have taken her husband home and shown him just how happy she was to still have him in her arms. But since they were on strict orders to take it easy, she'd have to be content with wrapping herself around him while they caught a few hours of sleep.

• • •

"Sheriff. Sheriff?"

Gray cracked an eye open, and his head pounded at even the small bit of morning sun that made it past his eyelid. "What is it?" he ground out, his mouth feeling like he'd just licked all the dust from his boots.

The doc crouched beside his bed, peeking beneath his

bandage. But when he went to pull Gray's eyelids up, Gray swatted at his hand.

"I'm fine. And awake," he said, groaning as he pulled himself upright. "Sorta."

He glanced beside him, instantly wide awake the second he noticed Mercy was gone.

He grabbed for his clothes. "Where's Mercy?"

Doc stood back so Gray could tug on his boots and get the rest of his clothes situated. His head throbbed and his gut felt a bit queasy, but he tried to ignore it. He had more important things to do. Like find his wayward wife. The woman couldn't seem to help wandering off.

"She's across the street with Martha, cooking up some breakfast for you, I believe."

Gray calmed a little. He'd have preferred Mercy stayed by his side, but in the interest of breakfast... Though he did hope Martha was doing most of the cooking.

"How are you feeling this morning?" the doc asked.

Gray sighed and rubbed a hand across his face. "How do I look like I feel?"

Doc's eyebrow quirked up. "You look like hell."

"You're not far off." He stretched as well as he could without jostling his head too much. "Why'd you wake me?"

"Mr. Sunshine and the reverend haven't returned yet. We expected them by now, so we're gathering a party of men to ride out to Banff's ranch."

Any remnants of sleep were burned off in a rush of anger. And fear.

Gray reached down and grab his holster, quickly

buckling it around his waist and settling his guns into place.

He'd grown quite fond of the kid...though he'd certainly never admit it to him. The thought of something happening to him was more than—

"Doc Fairbanks!" a voice yelled from outside.

Doc and Gray both rushed through the clinic and out the front door. Jed, the man they'd left at Josiah's to keep an eye on things, sat panting on the steps of the clinic, holding his side. Doc immediately dropped to his knees to examine him, but Jed brushed him away.

"I'm okay, Doc. Just winded. I had to race here from Banff's."

Doc's eyes widened.

"Why? What's happened? And where are the preacher and Sunshine?" Gray asked, hardly giving Jed time to answer.

Jed shook his head. "Mr. Sunshine and Reverend Connelly showed up first thing this morning, but Mr. Banff was ready for them. Someone must have tipped him off. He either has someone in town who's been watching, or he was prepared just in case his last gunman didn't work. But he was ready when they came to get him. They ambushed them. They never had a chance."

Gray's blood ran cold, and his hands gripped the butt of the gun on his right hip. He barely noticed he was doing it, but the smooth metal felt good in his hand. Comforting. He took a deep breath and let it out slowly, but he kept his hand on his gun.

"Are they..." the doc asked.

Jed shook his head, and relief washed over Gray.

"They're alive. But injured. The men beat the hell out of them. And Banff's had them tied up all night. He's coming here and he's gathering everyone up. He'll have at least a dozen men with him, plus Mr. Sunshine and the reverend as his hostages. I've never seen him so angry as when they told him he was under arrest. I don't know exactly what he's planning," he said to Gray, "but he's mad enough that he might try anything."

Gray nodded slowly. "Then we'll just have to be ready for him."

Jed nodded and leaned back against the railing. His breaths were coming easier, though he still dragged in huge lungfuls of air with each one.

Gray's mind worked furiously, discarding one thought after another. He'd never had to come up with anything too elaborate before. People either steered clear of him or came at him one-on-one. And so far, he'd always been the one to walk away.

But that wasn't going to work this time. Banff would never have the guts to face him one-on-one. And Gray was fast, but even he probably couldn't take down a dozen men before someone got a lucky enough shot. Plus, they had hostages. Men Gray didn't want harmed.

He sighed. He'd enjoyed having friends more than he thought he would, but life, or at least to-the-death fights, was a little easier when his opponent didn't have so much leverage against him.

His gaze jerked to the General Store. Mercy. She had to be kept away from the coming fight at all costs. What were the chances she'd forgive him if he locked her in one of the cells until it was all over?

Well, standing around making his head hurt with all the thinking wasn't solving anything.

"Jed, run across to Mrs. DuVere and send her—"

"I'm already here, Sheriff. What's going on?" he heard Mrs. DuVere say.

Gray glanced up in surprise, his mouth open to question how the hell she'd known—

"Samuel is still gone, and poor Jed here looks like he's about to pass out. I put two and two together."

Gray shook his head, gracing her with a small smile. "Your arithmetic skills are truly remarkable, Mrs. DuVere."

She waved him off, though the smile she gave him was pleased. He filled her in as quickly as he could. "I need you to spread the word to the townsfolk to stay in their homes..."

She was already shaking her head. "We told you last night, Sheriff. You belong to this town, and we take care of our own. If there's a fight coming, then we'll be behind you all the way."

Gray swallowed against the sudden lump in his gullet. "I appreciate that," he said, pausing to clear his throat, "but the last thing I want is to give Banff and his men more targets. If"—he held up a hand to stop her argument—"there are men who are armed, who know how to use their weapons, and who understand the dangers and are skilled enough to not become targets themselves, then...I would appreciate the help."

That had been more difficult to say than he'd thought. But if he was going to be a part of this community, then he needed to start accepting all that went with it.

To a point.

"However," he said, and Mrs. DuVere turned back to him, eyebrows raised in question. "That does not extend to my wife. I don't know how you'll manage, but do what you can to keep her indoors, away from any windows, and well away from any danger. If you can figure out a way to lock her in a closet somewhere, I'd be most obliged."

Mrs. DuVere laughed. "Oh, honey, we both know the chances of that happening are pretty slim."

He sighed deeply. "Just…try. Tell her she has more than just me to think about now."

She nodded and walked away.

Gray rubbed a hand over his face and then glanced at Doc. "You still got that gun, Doc?"

Doc nodded grimly, and Gray pursed his lips. "Then let's gather who we can and get our men back."

# CHAPTER TWENTY-EIGHT

Mercy paced the parlor at Mrs. DuVere's, trying to calm herself. But every time she thought of Gray marching out to meet Josiah while she was hiding behind the drapes—she couldn't keep still. Part of her wanted to run out into that street and throw herself in front of her husband. The other part couldn't forget the fact that it was no longer just herself she'd be putting in harm's way if she did.

"If you don't sit down soon, you're going to wear a hole in my carpet," Mrs. DuVere said.

Mercy flounced onto the sofa with a huff. "I don't know how you can keep so calm. I know you're worried about the reverend."

Mrs. DuVere nodded. "Yes. I am. But making myself sick with it isn't going to help anyone. He's not even here yet. Once he is...well..." She stood and went to a cabinet in the corner of the room and pulled out a heavy, polished shotgun. "I reckon I can pick off a man or two if necessary."

Mercy's lips tugged into a smile. "Got another one of those?"

Mrs. DuVere chuckled. "No. But you can help keep a lookout. As long as you stay away from the windows when the shooting starts. And don't tell your husband."

"Deal," she said. It was better than sitting around doing nothing or hiding away with the rest of the women.

"How much longer do you think—"

The faint sound of shattering glass had her frozen in place, ears straining for other sounds.

"Did you hear that?" she whispered to Mrs. DuVere, who nodded, holding her finger to her lips.

She crept closer to the door, quietly leaning against it so she could put her ear to the wood to listen. Her forehead creased, whether in a frown or because she was concentrating, Mercy wasn't sure. She was about to creep closer herself when the door burst open in an explosion of splintering wood.

Both women screamed as Mrs. DuVere fell, knocked backward by the blow. The shotgun went off, firing into the ceiling.

Mercy didn't know where to look. Mrs. DuVere lay unmoving on the floor, a trickle of blood coming from her head. She was still breathing, though that was small comfort, because two men were pushing their way through the remnants of the door, shoving Mrs. DuVere's body aside.

One of them had the presence of mind to grab her shotgun as he passed. The other stalked toward Mercy, his face a mask of evil intent.

"The boss wants a word with you," he said.

Mercy backed up, her eyes darting about the room for anything she could use as a weapon.

"Your boss needs to learn how to take no for an answer," she said.

She lunged for the heavy lamp on the end table just as the man lunged for her. Her fingers wrapped around it, but his arms were about her waist, lifting her off the ground before she could hit him. She tried to bring it down on his head anyway but only succeeded in hitting his arm.

It was enough, however, to make him howl in pain and release her. She swung the lamp around again and hit him in the side of the head as hard as she could. He staggered and went down, and she grinned in triumph.

And didn't see the fist of the other man swinging toward her face until it was too late.

• • •

Too many things happened all at once. Gray and Doc were standing in the front room of the clinic, trying to come up with some semblance of a plan when a shotgun went off across the street. But as they ran outside to see what had happened, Frank and his son raced into town, their horses' chests heaving.

"Banff and his men are nearly here, Sheriff!" Frank said. "They must have circled around and come in from the south. We was watching the road and didn't catch sight of them until they'd nearly passed us."

Gray's heart hammered in his chest. Banff was nearly on top of them. But that gunshot...

He looked back toward the tavern but didn't take two steps before Banff and his men arrived in a cloud of dust.

Gray glanced at Doc, who shook his head. Jed might have been able to round up a few men, but some lived farther out of town. And the ones who were nearby hadn't shown their faces. His heart sank. Perhaps the night before had just been a show. Or perhaps they'd meant what they said at the time. But they'd only been faced with one assailant. It was a different matter when faced with the man who'd terrorized them all for so long, along with an armed posse of his men.

Banff dismounted in the middle of the street and jerked his head at some of his men. Then he fixed Gray with a cold, arrogant stare as Sunshine and Preacher were brought forward, their hands bound in front of them. A ridiculous way to tie a prisoner, but they'd probably been allowed to ride their own horses and needed to be able to hang on. A necessity. And one that left them with some amount of mobility. Thank heaven for a tiny stroke of luck.

Gray fixed them each with a stare. Their faces were swollen and bloody, but their eyes were twin flames of fury. His gut twisted with rage, his heart anguished over what they'd obviously suffered. But their spirits hadn't been broken. They'd watch for an opportunity. Gray just had to give them one.

He straightened his back and fixed his attention on Josiah. It was time to end this.

Then Josiah smiled, his bug eyes turning to Mrs. DuVere's.

The door opened…and a man exited, his hand wrapped around the back of Mercy's neck as he pushed her forward. A gag had been shoved in her mouth and wrapped around the back of her head, and her hands were bound behind her back. As the man shoved her again, she stumbled, falling to her knees in the dirt beside Sunshine.

Gray's vision filled with red as he took in Preacher,

Sunshine, and his Mercy, on their knees in front of Josiah and his men. Each with a gun pressed to their head.

"Even you aren't fast enough to save them all," Josiah said, each smug word dripping like acid in Gray's ears.

He ground his teeth together so hard, he wouldn't have been surprised if they'd cracked.

"Now that I have your attention, Sheriff," Josiah said, sneering on the last word, "you and I are going to come to a little arrangement."

A glint of the sun off metal drew Gray's eye to the roof of the general store. Martha crouched low behind the chimney stack, a rifle in her hand. Movement farther along the roof meant someone else was up there with her. Probably one or both of her grandparents. Either way, he had a set of eyes and at least one weapon trained on the men below. That they didn't know about.

The tightness in his chest eased a fraction. Enough so he could breathe. Think. He looked back at Josiah and hoped his face didn't betray the turmoil that was going on beneath the surface.

"I don't think there is anything to arrange, Banff. Other than your surrender, that is. I believe a white flag is usually involved. I have a handkerchief if you'd like to borrow it." He patted at his chest before pulling it from a pocket, grimacing a little. "It's not completely clean, but it'll do."

He waved it at Josiah, who growled, his cheeks flushing red with anger. "You need to keep that yapping mouth of yours shut!" he spat out. "Keep it up and we'll be arranging your funeral instead of your immediate departure from town."

Gray raised his brows. "You'd arrange a funeral for me? That's awful nice of you. I'd like daisies, if possible. I guess that means if I win, I'll have to do the same for you. Do you like daisies?"

"Shut up!" Josiah shouted.

His men shifted nervously. Either because their boss was obviously losing his temper or because Gray seemed so completely unaffected by the scene before him. Most of them had lost the smug looks they'd started out with and had expressions ranging from confusion to outright fear.

Because only a madman—or a stone-cold killer who was very good at his job—would be so unconcerned about being this outnumbered with several supposed loved ones in his enemies' hands.

He had to keep the fact that his stomach churned with every second Mercy knelt at their feet to himself. Keep them guessing. Keep them scared. And he had to keep Banff distracted long enough to get in a good position. And long enough to allow a few more townspeople to get into place. If they were coming.

He slowly stepped off the porch of Doc's clinic, moving out farther into the street. Josiah's eyes narrowed, but Gray took care not to move toward him, and he kept his hands held slightly up, enough so the men could see he wasn't going for his guns.

The drapes on the second floor of the tavern moved slightly, and Gray thought he caught sight of Mrs. Du-Vere's brilliant jewel-colored gown. If the woman also had a gun in her hand, he'd buy enough drinks to keep her tavern in business until the day he died. Even if he never drank them. His one escapade into drunkenness had been more than enough for him.

Josiah's face twisted in anger. "I tried to go about this the nice way, Sheriff," he spat out. "I was willing to pay your little bitch of a wife good money for land that should be rightfully mine. But she had to be difficult!"

The man holding the gun on her nudged her head hard, pushing her forward enough that she fell into the dirt.

Rage flashed through Gray again, and he clenched his fists to contain it. He had to bide his time. Wait for the right moment. Josiah was trying to get in his head. Trying to enrage him so he'd make a mistake.

And he was doing a fantastic job.

But he couldn't let him see it.

Sunshine reached out to help Mercy back up as best he could with his hands bound together. The men watching them allowed him to get her upright, and then his captor shoved at him with the tip of his pistol until he had to let her go.

Gray sucked a deep breath in through his nose, trying to will himself into that calm, quiet place that he needed in order to get them all out of this alive. Though at this point, he wasn't sure that was possible. He'd do what he could, though. As long as Mercy walked away. The men, too, if he could. But, the devil take it, he'd sacrifice them all to save her.

"You're absolutely right," he made himself say. *Keep up the small talk. Keep them confused.* "My wife *does* tend to be difficult. Had problems with her myself," he said.

Mercy made a strangled noise behind her gag and glared up at him. Even bound and gagged and held at gunpoint, the woman was a gutsy little spitfire who refused to take his shit. God, he loved her.

"I'd be happy to give her a stern talking-to if you'd like me to get her off your hands," he said, taking a step toward her.

Several of Josiah's men aimed their guns at him and he stopped, hands up. "Just thought I'd offer."

"The only thing I want you offering is the deed to that property. The speed with which you sign it over will determine how quickly or slowly I let you die. And who I send to die with you."

Movement near the jailhouse caught his attention, and he looked over to see Frank inching his way up the stairs to Sunshine's apartment. The fact that he was literally tiptoeing would have made Gray laugh on any other day. Today, he just hoped the man could make it to the top without being seen. And, once there, could make it to the roof or the window or wherever he was planning on going with the ancient shotgun that he had clutched in his hands.

"What's going on here, Sheriff?" Tom said, coming from the direction of the smithy with a heavy hammer in each hand.

Josiah sneered at him. "Are you planning on fighting bullets with your hammers, blacksmith?"

Tom shrugged. "I'm not planning on anything, Mr. Banff. Just thought I'd see what all the fuss was about."

Frank's three brothers slowly approached from the alley behind them. One held a pitchfork. The other two were unarmed but stood with their arms crossed behind Gray.

Josiah's eyes darted among them, growing more agitated by the second. But when no one else approached, his scornful expression returned. "A pretty poor showing for the beloved town sheriff."

Gray shrugged. "These men are here because they are loyal friends. Yours are here because they are being threatened or paid. I'd rather trust my back to my friends."

Each of the men beside him stood a little straighter, and Gray's heart warmed at the sight. He wasn't alone in this.

Gray met Sunshine's gaze, then Preacher's. Gave them a tiny nod. They each straightened, watching him, poised to spring into action the second they had a chance.

"Enough!" Josiah finally shouted. "Clear the streets! Send them away, Woodson," he said, jerking his head at the men with him. When Gray didn't make a move, Josiah marched to Mercy, pulled a gun with his uninjured hand, and jabbed it into her head hard enough that she cried out. "Send them away or she dies. *Now*."

Utter stillness swept over Gray, creeping into his very consciousness. Bringing him back to that place he'd never wanted to go again.

"You've got till the count of five!" Josiah shouted. And he began his countdown.

Gray's breath slowly left his lungs. He counted along with Josiah. And when Josiah reached three...

Gray pulled his guns and fired.

*Bang!*

*Bang!*
*Bang!*
*Bang!*
*Bang!*
*Bang!*

It happened so fast, everyone stood staring, dumb-struck, at what had just happened.

The man holding the gun on Mercy had been struck in the shoulder and was lying on the ground, howling in pain. The one holding Sunshine had taken Gray's bullet in his thigh. The man next to him got one in the arm. Two others behind them also went down as they got hit in their pistol hands.

And Josiah…as much as Gray had wanted to put a bullet straight through his chest, he didn't want to murder a man in front of Mercy. He would have, had there been no other way. But Josiah, when it came right down to it, was a miserable little coward who didn't deserve a quick death. Gray would much rather he suffer a long, long life in prison.

So instead, he'd shot him in his thigh.

Josiah gripped his wounded thigh, putting all his weight on his other leg, and looked around him, sputtering in disbelief. A couple of his men started to raise their guns again, but Gray waved a finger at them. "Boys, I've got more bullets."

They holstered their weapons.

"You might want to rethink employers, gentlemen," Gray said. Then he pressed his fingers to his lips and whistled.

Martha and her grandparents stood up, brandishing

their guns. Doc moved from where he'd been standing behind the post on his porch, his rifle trained on Josiah. Mrs. DuVere and Frank also showed themselves, Mrs. DuVere shoving her shotgun through the window that Gray hadn't even noticed she'd broken.

And then one by one, more people stood. From every rooftop. From behind every barrel and post. From every alleyway.

Gray watched them all in amazement, his throat growing tight. They'd said they take care of their own. And they had. Damn it all, they'd all shown up when he'd needed them. Nothing could have proven to Gray more that he was finally home.

Josiah's men looked around. And almost as one, they seemed to realize it was over. They were outnumbered. Several just turned and ran, remounting and riding out of town as fast as they could.

But Josiah still stood beside Mercy, watching his plan fall apart, his gun still drawn, helpless rage mottling his face.

And Gray saw the exact moment the man decided to go down shooting. Josiah's gaze turned back to Mercy. His gun raised.

A shot rang out.

And Josiah screamed, dropping to the ground and staring at the bleeding hole in his hand.

Gray walked toward him, kicking his gun out of the way, and Josiah's eyes widened with terror. But Gray turned, ignoring him completely so he could drop to his knees beside Mercy. The other townsfolk swarmed them, helping Sunshine and Preacher, and Doc moved in to check on Josiah.

Gray disregarded all of them. He gently pulled the gag from Mercy's mouth and kissed her as softly as he could. "God, I love you," he said, pressing his forehead to hers.

"I love you, too," she said, leaning in for another kiss. "And I'd love to sit here kissing you all day. But…do you think you can untie me first?"

He sucked in a breath, and she half turned so he could see her hands. He…didn't even know what to say. It had just slipped his mind for a second… Oops?

He quickly untied her hands and rubbed his hands up and down her arms. And then groaned, releasing some pent-up frustration. "I swear, if you ever scare me like that again, I'm going to put you over my knee and spank you."

Instead of looking properly chastised, her eyes lit up with a mischievous curiosity, and he blinked at her in shock for a few seconds before shaking his head and muttering, "You are impossible," under his breath.

"Yes, but you love me anyway," she said, having heard him despite his taking almost no care to keep her from doing so.

"Heaven help me, I do."

He pulled her to her feet, his hands searching her, trying to make sure she really wasn't injured. "Are you okay?" he asked, cupping her face.

She nodded, and he leaned down to kiss her again, his heart thudding in his chest. He pulled her into his arms, and she buried her face against him. They held each other for a few moments, and then she took a long, shuddering breath and shook her head.

He looked at her, brows raised in question. "What?"

"I guess there went your retirement."

His laughter rang out through the street. "No way. That will be the last time I ever pull those damn guns. I'm retired."

# EPILOGUE

Gray forced a smile and waved goodbye to yet another neighbor who'd dropped by to *ooh* and *ahh* over the town's newest resident and leave a food offering with her exhausted parents.

He peeked under the napkin covering the basket and sniffed.

"Who was that?" Mercy asked, walking with a slight bounce as she cradled their newborn.

Gray glanced up, his breath catching at the sight of his girls. He cleared his throat. "Frank and his wife. It looks like…" He took another sniff. "Meatloaf. And potatoes and biscuits and corn and…there might be a pie in there." He frowned and Mercy laughed.

"What?" she asked.

"We've had people coming by day and night for two weeks. How much do they think a man can eat?"

Mercy snorted. "Never thought I'd see the day you would complain about having too much food to eat."

Gray raised an eyebrow and swallowed the piece of biscuit he'd just crammed in his mouth. "I wasn't complainin'. Just curious."

"Um-hmm. They are only trying to help out. Lord knows I don't want to be cooking right now. Maybe if this little lady would let me sleep for more than two hours a night," she said, giving their daughter a smile so full of love and sweetness that Gray had to clear his throat to get rid of the sudden lump.

"Yes, well, if I see one more apple pie, I'm going to cram it down their—"

"Gray!" Mercy said, laughing.

He shrugged and went to put the food in the kitchen. He came back holding some sort of wooden contraption that looked like a two-pronged fork with a ball stuck between the tines.

"And what is this thing?" he asked, handing it to Mercy.

She grinned and took it from him, shaking it in front of the baby's face. "It's a rattle, silly. Haven't you ever seen baby toys?"

He shrugged again. "Never really spent much time around babies."

"Hmm well, we're definitely going to change that. Here," she said, handing him his daughter. "You take her for a while."

Gray opened his mouth but didn't object, though that was always his first instinct. She was just so…small. And soft. He was afraid he'd squeeze her too tight or drop her if she squirmed. But she settled back into his arms with a contented coo, blinking her big blue eyes a few times before settling back into sleep.

Mercy draped her arm around his waist, resting her chin against his shoulder. "We still need to come up with a name for her," she said. "Can't keep calling her Baby her whole life."

"We aren't calling her Apple," he grumbled, still ready to smack Jason for the mere suggestion.

Mercy laughed. "What about Mela? It means apple in

Italian, according to Mrs. DuVere."

He actually didn't hate that but would still object just on principle. He drew a finger down her down-soft cheek. "What about Daisy?" he said quietly.

"Daisy?"

"It was my mother's name," he said, holding his daughter a little closer.

Mercy turned and pressed a kiss to his shoulder. "I think that's a beautiful name." She took their daughter's finger as she started to fuss. "Daisy." She kissed her forehead. "It's perfect."

She smiled up at him, and he leaned down to press a kiss to her lips, releasing her only when Daisy began to fuss in earnest.

He shifted, frowning. "Did I squish her?"

Mercy shook her head. "No, she's fine."

"Hmm. Well, maybe all she wanted was someplace nice and quiet to sleep but no one will leave her alone. Someone seems to drop by every time I'm...I mean she... is getting ready to nap."

Mercy laughed and lightly pushed him toward the door and his rocking chair on the porch. "Go on. You two rock on the porch a while. I think you could both use a nap. You're both cranky. I've got a few things to do."

She waved, grabbed a basket and her shotgun, and headed toward the orchard.

Gray settled into his chair and began to rock, hoping Mercy didn't get into too much trouble when she was off shooting targets or causing some other mischief in town.

"Your mother is a real handful," Gray said to Daisy.

She belched softly and settled back into sleep.

He nodded. "My sentiments exactly." He kissed her gently on her forehead and then pulled his hat over his eyes with a sigh, snuggling down in his chair on the porch with his little Daisy for a nice nap.

This retirement thing wasn't so bad after all.

# ACKNOWLEDGMENTS

Huge massive thanks to Liz Pelletier, my incredible editor and publisher, who fell in love with Gray just as hard as I did. Working on this story with you has been more fun than I could have dreamed. My undying thanks also to Lydia Sharp, who was always there with encouraging texts and emails no matter how many times I pestered you, and whose input on this story has been invaluable. And to the dream team at Entangled, Jessica, Riki, Debbie, Curtis, Meredith, Heather, Katie, and all the amazing people behind the scenes—thank you so much for your hard work and support from start to finish and in between. To Elizabeth and Toni—thank you for making this book gorgeous inside and out! And Toni, thank you especially for being a true friend and support for the last decade plus. You've been there since the very beginning and knowing you were a part of this book makes it even more special.

Thank you to my wonderful agent, Janna Bonikowski, for all your support, guidance, and hard work on my behalf. And for always reading my novel-length emails and responding with a laugh and a smile. I love that you get me as well as you do.

To Tom, who keeps things running when I am overwhelmed, who started doing yoga just so I'd have someone to do it with, and who is always there to support me no matter what. I love you, babe. To Connor and

Ryanna, who are growing up way too fast. I'm glad you can now drive yourself where you need to go and am extremely grateful you still find running to the store for me fun. You are my rocks and my world. If you'd grow up a little slower that would be great. To Kyelie, Andy, Matt, Mindy, Axton, Casen, Novalee, and Alix, I love you all so much! Thank you for always supporting me and cheering me on. To my parents, siblings, and family who have loved and supported me from day one—you'll never know how much it means. Thank you all! And to all my readers out there—you guys are why I get to do what I do. Thank you for all the love and support!

*Enjoy two stories in one! From an arranged elopement with one of London's famous actors, to a story about the resurrection of first love after being widowed—this Regency romance collection is perfect for* Bridgerton *fans.*

# The BRIDES of LONDON

## VANESSA RILEY

***The Bittersweet Bride***: Widow Theodosia Cecil needs a husband and needs one fast to protect her land, so she places an anonymous ad in the paper. She's delighted she spends her remaining weeks exchanging flirtatious letters with the perfect man... Until she meets him and realizes he's the son of the man trying to steal her land.

***The Bashful Bride***: When sparks fly between timid heiress Ester Croome and a handsome actor, they're quick to elope. But when she discovers there is so much more to him than meets the eye, in order to save the marriage the shiest woman alive must publicly woo the most desirable man in England...her husband.

# HIGHLAND WARRIOR

by Heather McCollum

Joshua Sinclair was once the fiercest and most notorious warrior of the mighty Sinclair clan of Northern Scotland. But now there's nothing and no one that can make him take up arms again. Except a beautiful woman, it seems.

When Kára Flett, daughter of a fallen Norse chief, finds herself unexpectedly sheltering the strongest, most brutal warrior in the land, she throws together a risky and outrageous plan to bring him to her side. Threats of violence bounce right off him. Offers of gold seem to entice him even less. Desperate enough to use the pleas of the village children to sway him, she's shocked when he's completely unmoved. There's only one tactic left for her: seduction.

Her hasty proposition falls completely by the wayside, though, as she and the Highlander come together in a carnal inferno. But bringing him into her life also brings his enemies to her clan's doorstep—the very clan Kára is trying to protect. And as their feelings deepen, Joshua will have to decide between duty and love once and for all.